# GRANGER'S DEMISE

A Novel

Books by Teresa Pijoan from Sunstone Press

*American Indian Creation Myths*

*Dead Kachina Man*
A Mystery

*Granger's Threat*
A Murder Mystery Laced with a Web of Lies and Familial Contempt

*Granger's Return*

*Healers on The Mountain*
And Other Myths of Native American Medicine

*Myths of Magical Native American Women Including Salt Woman Stories*

*Native American Creation Stories of Family And Friendship*
Stories Retold

*Pueblo Indian Wisdom*
Native American Legends and Mythology

*Water Stories of Native American And Asian Indians*
Legends of Rain, Rivers and Lakes

*Ways of Indian Magic*
Indian Legends from the Tewa

# GRANGER'S DEMISE

A Novel

## TERESA PIJOAN

SUNSTONE
PRESS

SANTA FE

This is a work of fiction. Names, characters, places and incidents are either the product of this author's imagination or are used fictitiously and any resemblance to actual persons, living or dead, business establishments, events or locals is entirely coincidental. The publisher does not have any control over and does not assume any responsibility for the author or third-party contents.

Any faults found in this work belong to the author.

Sunstone books may be purchased for educational, business, or sales promotional use.
For information please write: Special Markets Department, Sunstone Press,
P.O. Box 2321, Santa Fe, New Mexico 87504-2321.
Printed on acid-free paper
∞
eBook: 978-1-61139-786-4

---

Library of Congress Cataloging-in-Publication Data

Names: Pijoan, Teresa, 1951- author
Title: Granger's demise : a novel / Teresa Pijoan.
Description: Santa Fe, NM : Sunstone Press, [2026] | Summary: "The ugly
    truth comes to light and is laid bare, proving that blind love can have
    devastating results"-- Provided by publisher.
Identifiers: LCCN 2025049293 | ISBN 9781632937773 paperback | ISBN
    9781611397864 epub
Subjects: LCSH: Families--Fiction
Classification: LCC PS3572.A4365 G726 2026 | DDC 813.54--dc23/eng/20251125

LC record available at https://lccn.loc.gov/2025049293

---

**WWW.SUNSTONEPRESS.COM**
SUNSTONE PRESS / POST OFFICE BOX 2321 / SANTA FE, NM 87504-2321 /USA
(505) 988-4418

Thanks to Cat Galindo, Karla Rueda, Itzel Osorio, Nicole D. Garling, Joseph E. Garling, Claire M. Connally, Lillian M. Connally, Diana Godinez, Cindy Claunch, Jorge Sedas, Devin Casamero, Randy Pijoan, Millie DeFabio, Shantelle Torres, Carolyn Herem, Miriam Lucero and LoreDonna Silveria. Zeus and Daisy help with meditation as we hike up the mountains, also Wally and Oscar who keep the bed warm at night.Also, Madeline Garnaat, Jonathan Larrañaga.

Special thanks to:
John D. Pitcher, M.D., who continues to try to save my eye and my vision.
Athanasios K. Manole, MD for keeping my body upright, hiking, rappelling and going strong.
This work has been published by the Magical Mystery Men. You two are the best.

Edited by April Fitzer.

This book is dedicated to Diana Godinez who sees beyond the obvious.

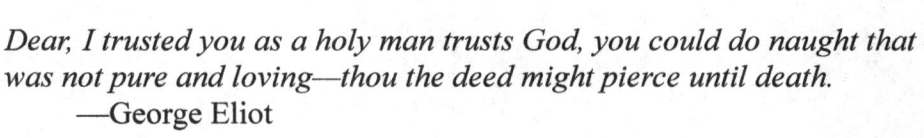

*Dear, I trusted you as a holy man trusts God, you could do naught that was not pure and loving—thou the deed might pierce until death.*
　　—George Eliot


*Do not speak unless by doing so, you improve upon the silence.*
　　—Spanish Proverb

# PREFACE

Marching up the aisle of students, came a man of late middle age. One might suggest his age to be in the late sixties or early seventies and they would be correct. This was a handsome man, wavy brown hair with a touch of red, greying at the temples. His moustache and goatee were carefully coifed. Each hair had the exact correct length around his mouth and down his chin. This man was perfectly proportioned and came forth as if brought out of the world of myth. His incredible assurance and arrogance were solidly noticed as he stood at the front of the classroom. Standing tall, he appeared to be on stage, waiting for applause from the audience. The gold framed spectacles were removed from his face to be moved to sit on the top of his head. His piercing brown eyes noticed the faces of the students who sat before him. The lecture hall had plush theatre seats, the lighting was focused on him and him alone and the acoustics were perfect.

An expensive brown-leather valise was placed on its side, flat on the desk at the front of the room. "Welcome to the world of healing. This is magical art, this knowledge will inform you of the ability to remain healthy, to keep others healthy and to bring about demise." He marched around the large wooden desk, picked up a marker and wrote his name boldly on the white board. As he wrote his name in large letters, his silky-smooth baritone voice said, "My name is Dr. Granger Pino."

Turning he continued to address his audience. "Some of you may have heard of me and if you haven't it would be wise to google my name to find out exactly who I am." The marker was replaced in the trough at the bottom of the white board. "My history is such. I shall make this short as we have much to cover in these five days." He returned to stand in front of the desk. "I was found guilty of killing my father. This isn't true. My father was a fine, strong man, who was also an exemplary doctor. He took medications to maintain his ability to treat his patients, to keep them alive."

Dr. Pino put his right thumb into his dark blue vest pocket. Bending to study his polished brown shoes, he continued, "What I did was relieve him of his suffering. For you see, he had become a vegetable covered with skin. A life no one would wish on any person who we love. As per his wish, before he became ill, I granted him an easy and painless death." Now he leaned against the desk, "This was an act of love and kindness, you see. As for the other incident, well, that was done out of ignorance. My mother's truck would not start. I attempted to repair it, not being a mechanic, I failed."

He stood upright and again marched with heavy foot falls back and forth in front of the desk. "Her truck stalled in the middle of a busy interstate with her inside of it. My mother is my love, my heart and this was something I would never want to happen, however, the cars racing down the interstate crashed into her little truck." At this he slapped his palms together. The students jumped, some laughed.

"No, no, this was not a laughing matter, no. Several people were seriously hurt never to recover. Some died. My mother survived and is doing well after months in the hospital." He stopped, staring up at the ceiling, "Again, I was found somewhat guilty for working on her truck thus causing this accident. This was not my intent. This was not my intent at all." Again, he leaned against the desk, "At this time I was practicing the art of healing and shared the office with others who were also, found guilty of murder and attempted murder. This was their own doing." Under his breath, he almost whispered, "I had nothing to do with their choices." Retrieving his arrogance, he smiled showing his perfectly placed, perfectly white teeth under his perfectly trimmed moustache.

He rubbed his hands together, "All of this cost me six years in the prison system." Shaking his head, he continued, "I survived and have dedicated myself to the teaching of herbal teas and cures, explaining the use of herbs for good health and spreading the word of Buddha." He turned to the desk, opened his valise to remove a yellow legal pad and handed it to the first person in the front row. "If you wish to remain in this class, please sign your name, your phone number and your student I.D. number. Those of you who wish to leave, please, do so now. Let us begin."

His laptop was pulled out, the lights were dimmed and the class proceeded as expected. Once the lights were turned back on, Dr. Granger noticed the audience had radically shrunk. He had been promised a class of at least thirty and truly when he entered almost all the seats were filled. As he viewed the plush theatre seats now, there were only nine students watching him. One of which, was a woman in her late fifties or sixties with mango colored hair with ends that appeared to have been dipped in purple paint. Her large three ring binder was quickly closed as she noticed him watching her.

"Dr. Pino, might I have a word?" The first impression he had of her was her large bulbous nose set between two faded cornflower blue eyes. Wrinkles were etched into her face around her mouth, under her nose and around her small eyes. She put out her hand, he did not comply. Each finger on each hand was laden down with rings. Rings with stones, rings with plastic baubles, one ring with a chain reaching a silver bracelet on her wrist. Her fluffy white poet's blouse was loosely open to show her cleavage of black spots and wrinkles as well. Her skirt was tie-dyed in the same wild colors as her hair.

"Dr. Pino? Dr. Pino, may I ask you a question, please?" Realizing that she was still speaking, he stepped back and answered, "Yes, please, what is your question?"

Her voice was not sharp edged rather it was flat, "I was wondering if you make house calls?" Her face blushed revealing a field of freckles, "It's my grandmother, and you see, well, she's not well, or perhaps that's not right." The woman quickly turned to see if anyone else was in the lecture hall with them. Turning back, she asked in a more forthright manner, "The problem is, my grandmother is too healthy. She is old, very old and as you spoke of your father and his situation, well, perhaps I am in the same situation."

Dr. Pino lifted his closed valise from the desk, "Your grandmother is dying slowly? Is this what you're telling me?"

"Well, no, not exactly. You see this is the problem. She just won't die." The woman searched his face as if hoping he understood. "She is not ill. She is at the peak of health actually. Well, no, that's not true either. She has horrible arthritis, but she is fully knowledgeable and busy."

She again put out her hand with the ringed fingers, "Please, my name is Karen Sullivan. I have wanted to take your class for ages." The notebook in her hand was shoved under her arm, "You see, I would be more than willing to pay you." She fell into a step beside him as they walked up the aisle of theatre seats to the double doors. "I did research on your history, and I know what you can do and how you can do your magic. I am more than willing to pay you a handsome sum if you help me." When they opened the double doors of the lecture hall, she put out her hand to stop him, "You do know you are going to lose this class since you do not have twelve students here." Her manner now became smug, "If you need money, I will be more than happy to pay you for your knowledge."

Her hand was now on her hip. Dr. Pino walked through the open double doors. The bright hall lights stopped him for a minute as he noticed she was handing him the attendance sheet with all the students' names and phone numbers written on the yellow legal pad. "Here you go, you probably should turn this in at the office." Using her index finger with the plastic face of the Tanzanian devil, she pointed to her name on the paper with her phone number and her address. She mouthed the words, call me. Turning on her heel, she walked down the hall swinging her hips in rhythm to her step. Dr. Pino noticed the thick hair on her legs and the bright yellow crocs on her bare feet.

The academic secretary stared up at Dr. Granger Pino, "You do realize that you needed at least twelve students to qualify for this class? As it stands right now, I will have to remove you from our calendar of classes. You will no longer be teaching here, and the principal will need to speak with you. Would you please take a seat, I'm sure she can see you right now." The secretary walked to the backroom of the main office. She quickly returned, pointing at him to go through the door behind her desk.

This room was expansive. There was a huge conference table in the middle of the room with at least twenty chairs around it. The table was polished wood with a shine to make a silversmith jealous. Dr. Granger Pino peered around the corner of this cavernous room to find a small woman sitting at a large desk with a computer and a monitor. She quickly stood to put out her hand, "Dr. Pino, I presume. We seem to have quite a few of you around here. I gather you must be Sophia's brother? Am I right?"

Dr. Granger Pino's face reddened at the sound of his sister's name and nodded in agreement. The Principal then stated, "I am Dr. Ortega, the head of this huge institution. From what Silvia, my secretary, has informed me your class did not make the numbers. Also, I would like to add, when we checked your credentials, we found you have no degrees, only a certification from a Chinese Medical clinic. Unfortunately, your class would have been cancelled anyway since we are an accredited institution." She took a breath, "Please, forgive us for not notifying you sooner, but we just received this information. Thank you for your interest in this university. Have a good day." The woman sat back down at her desk to completely ignore him.

Granger turned on his heel, his head down as he took deep strides, leaving the building. Under his breath, he said, "Strong men do not cry. Damn!" Weaving in and out of parked vehicles, he finally came upon his polished gold Mercedes. A tall man stood leaning against a truck parked beside the Mercedes. The man approached Granger, "Excuse me, Professor, but I have a bone to pick with you. In class today, you talked about Buddhism and selflessness and yet when I arrived this morning to park next to you and your gold Mercedes, I could not believe you would spout such hypocrisy!" Pointing at the polished gold vehicle, he continued, "I dropped your class because you let us know what a phony you are! Aren't you ashamed to be so hypocritical in your beliefs?"

Granger lifted his head high, "This Mercedes was a present given to me from my mother. It would've been rude of me to deny her the pleasure of accepting her gift. Please, move out of my way. I have a meeting to go to right now." The man walked around the Mercedes whistling, "Yeah, I bet you do." He jumped in his truck and sat there watching Granger get in his Mercedes. Granger slowly and carefully placed his valise on the passenger's seat as he slid onto the driver's seat. "Damn, damn and damn again! I need to get out of here!" He started the engine, backed out carefully and drove off the campus.

Once on the main highway to Calavera and his mother's farmhouse, he broke down. At an exit ramp, he pulled over to get out of his blessed car. Walking onto the dirt and into a group of Russian olive trees, he slapped his hands together, "I am important! Oh, Mama, help! What am I going to do now?" He kicked the base of a tree with his well-polished shoe, "I need a thousand dollars! I can't keep taking my mother's money. She's just about out of cash. Guess we'll have to sell her farm and get a place out of state. I can't stay here anymore, not anymore, no, not anymore."

13

# 1

Edna stared at the ceiling. Squinting her ninety-two-year-old eyes, she could make out faces from her past in the paint swirls high above her head. The scent of the pine cleaner permeated everything in this room. Edna shifted her right shoulder. Her hospital bed was lumpy. It took time to find the right area to relax. "Hey, Bradly, I'm still here. Doesn't appear that I will be coming to meet you anytime soon." Edna opened her right hand to flex her fingers, open and close. Her plump sausage sized fingers were not able to make a fist. Osteoarthritis had swollen each joint of each finger deformed with pulsing pain.

Straightening her arm and then bending it repeatedly, she listened to the popping and grating of the bones in the joints. She spoke to the ceiling, "My fingers keep going numb. You used to rub my hands and feet, remember?" Using her left hand, she felt for the pink sponge curlers in her grey hair. The stylist told her to use the curlers, not to get a perm because it was thinning her fine grey hair. The last thing Edna wanted was to meet her loving husband in heaven with a bald head.

The hospital bed squeaked as she shifted her thin body for a more comfortable position. Edna had moved all of her clothes into the front dining room along with her late husband's hospital bed. Her legs were no longer steady enough for her to go up and down the steep stairs to their old bedroom. When she started to use the bedroom porta potty near the bed, she asked a friend to help her keep the lower room clean. Her friend had a maid who came over to Edna's twice a week to scour the floor, wash the walls and clean out the porta pot. Edna felt safer being downstairs for she could hear anyone coming to the front door or trying to get in the back door by the kitchen. The comfortable laminate wood floor was easy to clean and gave the room a larger appearance.

Edna sat, felt around the floor for her slippers with the skid proof bottoms, stood to pull down her grey sweatshirt with an orange cat motif on the front. Humming to herself, she straightened the bed, tightening the bottom sheet, pulling up the top sheet to have the quilt placed neatly

15

over the top with a fold just under the pillows. It was very quiet during the day. At times, Edna felt alone in the world and would quickly go outside to make sure the world hadn't disappeared completely. What a relief it was to see cars going by, children playing in their front yards, with birds chirping and airplanes in the sky.

Suddenly, there were three loud knocks on her front door that shifted her attention. Edna turned quickly, almost losing her balance. Righting herself, she called out, "Yes?" The heavy wooden front door swung open unprompted by her. Two people entered the front hall. Her vision being limited prompted Edna to hurry out of the dining room, closing the door behind her. A woman of older middle age and a man approximately the same stood awkwardly staring at her. Edna put her hand out to the woman, to say sweetly, "Karen, how lovely for you to visit! It is nice when family remembers do politely look in to be sure their elderly relatives are still alive."

Edna's smile worked at being sincere. "Do come in, introduce me to your friend, but first let me put the kettle on for tea." She slid her feet in the fluffy slippers to move around the two of them into a hall. Dutifully Karen and her friend turned to follow.

Karen stopped in the hall before a doorway leading into a dark room. She reached inside to flip the light switch. A large room loomed in front of them. The floor was covered with large Persian rugs. They covered the entire floor from door to walls. In the center of the room was a long L-shaped couch covered in Persian tapestries and large pillows with floral designs. Two Elizabethan wing chairs were placed side by side in front of an open-mouthed empty fireplace with numerous photos in silver frames on the mantel piece. A portrait of a youthful Edna was painted in oils over the fireplace.

The floor to ceiling windows faced out overlooking a huge expanse of lawn and garden now overgrown. The left side of this huge room held a grand piano placed in front of a floor to ceiling bookcase filled with books all leather bound. Portrait oil paintings were hung tastefully on the other walls with empty eyes staring at the couch and piano. A life size human statue stood between the two tall windows. Karen whispered, "That is a statue of my grandfather. As you can see, he was a formidable man. It was made for him when his first successful play opened on Broadway. He was very famous."

Edna's frail voice echoed down the hall, "Hey, are you two coming or should I find you?" Karen shook her head, "We better go. Grandma does not appreciate people who do not do her bidding, promptly!" Walking ahead of her friend, Karen entered the kitchen to find her grandmother pouring hot water into a China tea kettle. "Come, the water is hot." Karen's friend stood in the doorway leaning against the door frame. He was neither in the kitchen nor out of it. He watched the dynamic of the two women.

Karen moved quickly to the back door. Her hands wrapped around a red walker standing near the coat rack. "Grandma, I didn't know you used a walker." Karen pushed her shoulder length hair behind her ears. The strange mango color gave Karen a washed-out appearance. She questioned her grandmother, "I thought you only used a cane now. Are you using the walker, too? You know, you need to be careful with walkers they can give you a false feeling of security." Karen shook the walker, "I know of people who have fallen and broken their hips while using these walkers." Karen dropped the walker onto the floor with a clatter. Shaking her head, she spoke to her grandmother, "You do know if you break a hip there is a seventy percent chance you will die soon after."

Edna had her back to the two of them as she spoke, "You can sit down. There is no reason for you both to stand."

The kitchen was painted a soft bird's egg blue. White lace curtains rose and fell as the breeze came through the open window over the deep porcelain sink. Cornflower blue tile covered the counters and was lined with white and blue smaller tiles to give the room an open feel to it. The stove was an old porcelain stove with covers over each burner and with blue dish towels hanging from the oven door. The kitchen smelled of burnt toast. The light over the kitchen table was covered with a glazed cornflower design. All in all, the kitchen was cozy and warm.

Karen pulled out a wooden chair from around the wooden table. She nodded to her friend. Hesitantly, he sat beside Karen on the wooden chair offered. Edna rattled some teacups and saucers onto a large wooden tray. A white pitcher was filled with milk as a white China sugar bowl was put on the tray. It had lumps of sugar in it. "Tea is ready. Here we go." Edna placed the tray on the center of the wooden table to say, "Help yourselves. Sorry, there are no biscuits. No one has been able to do my shopping as of late." She gave a wrinkled smile to Karen.

"Grandma, this is my friend and my professor Dr. Granger Pino. He is giving a class on healing herbs. Since you are always going on about 'the good old days' and their 'natural cures' I thought you two should meet." Karen pushed back her shoulder length orange mango hair with purple ends. She handed Granger a tea saucer with a matching teacup to ask, "Shall I pour?" Edna nodded approvingly.

Granger smiled at both the women in a smug and self-satisfied way. He noticed Edna had a wonderfully expressive face and there was a sort of radiant vitality about her that challenged attention. Slowly, he lifted the teacup filled with tea to his nose, sniffing it artfully. His well-trimmed moustache moved with each sniff. A snarky expression appeared on his face as he gently returned the teacup onto the saucer. The tea was untasted. He shook his head, "This tea has been processed. Certainly, this is not good for you." He pushed the saucer with the tea cup on it away from him onto the middle of the table. Both of his hands returned to his lap. His face was expressionless. He had a splendid set of white teeth and deep warm brown eyes. His manner, however, was much cooler than the tea.

Karen stared down into her lap.

No one appeared to have anything more to say. Finally, Edna cleared her throat to speak up, "How pleasant of you to visit me with my granddaughter, Dr. Pino. Perhaps you don't know the history we have." Edna tugged down on her sweatshirt as she spoke, "My lovely granddaughter was born out of wedlock, you see. No one wanted her. She was a colicky baby, crying all the time, was hesitant to be potty-trained and oh, my, what a handful she was." Edna checked the tea in the tea pot. "Well, I love children, so I took her in as my own. I drove her to school. We sent her to a very expensive school, don't you know? We paid for her to have braces on her teeth and go to a private school."

Edna stood to rummage through a chest at the side of the kitchen door. "Here we go. This was Karen when she was little. We had to pay for her braces and her horse." A photo album was placed in front of Dr. Granger Pino. "Go ahead, open it. Karen, show him your pictures." Edna's arthritic index finger pounded on the closed photo album.

Karen blushed, "Grandmother, this is embarrassing. I'm sure he doesn't want to see my baby pictures." She picked up the album and handed it back to Edna. Dr. Granger Pino said nothing, he stared at the two women quietly. Edna sat back down, hugging the photo album. "You see, Karen needed braces, and she wanted so many things that her grandfather and I would not buy her. They were silly things that would deplete our savings and her college money. We were thrifty and had hoped she would become so as well." The photo album was placed on the table to the side of Edna's teacup.

"Our Karen wanted the world, yet she would not help us, nor would she help around the house. For some reason our Karen wanted the world with no effort on her part." Edna put her hand on the table to reach out to Karen who ignored her grandmother. "She was a difficult child. I love you, Karen, regardless of what you tell people." Edna now looked at Dr. Pino, "Our Karen would tell people terrible stories about us. She would tell them that we beat her, which we didn't. We never lifted a finger to you, did we, dear?"

Karen shook her head. "But you both were very strict with me! Grandma, I think we should have our tea and not talk about our history. We came by to share information about herbs. Please, we're here just for a social call not a psychiatric evaluation." Her face was set in a grimace.

Dr. Granger Pino sat still staring at the teacup that had once been in front of him. He was older than middle-aged in a brown and grey tweed suit with leather patches on the elbows. His graying brown hair was thinning, his moustache and goatee were mostly white. His eyes appeared strained as his thick glasses had been pushed up on top of his head. His appearance was more of a retired professor rather than an active professor. His hands were well cared for: nails manicured and polished, soft skin, and a wedding band of gold on his left ring finger.

Once again, Karen cleared her throat, "Grandmother, we were really just passing by and I asked Dr. Pino to come in and meet you. I think it is amazing, well, you are amazing to be so elderly and still sharp and witty. Classes and work have been crazy busy, or I would've come by more often." Karen lifted her hand in an attempt to place it on the professor's arm but then thought the better of it to sip her tea.

Karen certainly was not much younger than her professor. Her faded blue eyes highlighted with black kohl did not enhance them. The long dangling silver earrings swung freely until caught in her hair. Karen's tight mouth was always in a down turned frown with etched wrinkles. The mango hair and turquoise silk top gave Karen a washed-out appearance. There was no color to her face. Her bulbous nose did not help her attraction.

Edna shook her head. One of her pink curlers came loose to dangle beside her right ear. She pulled the curler out to place it on the table beside her tea saucer. "I'm sorry to be under dressed, but I was not expecting company." Her teacup was lifted to her lips where she took a long draw of it. Then, without a word, she poured herself another cup. A drop of milk, one lump of sugar and a light stir turned the tea a gentle brown. The spoon was licked and placed quietly on the table.

Edna leaned back in her chair, "This is my favorite tea, and I have been drinking it all my life. I just had my ninety-third birthday, young man, obviously you have a purpose in coming here. I would like to know what it is. Are you interested in marrying my granddaughter? For if you are, you should know she has no interest in men." Then as an afterthought, Edna added, "and no interest in women from what I have been told."

Dr. Granger Pino studied Edna. Her eyes were sharp. Her tone and voice were strong. It was hard to believe the woman was still as testy as she appeared. Karen had waylaid him, telling him of the family's frustration in wanting their inheritance. The woman apparently would not die. This ancient woman was far from incapacitated and certainly not ready to pass on to the other realm of existence.

On the counter was a large 8x10 photograph of a man. He was smiling with sparkling blue eyes. His moustache was neatly trimmed above a slow smile, showing yellowed teeth. Edna noticed Granger staring at the photo, "That is my late husband. He is the love of my life. We converse daily about our opinions and issues. He was an actor and a professor such as yourself." She pointed to the far wall, which was covered with more photographs and awards. "My husband wrote several plays that were performed on Broadway and later were made into films. He was well known and very famous in his day."

Edna put the napkin on the table to smooth it flat with her hands, "At the time, we were so busy there was very little we could do about their lack of care. Now, I wonder if that was a mistake for my family seems to have forgotten my existence as well." Calmly, she nodded to Karen. "Do you remember when I wanted to write my memoirs?" Karen shook her head 'no.' Edna continued, "Well, you see, Dr. Pino, I wanted to write about my life with my fine husband including all of our artistic theatre tickets and such." Edna glanced at Karen, instead of judging her, she gave her a quick look that showed no feeling at all.

It appeared Edna did not press a negative point, but it was obvious that there was an ulterior motive behind everything she said, "You see it is strange that this is the first time that I have met you and yet there is a Donna Pino McGuire who comes to help me write up my memoir. Pino is not a common name, is it?" She studied his face.

Again, the face remained expressionless. Granger Pino cleared his throat. Stoically, he stated, "No, Pino is not a common name." Swallowing with difficulty, he added, "Donna is my sister's youngest daughter. My sister is Sophia Pino. I believe she works with Dr. Robert Glacie, the anthropologist."

The napkin in front of Edna was quickly placed in her lap. Looking up at him, she smiled, "Oh, yes, yes, I do know Robert. Dr. Glacie would give Donna tickets for me to go to some do or other at the university. Yes, I believe at one time I did meet Sophia Pino, but she had a different name?"

Granger Pino shifted in the wooden chair, "Yes, she was married to Geoffrey Vinder. They're divorced now. Both of her girls took her maiden name or our family name, I mean." His discomfort was more than obvious. His right foot began to shake, and his hands were wrapping one around the other in his lap.

Edna clapped her hands, "Oh, you are Dr. Walter Pino's son? I remember reading his obituary. When you get as old as I am you start reading obits all the time just to make sure your name isn't in one of them." She smiled at him. He did not smile back. 21

A pocket watch was removed from Granger's brown vest. Noticing the time or perhaps finding an excuse, he stated, "Sorry, but I really need to go. I have a meeting in fifteen minutes and it's across town. Please, forgive the intrusion." Wiping his hands on his pressed jeans, he stood. Placing his hand on Karen's shoulder, he added, "Karen, I am sorry I just remembered this meeting. Let's talk after class on Wednesday." Nodding to Edna, he turned and departed.

Hurriedly, Karen gathered up the teacups and the saucers to put on the tray. She added the pitcher of milk and the sugar bowl. Quickly, the tea kettle was placed on the counter and the tray was moved to sit beside the sink. "Grandma, it's been fun. Good to see you, gotta go to my next class." She pulled a backpack from the floor next to the front door where she must have left it when she entered. She was out of the front door like a shot as it slammed shut behind her.

Edna patted the tabletop, "That was definitely strange. They came, they sat, and they departed. Wonder if they have a term for such behavior in Latin." Putting her hands on the tabletop, she lifted her frail body to stand. The pink curler was picked up to be shoved into her deep pant pocket. "Maybe he doesn't like women with curlers." She shuffled back to the bedroom. "Or he expected to find a lovely house filled with treasures." Edna was tired. She went back to her hospital bed to take off her slippers. The dishes could wait.

Racing onto the street, Karen practically flattened Dr. Granger Pino who was standing by the front gate waiting for her. "Karen, that was most uncomfortable."

"Sorry, sorry, Doctor, sorry. I wanted you to meet her, so you'd know what we are up against. I will pay you ten percent if you could possibly help to hurry her along to the next life." Karen turned to stare back at the house. "Good, she's not looking. You never know with her. What do you think? Is there a way, an obvious way to help her be with her ever loving husband?"

Well, yes." Dr. Granger Pino smiled, "She certainly does love her tea, doesn't she. It so happens that teas are my specialty. You, on the other hand, need to come and visit her more or this will appear suspicious. You need to become her new best friend. Help her with her groceries, help her fix dinners and clean. Karen, for this to work, you will need to become a companion to her. Do you think you can do this?" Karen looked over her shoulder at the house. A curtain moved.

She took his arm, pulling him away from the house to the area where the cars were parked. The wind had picked up tossing dead brown leaves into piles on the cement. A single robin sang its song in a nearby tree. The street was quiet for the moment. Once the school buses started arriving, the neighborhood would come to life. Karen held her orange and purple tie-dyed skirt down as the wind swirled around them both. "I'll try to become her friend. She's difficult because she has her strong opinions and her ways. When we try to play a board game she always cheats, but I am the one criticized." There was a loud bang as a car backfired somewhere near them. They both jumped. Karen walked beside him as they moved through the cars in the parking lot. "Yes, I'll do this. How long do you think it will take before you have what you need to push her over?"

Dr. Pino stroked his goatee, "Not long, but we need to take our time. This was your first visit in some time. It would appear suspicious if she died tomorrow for instance. You would be the obvious cause. Let's give it a month."

*Granger's Demise*

"A month! That's too long! We have debts to pay! "Karen's wide angry eyes admonished him. Stepping in front of him, she asked, "Why not Halloween? That's in twelve days. What do you think?" Her mango-colored hair blew around her head in the strong breeze.

His right hand tenderly brushed a strand of her mango hair out of her face. "Halloween might be perfect. Lots of candy, lots of people coming and going. Yes, let's shoot for Halloween." He pulled his glasses down from the top of his head, wiped them with a handkerchief found in his jacket pocket to put them on his nose. "Halloween it is."

Wind blew empty plastic bags along the edges of the street. Dogs barked as joggers ran past the small front yards. A large plane scowled its way across the sky as the two people moved to a gold Mercedes Benz. Edna moved through the bedroom on her sore bare feet to open the white curtains and lift the window latch. Staring out onto the parking lot, she noticed Dr. Granger and Karen got into the same gold vehicle. "Oh, my, this is certainly suspicious. Think it's time to call Dr. Goldfarb Junior about my will."

Edna's gray hair was combed free as the pink curlers were placed in a clear plastic container on the bathroom counter. The curls sprang into action, light and fluffy. Proud of her hairdo, Edna moved to sit on the edge of the hospital bed. The bedside table was covered with prescription bottles, a glass of water and a telephone with a pencil and pad beside the phone. A heavy black phone, cradled in its base, was lifted. Arthritic fingers held the pencil with the eraser down to dial a familiar number.

Her voice was clear and sharp, "Roger Goldfarb please." Tapping the pencil on the side of the bedside table, Edna waited. Finally, there was a man's voice on the line. Edna could see him in her memory, a man of formidable standing in the community, he wore his hair in a prep school cut, his eyes a dark chocolate brown. "Roger, your assistance is needed. My granddaughter Karen was just here with a man called Dr. Granger Pino. They appear to be in a liaison of some sort. I find this questionable. Do you know anything about a Granger Pino and what he may want? He certainly struck me as being odd."

Nodding as she listened, a smile grew across her face. "Oh, yes, I see. Yes, yes, let's rewrite the will. Would you be able to stop by on your way home this late afternoon? Fine, fine. Shall see you then." Edna gently returned the black phone to its cradle. She spoke to the mirror as she stared into it, "Well, that certainly is a strange turn of events. It looks like Animal Humane is going to get most of my money. Thank you, Karen!"

Dutifully, the next day Karen arrived with a bag of groceries her grandmother had requested earlier. The two of them shared dinner and when there were no classes the next day, the two of them played a game of Chinese checkers. True to form, Grandma Edna would jump over pieces two or three times at strange angles. Karen noticeably praised her grandmother. Edna was ever so pleased to have the company and the attention from her granddaughter. When Karen was not there, Edna bragged about her to the neighbors and friends who happen to drop in from time to time.

As the groceries were being placed in the cupboards on the ninth day, Edna approached her granddaughter, "Karen, dear girl, I have a surprise for you. Wait here, don't go anywhere. I think you'll like this." Edna hurried into her bedroom to return with a large brown manila envelope. "Here you go! Oh, I'm so excited." She handed the large envelope to Karen. "Please, please open it!" Karen pulled out one of the kitchen's wooden chairs to sit abruptly.

Carefully turning the manila envelope in one hand, she flipped open the envelope with the other. "Grandma, what have you done now?"

Edna sat cautiously on the kitchen chair opposite her at the kitchen table. "Go ahead, open it!" The first item Karen pulled out was an airplane ticket. She stared at it in disbelief. Then she reached back into the manila envelope to pull out a short piece of paper with an itinerary on it. The first date was in two days. Karen read the information to stare at her grandmother, "What is this? Why are you doing this? Grandma, this is too much!"

Edna's smile lit up the room, "No, my dear, no. This is for you and for all your help over the last few weeks! You'll be staying with Nate at his huge mansion right outside of Salem. Now, you will think I'm trying to be a match maker, but no, I'm not the type. Nate is exactly your age. He is filthy rich. He has been divorced twice and has not had children – young or old. He does have a sailboat and a yacht. He is great fun, and he is excited to meet you and have you stay at his mansion on the beach."

"Grandma, this is match making! I can't accept this." She reached back into the manila envelope to pull out a check. "What is this for? Oh, my, for one thousand dollars! Are you crazy? What is this for? Are you trying to buy me?"

Edna reached across the table to her, "Karen, you have proven to me that you are a caring person. I always thought you were a selfish brat, but that was before. Karen, dearest, you have been beyond kind to help me. You have been ever so loving. Who knew you were such a thoughtful woman." Pushing her curly bangs from her forehead, Edna went on, "The money is for you to get a new wardrobe. Your hippie clothes are totally out of date even for me at my age. Also, you certainly must have debts you need to pay off before you go." Edna pointed at the airplane ticket. "Look, this is for Halloween or All Hallows Eve. I know how you love it." Edna's smile was filled with love, "You can buy a creative costume. Nate swore he would take you to all the best parties. Evidently where he lives, they have costume parties galore on Halloween."

Karen's face turned a dark shade of red, highlighting her bulbous nose. Her hazel eyes stared blankly at the items on the table before her. False tears welled up in her eyes, "Grandmother, I had no idea you were so lonely. I would have helped you long before this if you would have asked." She wiped her bulbous nose on her floppy blouse's sleeve. Edna pulled a tissue from her pocket and handed it to Karen. "Oh, darling, I have had the most wonderful time with you! I now know who you truly are!" Cautiously, Edna was up off her chair to walk around the table and put her wrinkled arms around Karen. "I feel so blessed to know you now."

Wiping her eyes with the tissue, Karen twisted away from her grandmother, "I cannot accept this. This is too much." All the items were carefully placed back into the manila envelope. "I cannot accept these. Please, take them back and get your money for these. Please, please, I can't accept this." She shoved the envelope to the middle of the table. Karen's hand trembled as she moved it away from the manila envelope. She whispered, "This is too much, too much, too much."

"Karen, dear girl, all the arrangements have been made. Nate has his driver pick you up in his limo and all the tickets for the parties have been bought and paid for by Nate. He's excited to see you and know you. Karen, everything is in place." Edna moved carefully around the table to return to her chair. She was confused.

TERESA PIJOAN

Vehemently shaking her head, Karen pleaded, "I have classes and a final. I have work to do and I can't up and run away. This is very kind and thoughtful of you, but I can't accept this."

Edna gave Karen her most pleasant smile, "This is all arranged. Dr. Pino has agreed to give you the final exam this Friday in his office. He assured me that you already have an 'A' in his class or workshop or whatever you call it. Everything's arranged."

"But, but, you, what about your food? What about someone to help you change the sheets and cook your food? Who's going to help you if I'm not here?" There was noticeable perspiration on Karen's brow. "I can't just leave you, right?" Mango colored hair fell in her face as she frantically shook her head.

Pleading, Edna put her hands to her chest, "My dear girl, I had my life figured out before you started coming to help me, I can carry on while you're gone. Do not worry, someone recommended a senior care person to come and help. You go and have fun!"

Mango hair was pushed back behind her ears as Karen's voice became stern, "Grandma, you're doing this again. You're planning my life without asking me first. I am fifty-nine after all. I can make my own decisions. You push and push and push until I finally say 'yes' to something I really don't want to do." She stood up to push the chair back under the table. "Did you even think if asking me first? Were you so sure you would believe I would want to do this?" The manila envelope was picked up and put onto the kitchen counter. "If you don't want me around you could just say so!" Karen stormed out of the kitchen, down the hall, through the front door to slam it as hard as she could.

Sitting in her tiny Volkswagen bug, Karen burst into tears. She slammed her palms against the steering wheel, "Damn, damn, damn, damn how could she do this to me? God, how I would love to go! Why is she doing this to me?" Karen forged in her oversized leather purse for her cellphone. Quickly dialing, she waited impatiently for an answer. "Hello, oh hi, listen I'm in a fix. Grandmother just gave me a ticket to Salem, Massachusetts. She set up my reward vacation not only with an airplane ticket, but with a cousin I don't know to stay in his mansion, go to parties with him, and a check for one thousand dollars! This is all supposed to happen in a matter of days!"

She tilted her head to say, "What? You want me to go? Won't this ruin our plans? Why would you want me to go?" Again, she listened intently to answer, "I turned it down. I turned the whole charade down. She's doing what she did to me when I was younger. She wants to plan my life!" She paused to reply, "Oh, all right. No, I'm here in the parking lot." Trepidation and anger filled Karen's emotions. Tears were wiped with the back of her hands. The car keys were pulled from the ignition. She grabbed her oversized leather purse to step out into the oncoming wind. "Damn, and damn again." Not knowing how to respond or take back her emotional tirade, Karen rang the doorbell.

Edna stood back to let Karen into the front hall. Edna did not say a word. Nodding to her grandmother, Karen walked into the kitchen, picked up the manila envelope, dropped it into her purse and turned to give her grandmother a hug. "Thank you. I'm sure I'll love this trip." Edna stood frozen in awe. Karen let go of her grandmother to whisper, "I'll see you tomorrow. Thank you." She went out the open front door, walked to her small vehicle and drove away in the blowing fall wind.

As Edna closed the front door keeping the weather out, she muttered, "You are most welcome." As she shuffled to the bedroom, Edna looked up at the ceiling, "Karen's sixty-one if she's a day. Not sure what her problem is?"

Karen's trip to Salem passed quickly. The five days she was there were filled with a whirlwind of social appointments, parties and nighttime engagements. Nate was not only wealthy, but incredibly handsome. His affection for her remained purely cousin-like because there was no romance or infatuation between the two of them. Karen was sure he was gay and was totally relieved.

Every night Karen called her grandmother. A caregiver, Mrs. Ulibarri, showed up the evening Karen had departed. Evidently the woman loved to play board games and did not speak English very well. A white bag with loose leafed tea arrived the night prior to Karen's return. The caregiver knew enough English language to read the label as tea leaves. Mrs. Ulibarri carefully made the tea as per Edna's direction for their usual board game time at four o'clock in the afternoon. Edna had informed Mrs. Ulibarri this was the civilized time for tea and light sandwiches. The tea was served to Edna while Mrs. Ulibarri had her usual diet drink. Mrs. Ulibarri graciously let Edna win all five of their games.

As the clock showed six-thirty in the evening, Mrs. Ulibarri put the board game on the shelf and cleaned the dishes. This was the time

Mrs. Ulibarri was preparing Edna for the night. The portable potty was cleaned out, clean sheets were tucked in at four corners, Edna's water glass was filled with fresh water on her bedside table and the black phone was disconnected from the kitchen to be moved to the bedside table and plugged in the bedroom wall socket. Mrs. Ulibarri, once done with these chores would be able to return home. Edna graciously paid Mrs. Ulibarri for her week's work and wished her well as she closed and locked the front door. Nights were lonely for Edna, yet she did enjoy her conversations with her late husband who stared down on her from the ceiling.

As Edna, in her freshly washed nightgown lifted to repose on her hospital bed, she noticed that the sheets smelled lovely and were soft to touch. Raising the back of the bed with the remote, she took her book of famous sayings, put on her reading glasses to pull the marker from the book. By ten thirty, Edna knew something was terribly wrong with her body. She started to sweat. Stumbling off the bed, she leaned forward to balance her body using her hands against the walls. She staggered to the front door, unlocked it and tried to open the door to call for help.

Then she started to shiver, and her body shook uncontrollably. Returning to the bed, she leaned over grasping the far railing of the hospital bed, to use all her strength getting onto the bed. She gave a deep sigh and tried to relax. Her body was wet with perspiration. As she leaned down to pull the sheet up to her chest, suddenly her body heaved. "No, no, no! I do not get sick! No, I refuse to be sick!"

Lifting her right leg over the side of the bed to stand, she fell face first onto the floor. Her body heaved again. This time, yellow sticky acid flew out of her mouth covering the right side of her face. Her feet started to jerk uncontrollably. Using her left hand, she tried to push herself to sit upright. Her arm would not hold her weight. Reaching over her head, she pulled on the telephone black cord. The telephone fell inches from the top of her head. The cradle dislodged from the headset of the phone. Again, she pulled on the cord. The phone's cradle landed on her shoulder. Her fingers were randomly dialing numbers.

A woman's voice answered, "How may I help you?" Edna whispered through her tears, "Help, help me, help..." There was silence. Then the woman on the other end of the phone asked, "What is your name? What is your address?" There was no answer. All was quiet. The woman on the phone hung up in a huff. Now, Edna was able to meet her loving husband.

At ten o'clock that next morning, the Meals on Wheels lady arrived with a doughnut and a round container of two scrambled eggs and two piecess of fried bacon. The sliced cantaloupe with strawberries were in a separate container. Knocking on the door, it swung open with no one to greet her. Edna was found on the floor beside her hospital bed. The black telephone cord was grasped firmly in her frozen left fist.

The ambulance arrived twenty minutes later at which time Edna was legally and medically listed as 'extinct.' Karen's cellphone number was found stuck to the stainless-steel refrigerator door. The inspecting detective immediately called her. Karen's response was one of shock, horror and hysteria. Karen was not considered a suspect in that she was over one thousand miles away surrounded with witnesses. Karen let the police know she would contact other family members. This was a relief to the police chief who had arrived with the ambulance. The medical examiner questioned cause of death; a full autopsy was to be performed. As per the request also found on the kitchen refrigerator door, Roger Goldfarb attorney of law was informed. He promptly set a date and time for the reading of the will.                                          29

## 2

K aren flew home to attend the funeral. Saint John's Episcopal Church was flooded with people who had loved, known, or wanted to remember Edna Sullivan. Actors arrived to say their praises not only for Edna, but also for her husband. A professional harpist was present who had gone to school with Edna. She cried profusely as she strummed the harp's strings. Karen was amazed and lost seeing so many people. Mrs. Ulibarri attended the funeral with all her eleven family members. Flowers overflowed on the altar where the cremated ashes were placed next to her husband's ashes. These were to be spread out over the small theatre where the two of them first met. A cherry picker truck had been rented by Mr. Goldfarb, attorney at large, to have the ashes thrown over the roof of the theatre.

The Episcopal minister gave a beautiful eulogy as he had known her socially. He had also baptized her two children. No one was sure where her son was as he had disappeared when Karen was only three years old. Karen's mother was killed in a head on collision. Karen had been left behind to be brought up by her grandmother and grandfather.

As the funeral service ended, there wasn't a dry eye in the church. Mrs. Ulibarri, with the help of Mr. Goldfarb, had set up a tent behind the church with food items and drinks. It was a pleasant day filled with beauty and sadness. Dr. Granger Pino was nowhere to be seen.

As people walked to the parking lot, Karen mentioned how she was flummoxed by Goldfarb's lack of response upon learning of her grandmother's demise. She mentioned this to several people around her, "Mr. Goldfarb did not appear to be surprised at my grandmother's death. He was acting most suspiciously." Karen's father arrived. He was wearing a tattered blue parka, and his pants appeared to not have been washed for several weeks. His face was drawn with a shaggy beard and gray shaggy hair tied back in a ponytail.

Four days later was the reading of the will. Edna's younger sister arrived in a handicapped van in that she was wheelchair bound and had numerous medical issues. Edna's younger sister flew in from California. She was the only person there who was dressed in black with a sullen expression of loss. Two men arrived. One older man was in a new suit, polished shoes with a trimmed beard and his ponytail of gray hair neatly in place. The other man was a tall man as well. Pulling out a chair for the other man, who was dressed in a nice suit, a shiny new parka and well-polished shoes. This man carefully sat in the chair as if he hurt. His eyes were down, his mouth a straight line of tension and his hands were held tightly together as if in prayer. The standing well-dressed man nodded to Mr. Goldfarb as he quietly took a seat in the back of the room.

Mr. Goldfarb, attorney at law, had chairs placed in rows, in a semi-circle in front of his desk. The chairs were made of expensive dark wood with green velvet cushion seats. His desk was made of black walnut wood dressed with a green ink blot cover. Floor to ceiling heavy green drapes were pulled to cover the windows, giving the room a forlorn feel to it. The only light in the room was on his desk. Mr. Goldfarb Junior stood as he welcomed Edna's family into his official sanctuary. He was a tall man well over six feet tall. His thick reddish-brown hair was cut in a prep school fashion. He wore a dark navy-blue suit with polished black leather shoes. His expression was professional, and his voice was deep and stern. As Karen entered the room, she moved to an empty chair at the front of his desk.

A large platter of cinnamon toast and a tea pot were placed on a table at the side of the room. White Styrofoam cups were stacked beside the tea pot. This was offered to the family and guests as they entered. The last person to enter was Donna Pino McGuire. Sophia Pino's youngest daughter. No one from Edna's family recognized or acknowledged Donna's presence. Karen had no knowledge of Donna being in the room.

Mr. Roger Goldfarb, Junior attorney at law, motioned for all present to please sit and make themselves comfortable. There was total silence as the will was read out loud by lawyer Goldfarb. Quietly, Karen and her estranged father remained sitting as statues. The first person to receive a financial gift was Mrs. Ulibarri who was given a check for five hundred dollars. She graciously accepted this thoughtfulness with a nod of her head. Mr. Goldfarb continued, "To my doctor, Dr. Evangel I bequest to him my Queen Ann chairs and two airplane tickets to anywhere he and his wife would like to visit in Europe. This money has been set aside in escrow." On and on the reading went until it came to Karen. In his deep voice, Dr. Goldfarb read out loud, "To my granddaughter Karen I leave one dollar. It is time for her to make her own way."

Karen started to cry. "I'm going to be sixty-three next week and I'm broke!" Staring at Mr. Goldfarb, she continued, "I'm going to die! I have no money! None! What am I going to do? What!" Tears flowed down her face, spreading black mascara smudges on her cheeks.

Mr. Goldfarb handed her a box of tissues. Greedily she took the box only to throw it at him. "No, I don't need tissue! I need money! Damn that woman! Damn her to hell!" Mrs. Ulibarri knelt beside Karen putting her arm around her shoulders, "You don't mean that. You're just upset. Things will work out, you'll see." Karen shoved Mrs. Ulibarri away from her. "Leave me alone! All of you leave me alone!" Stepping over Mrs. Ulibarri's fallen body, Karen stood facing the room.

"No! No! How could she do this? I took care of her these last weeks! I fixed her food, wiped her bottom and did what she asked, and this is how she repays my kindness? She swore she would help me out with my debts! She swore to me!"

A deep stern voice came from the back of the room. The late arriver in the new suit stood, "Karen, sit down and be quiet. Show some respect if not for your grandmother then for yourself. You are acting like a fool. Sit down!

Mr. Goldfarb continued, "To my son Justin Sullivan, I leave our house, the house he grew up in and deserted. It is to be his house with property taxes paid for the next twenty-five years out of an escrow account set up in his name. Also, Justin is to receive a monthly stipend of six hundred dollars a month for his personal needs. His father's car is for his use and the insurance is paid for and will be paid for out of the escrow account. Justin, welcome home, dear." Karen turned in her chair to glare at the man. "You! You're my father who deserted me!"

Continuing on, Mr. Goldfarb held up another typed page, "Donna Pino McGuire is receiving a sum of five thousand dollars as a scholarship fund for her daughter Fleur. Also, Ms. McGuire is to receive a sum of eight thousand dollars to be used as she sees fit to better her life."

Mr. Goldfarb put this last piece of paper down, placing it in a brown folder, he announced. "This is the termination of the reading

TERESA PIJOAN

of Edna Sullivan's will. Thank you for coming. Those of you who are receiving monies, please stay behind for you will need to sign papers validating your agreement to accept checks made to you by this office in Mrs. Gilbert's name."

Jumping up, out of her chair she angrily strode over to Donna who was sitting patiently in the back of the room. Karen pointed her finger directly into Donna's face, "You, you are a liar, a thief and a murderer! You were the one who killed my grandmother! You are going to jail! I swear to you, you shall pay for what you have done!" The small cloth purse sitting in Donna's lap was grabbed by Karen who quickly turned it upside down spreading all the items on the floor around Donna's feet. Karen glared at Donna to say through clenched teeth, "I shall kill you! You, bitch! I shall kill you dead!" She tossed the purse on the floor at Donna's feet to storm out of the room.

Mr. Goldfarb watched in silence. Karen's father stood tall in his new suit as he nodded to Mr. Goldfarb. The two men spoke quietly. Papers were signed, exchanged with a handshake and a smile. Justin Sullivan discreetly departed the room. "Ms. McGuire, I will need your signature here and then I will be able to give you your check and the number to the escrow account. Edna thought you were wonderful and patient with her. She wanted to thank you for your help in writing her memoirs."

Ten minutes later, Donna Pino McGuire stepped out of the lawyer's building into the blinding bright sun. Bird song sang out as she went down the steps. The wind had finally stopped. Piles of dried leaves did not move as she walked to her dark blue truck. Donna carefully placed her small purse on the passenger seat of the truck. Windows were closed, doors were locked as Donna started the old truck. What a thoughtful kind elderly woman Edna was! How kind of her!

# 3

Sophia stretched in her cozy bed. She was covered in cats. She heard the cellphone chirping in the kitchen. Sliding her feet into her cozy grey slippers, she hurried to the kitchen, tripping over an orange cat who was meowing. The phone was in her hand before the last ring. "Hello?"

"Hey, Sophia, it's Robert Glacie, your boss. Do you have a minute? You sound as if you were running." The deep voice of the U.S. History professor at the University cleared his throat as he waited for her answer.

"Yes. What's up? How's that old truck of yours doing?" Sophia smiled to herself as she remembered all the times Robert's old blue Ford truck was found dead by the side of the road with one problem or another.

"Truck is fine, thank goodness. Listen, would there be a chance you could take my U.S. History class tomorrow at ten in the morning? I've just become engaged to a beautiful young woman and I need to be with her in Colorado Springs tonight. You're my first choice to sub my class and since all the students love you, are you up for it?"

Laughing, Sophia said, "Yes, absolutely. Can you email me your notes since I'm way out here in the outback? Your notes are great and precise. I don't have to give a quiz or anything, right?"

"No, and yes. I will email you my notes and do have fun with them as I know you will. No quizzes or tests are to be given. This is full class of seventy or so students in the lecture hall 101 in the Academic Building." There was a pause as Robert blew his nose, "Oh, and by the way would you be able to come to my wedding?"

Hesitantly, Sophia asked, "Robert, you want me to come to your wedding? I'm sure I don't know the bride. Also, you sound as if you have a cold. Should you be getting married with a bad cold?"

Robert blew his nose, "Sorry, no, it's not a cold. I'm allergic to my neighbor's long-haired cat. He is going to house sit for me and he had to bring his cat with him. It will take me a week to get all the fur out, but it's worth it. He loves my dog and my dog doesn't mind his cat so all is good." There was a loud sneeze.

Moving the cellphone away from her ear, Sophia thought to ask, "Where is the wedding being held and what should I bring? I mean, you are a dear friend, and I want to support you. Please, tell me more?"

Clearing his throat, he explained, "The wedding is taking place on Pike's Peak in Colorado, by Colorado Springs. Karen is my bride-to-be, and she is a love. We just met and she's my dream woman. Evidently, she knows your brother, and I won't hold that against her, and you shouldn't either."

Sighing, Sophia queried, "Why Pike's Peak for heaven's sake?"

Huffing, Robert said, "Well, she wants to learn how to rappel. Oh, bring your gear. Even though the snow is deep up there this time of year, we can still rappel over on the west side. Evidently, there is a glorious drop with incredible sights. You should bring really warm winter clothes as well. The wedding is being officiated by one of my students who is a practicing minister. This will be great fun! You'll love it as you love the outdoors."

A black and white cat walked into Sophia's kitchen howling as it rubbed against Sophia's ankles. "Robert, are you sure you want to get married so quickly? Do you really know this woman? How old is she, first and second, what is her full name and what does she do?"

"I knew you would ask. I thought my first and only wife was my true love forever and forever. Karen is different. She has orange hair and is....I would say, a full-fledged hippy type. She loves Stephen dog and is great in bed and knows how to cook flan. Her laugh is contagious. Oh, Sophia, you will love her! Trust me, I know what I'm doing."

"Fine, Robert, but how old is she? Remember you are seventy-two years old and not a spring chicken. How old is she and what does she do to live independently at this stage of life?"

"Okay, okay, she's sixty-three, but she looks forty. She speaks kindly of her parents. Especially of her grandmother who just died. Her parents are coming to the wedding as well. I haven't spoken to them yet, but Karen says they are lovely people and want what's best for her. Please, Sophia, trust me! I know what I'm doing."

"Robert, I will take your class tomorrow, which will end at eleven forty-five. When is this wedding and will I have enough time to load up all my gear and get to Colorado Springs? Where should I meet up with you guys?"

Robert sneezed into the phone, "Sorry, sorry, it's that cat. My nephew Timothy is flying in tonight from back east. He's the only family I have, we have that is. It's just him and me. I asked him to call you when he comes in and he will pick you up at your farm around noon. He will drive you and your gear to Colorado Springs. He has all the info, don't worry."

"Let me get this straight, Robert. You were so sure that I would say yes that you set all of this up before you called me? Wow, what a hutzpah! What if I said I wouldn't participate in this crazy scheme?"

"Come on, Sophia, how long have we known each other? I got you your first teaching job at the University eighteen years ago when you retired from research. You really don't think I know you?"

Three more cats came into the kitchen. As Sophia was speaking with Robert, she was opening cat food cans. Now there were six cats sitting in her kitchen staring at her as she spooned dollops of food into cat-tin dishes. "Robert, send me the class notes, and I'll see you with Timothy in Colorado Springs. Now you owe me big time!"

Robert laughed as he clicked off. Sophia shook her head as she spoke to the cats, "You do know your mother is a push over. I better call Donna and see if she can fit in house sitting." There was a bark at the back door. The cats' dishes were placed in their proper places as the cats chowed down.

Two large metal bowls were lifted from the floor to be placed on the kitchen table. A freshly cooked bowl of ground turkey was removed from the refrigerator along with two hard boiled eggs and a container of rice. The dog bowls were filled with their goodies along with one scoop of dry food from a container on the floor next to the cupboards. The barks grew louder when they heard the lid on the dry food lift. Sophia took the bowls to the backdoor. Her foot held the wild canines at bay, while she placed their bowls on the ground. One on each side of the door. Quickly, she closed the door behind her.

The day was glorious. A large flock of cranes flew overhead, heading to the river. The high clouds were scarce, and the wind was quiet for once. Sophia hugged herself in the cold weather. Then she bent down to pet the dogs, rubbing thick fur as they stared up at her for more food. "No, that's all you get for breakfast. Let me change into something warmer and we'll go and feed the horses." Slowly, she opened the back door. The cats were sitting in a row waiting for her to open the door.

One by one the felines ran outside as the two dogs came inside to clean up the cat bowls. "Tucker, Sassy, you wait in the kitchen until I'm dressed! You two in here!" she was firm in her orders. Sophia hurried into her bedroom to change into her warmer clothes and boots. The horses were fed their two flakes of alfalfa with one scoop of grain. As they ate, she walked into the stalls, around the horses and opened the back gate to allow them to run into the arena. Geese flew over her head honking in unison. Birds scurried when she walked toward them. They were searching for grain in the wet manure. After mucking out the barn and breaking the ice on the water trough, Sophia went inside to fix her breakfast and check her email.

Heating her hands around a hot cup of tea, she read her email. "Oh, this will be great. We can have the doers and the shafted." She printed Robert's notes, left them on the kitchen table next to her fried eggs, hot cinnamon toast and one sliced tomato. "Today, I shall have to get things in order." After her call confirming that her youngest daughter Donna was able to farm sit for her, Sophia started packing her backpack with her necessaries. Shaking her head as she packed thermal socks, she said to the room, "This woman knows Granger. This is terrifying. I will say nothing, nothing, nothing, yet this is something to watch!"

Thursday morning, Sophia walked down the main aisle of the lecture hall noticing the students. Many had their notebooks out, some were studying their cellphones, and others were chatting and laughing. Her valise was placed flat on the table at the front of the room. The attendance sheet was taken to the last person in the hall. Students turned to watch her walk back to the front. "I gather that most of you have read the notice on the door regarding my reason for being here." Taking a black marker from the lip of the white board, she wrote "Sophia, your history storyteller." Some of the students clapped.

"All right, now, let's see. Today we are going to build an oligarchy. We shall need three people to be the proper antagonists, and one person to be the protagonist and four people to be the victim starters and the rest of you are the victims. This is how it is going to play out." Lifting a fat group of papers from her valise she placed them on the lip of the white board. Every seat in the lecture hall was filled. Sophia walked down the aisle. She stopped and pointed to a young man in his twenties. "You, sir, shall be our protagonist. Would you mind stepping to the front of the room in front of the white board?"

He laughed, walked around the other students to greet her. "My name is Tim Dunn. It would be my pleasure, Ma'am." Sophia immediately flinched, "Listen all of you, please call me Sophia, but please, please, do not call me Ma'am. I am no one's Ma'am, therefore, you do not need to call me such. Let's keep this light, shall we?" Tim put out his hand to her, "Yes, Sophia, I'll see you up front." She shook his hand. Pointing to another student, a woman who appeared to be in her forties, she asked, "Excuse me, would you please be the wealthy woman behind this endeavor?"

The woman shook her head, "If it's all right with you, I'd rather watch." Sophia smiled, "Yes, no problem." She patted another woman of about thirty on the shoulder who was sitting on an inside seat, "How about you? Are you up for a radical play?" The young woman stood up immediately, "Yeah. My name is Maddie Gonzales, and it would give me great pleasure to work with Tim." The other students laughed. Sophia walked to the front of the lecture hall to pick out another student. This was an older woman who appeared to be in her sixties or seventies. She put her books on her seat and walked to the white board to stand next to Maddie and Tim.

Sophia returned to the whiteboard. "All right, before we jump right into this production, let's review what Dr. Glacie was expounding upon in here." She picked up the black marker and wrote 'oligarchy' on the board in large letters. "Our government was once a democracy. A democracy is defined as what? Who can tell us?" A perky young man in the front row raised his hand, "It is government by the people, for the people and works for the people. A government chosen by the people to represent them fully."

"Bravo! Who knows what an oligarchy is?"

Another student in the left middle side of the lecture hall stood to explain, "An oligarchy is a country run by the few who are rich and powerful. The people lose all rights and all choices for these are made by the rich and powerful who were not chosen by the people but are the ones who control the people."

Rolling the black marker between her palms, Sophia said, "Exactly. Now we are going to find out just how that works. Tim over here is a

39

charismatic man. He has a middle income, but his rich aunt has a friend with a goal. This aunt, who right now is of little importance aside from knowing the other woman, introduces her nephew to the rich woman." Sophia had Tim step forward along with the older woman. Putting her hand on the woman's arm, she asked, "We didn't get your name?"

Smiling, the woman said softly, "I'm Alexis Cook. I'm sixty-nine and proud of it." Sophia put out her hand, "Hey, we're the same age and we don't show it, right?"

"Right. Now I'm the rich aunt. What do I do now with this young kid?"

Tim shook his head, "Hey, I'm charismatic, don't mess with me."

The class laughed. Sophia continued with her presentation, "There are patterns in life with causes. In order for things to be set in motion, this cause needs to have some form of legitimacy. These causes do not happen on their own, nor do they happen in a vacuum. In order for this cause to strike issue with the many, there is a need for people to make this happen. One person, ten persons, a few hundred people who are capable of being and setting in motion a cause."

Sophia wrote on the white board, "Look back at 'World War I and then check out World War II.' Charismatic leaders who basically had no financial ability took power. How did this happen? We'll walk through this." Again she wrote on the white board, "Rebellion. There must be a need for rebellion. Either starving masses or a huge population that is uncomfortable with the present form of government. An innate desire for radical change."

She wrote again, "Disappointment. This can be due to Inflation, depression, lack of jobs, with poor social economic population with illnesses on the rise. The importance of rebellion is for the population to be illiterate or misinformed or not informed at all of what the government is doing. This unrest leaves the population vulnerable. All sorts of things can cause rebellion, a desire for freedom, freedom of speech, freedom of religious worship, again a series of related patterns.

This leads a huge population of people to embrace emigration to other countries, to form new religions, very often as full of tyranny as the forms of religion they had desired to leave behind. It's the magnetic power that a very few men have. This charisma can lead youth or people with little education to follow and make extraordinary achievements."

Sophia went to the whiteboard to write, 'Revolution.' Taking

Maddie aside, Sophia continued, "One person with a wealthy bank account achieves more wealth by gathering a group of wealthy people to follow their beliefs."

Sophia walked over to Tim, "Here comes our charismatic leader. He's young, he's smart, but not too smart for he needs to be manipulated. He's someone every young person wants to become." She pushed Tim forward, "His voice becomes the voice of rebellion."

Taking Tim by the hand, she led him into the middle of the lecture hall. "Now on this side of the room, we have the angry population. You guys are all poor, unemployed and can't get anywhere in life. You listen to him and believe he can guide you to a better lifestyle and perhaps make you rich, but you must rebel. Right, Tim?"

Standing tall with his chin in the air, he called out, "You guys follow me, and I'll make you so rich you won't believe it! Follow me, gang." Sophia nodded, "Yes, he has money for all of you if you follow him, right Tim?" Lowering his voice, Tim expounded, "Damn straight! You guys are going to get rich. I'll make you rich! I am the chosen one!" Raising his hands with his arms open, he called out, "You are my people! I love you all!"

Alexis called to Tim from the stage, "Hey, you're my puppet, get back up here. I'm the one calling the shots. Get yourself back here, young man!"

Sophia clapped her hands, "Exactly. Alexis, you're the one with the money. Tim, you don't have a penny to your name. You were picked by Alexis to be the voice. You better do what she wants." Tim trotted back to stand next to Alexis.

Maddie made a face, "Hey, what about me? What role do I play?" Alexis put her arm around Maddie's shoulders, "You are the one who makes all the money for this guy. You ask for donations; you plan the parties where the rich pay ten thousand dollars for a dinner plate or a day with this great person called Tim."

Sophia walked onto the stage by the white board, "Right. Maddie, without you none of this would happen. Class, do you see how these three are all interconnected? Each one is vital to this role of revolution." Pointing the right side of the lecture hall, she reiterated, "You are the followers of Tim, right?" The students all clapped and pointed to Tim. Sophia went on, "But what about this side of the room? What do these people do? Does anyone know?"

TERESA PIJOAN

A woman in bib-overalls stood up, "We're the ones who don't want a revolution. We want to solve the problem logically and without bloodshed." Another student stood, this young man had a goatee and long blonde hair, he said, "We are the ones who aren't fooled by those guys. Besides, we have money and don't need to rebel. Right?"

Sophia wrote on the whiteboard and circled the word, 'Power.' "There needs to be something behind all of this and that is power. Power comes with backing and backing must have money. In order to produce an army, one needs soldiers that will blindly follow with armaments, tools to secretly communicate and the ability to move things from one place to another without notice. All of this takes up a lot of money and with this money comes power. Unquestioning soldiers are in place those who will follow blindly and with enthusiasm."

Pointing to the word Oligarchy on the white board, Sophia went on to explain, "Alexis has the money and thus she has the power. Alone, she cannot achieve her goal. Her money could be used up in a heartbeat. She needs to have a steady flow of income, a surplus of money for propaganda and advertising. All of this can come from other countries. Countries that want your country to fail, to falter and lose their governmental power.

"Thus, she needs Maddie who will buy low and sell high, those who want to be known as rich and powerful. Those who will hobnob with Tim and want him to benefit them financially if he wins. All this needs startup money for Alexis who gives the power to Tim. Maddie continually works this being paid well by Alexis.

"Tim is the people's leader. He's not all that bright, but he follows orders and gives orders with a silvery tongue. He's paid well, too. The followers follow blindly. Their reward is a compliment from Tim. Those who follow in Tim's close circle can receive goods for high paying jobs."

One of the students on the left side of the room stood up, "Yes, but what can we do to stop all of this? We don't approve of them or what they're doing. What are they doing?"

Clapping her hands, she asked the right side of the room, "What are you doing over there?"

A tall older man stood, "We are overthrowing the government, taking Fort Knox and going to run things our way. We want to be rich!"

Walking over to him, Sophia shook his hand, "Bravo, yes, all of you want money and power, too." Then she walked to the other side of the room, "How are you going to stop them? Remember with money comes power. If the people do not have the money, do they have power?"

The student with the goatee answered, "We can stop them with knowledge. We'll educate them and they'll know they're following the wrong side." Sophia walked to him and shook his hand, "Yes, that's a start. This is, however, how an oligarchy starts. It is by now already ingrained into the government, the culture and everyone's way of life. Tim will become a president and all the other millionaires behind Alexis will become his staff. You lose and they gain everything. You've lost. No matter if you vote, your votes won't count. No matter if you have a constitution, it no longer is followed. In a nutshell, you've lost. You have lost."

Glancing at the large clock at the back of the lecture hall, Sophia noticed there were eighteen minutes to go in this class. "Tell you what, why don't you figure out how to break this oligarchy? I'm going to let you ask questions to see how you can get to Alexis and her team."

The time flew by quickly. The final solution appeared to be the demise of Alexis, Maddie and Tim. One was done in with poison, another was shot with a gun and Maddie was bumped off with an overdose of bad drugs. When the class finished, the students stood and applauded. Sophia was handed the sign-in sheet. She turned the lights off as she walked out of the room. Two students met her in the hall, "Wow, Sophia, we really enjoyed your class today. Are you coming back to lecture in another class?"

"Thank you, but no. Sadly, I was involuntarily retired. Today was fun for me as well. Thank you for the compliment." The student Maddie walked beside her as she darted out of the double glass doors to the outside. Dr. Ortega quickly followed Sophia and the two students outside. "Dr. Pino! Dr. Pino! Please, I need a word with you!" Dr. Ortega all but ran to catch Sophia. "You are not welcome on this campus. You know this and I know this, so what are you doing here?" The principal's face was red from exertion.

Sophia turned to address her, "Dr. Robert Glacie asked me to take this class. He is in the process of getting married. Since we have worked together for years, he felt it appropriate. Do you have an issue with his choice?"

Dr. Ortega shook her head, "He needed to ask me first. There are other professors who are perfectly capable of taking his class besides you! You are not welcome here. Please leave!" She turned in a huff and scurried back into the building.

The other student beside Maddie asked, "What was that all about?"

Smiling, Sophia said, "My brother Granger sent her phony emails to get me involuntarily retired. There's nothing she can do when Dr. Glacie invites me to teach his class. He has tenure and is the head of the Humanities Department. Just ignore this."

The student put out her hand, "Hi, I'm Andrea. I loved your class. My boyfriend sent me google searches about your brother when he came to teach his class on healing herbs. He started with a full classroom and ended up with an empty class. It was almost sad."

Maddie spoke up, "Yeah, he spewed knowledge to us about being Buddhist while Andrea's boyfriend sent us news of his golden Mercedes with green leather seats. When Granger told us he had never been sick a day in his life, Raymond sent us news of your brother getting chemo in jail for prostate cancer. By the time the class was almost halfway done, most of the students walked. What a slimy hypocrite."

The three reached Sophia's old SUV. She put the key in the driver's door to unlock it. Maddie bent over appearing to be having some sort of fit. Sophia put her hand on Maddie's back, "Are you all right? Do you need help?" Maddie stood upright. She was desperately trying to hold back a laughing fit. She blurted out, "I can't help it." She giggled, "You're the one with the old beat-up vehicle, not your brother the Buddhist!" Tears ran down her face as she laughed. "Wow!"

Sophia patted the hood, "This vehicle is more than forty years old and is still running like a fine tooled watch." Andrea pulled Maddie aside, "You see, old age doesn't mean anything. If something works, it can work forever."

Smiling, Sophia answered, "Damn straight. Now, you will have to excuse me, I seriously need to get home to prepare for Dr. Robert's wedding." Wiping her eyes, Maddie let Andrea pull her back to the educational building.

# 4

Relaxed and relieved that the class had gone well, Sophia drove home to the South Valley. Her two pups—Tucker and Sassy met her as she walked through her front gate. "Hey, guys, today is a good day!" Patting them with loads of kisses, she quickly stood, "Oh, guys, I have to get everything ready to leave. You both be nice to Donna. I know she spoils you rotten, but please, make her feel at home!"

The front door slammed shut as the two dogs were barking a welcome. Sophia's youngest daughter Donna called out as she walked down the hall, "Mom! Where are you?" She soon found out as she turned the corner into Sophia's bedroom. Sophia was sitting on the floor holding one of her hiking boots. "Mom, what are you doing on the floor and why are your boots in a plastic bag?"

"Hi, Sweetheart, hey, thank you for looking after things while I'm gone. This should be an interesting adventure." Holding up one of her boots, Sophia explained, "I sprayed them with water repellant this morning. Putting them in a plastic bag afterwards keeps the room from smelling of repellant and helps to saturate the boots." Lifting one to her foot she promptly put one on. "Say, you're looking rather smart in your new scrubs. Are those the ones you got for your birthday?"

Donna came into the room and twirled, "Yes, I do believe the red satin shimmering material makes me look thinner. The animals like it as well for it doesn't show all the blood from the surgeries." Donna sat on the edge of the bed beside her mother, "Today was vaccine day at the vet hospital. We had eleven dogs and eight cats. Last Thursday, we had double the number. For free vaccines, you'd think we could vaccinate the whole county, but people just don't take advantage of this offer." There was loud honking in front of the house, bringing another cacophony of dog barking.

Donna stood to walk back to the front door. Sophia pushed on her other boot and stood up to finish rolling her clothes into her backpack. A man's deep voice was heard speaking with Donna. Sophia zipped up her backpack, stomped on her boots to make certain they were firmly tied and proceeded to the front room. There stood a tall man with a clean-shaven face in a red plaid shirt with thick trousers that had numerous pockets. He and Donna both turned as Sophia came to them, "I am believing you to be Timothy Turpin, the best man of this great adventure?"

"You would happen to be correct. And this lovely young woman is your daughter?"

Donna blushed, "Yes, I'm her daughter. Listen, you two get acquainted. I have to get back to the vet clinic. Mom, all I need is the spare key and the feeding directions. Would it be all right if tomorrow I rode Storm? He's looking desperate for some company aside from River Shore."

Sophia moved into the kitchen, "Here are the directions all printed out. As for Storm, it would be wonderful if you took him for a good long ride. River Shore may get all uppity, but that's life. Unless you want to halter him behind you? Although, he is so much bigger than Storm, perhaps not." Sophia reached into the glass cupboard, "Here is the key to the front door. The back door spare key is in the tack room hanging next to the tractor keys." Pulling Donna to her, Sophia gave Donna a firm hug, "Please, be nice to your sister while I'm gone. Please, be kind to my mother while I'm gone and do not stay up all night watching movies."

Smiling at her mother, Donna said, "Yes, Mom. Go, have fun! Oh, and Grandma did call me, she wants you to stop by on your way north. She said she has a surprise for you. And Mom, you be kind to grandma, okay?" Taking the keys from her mother's hand, Donna walked around her and Timothy, leaving the two of them staring at each other.

Tucker and Sassy were sitting watching the two humans. Sophia knelt down to them, "Hey, I love you both dearly, dearly, ever so! Please do not tear up any books while I'm gone." The two dogs smiled, wagged their tails and said nothing at all.

Outside in front of the garage, Timothy opened the passenger door of his jeep. The jeep was an older model. It was covered with mud. The windows had been cleaned or attempted to be cleaned with a dirty cloth and the windshield wipers had done a better job on the front windshield.

*Granger's Demise*

Reaching out for Sophia's backpack, he asked, "Do you want your pack in front or in the back?" Sophia put her hand up, "No, actually, I'm going to follow you in my vehicle. I learned early on in life that it is best to have your own transportation when dealing with the unknown."

"Oh, you don't trust me? Or you don't trust my driving?"

"Neither. I feel more secure when I have my own means of transportation. We have no idea what we are getting ourselves into, correct?" Sophia nodded to her older SUV parked next to the jeep. Her SUV was clean and waxed, the windows were spotless, and the tires were the only thing with a trace of dirt. "This has nothing to do with you or with Robert. This is my own personal hang up. Please, forgive me if this sounds selfish, for it is, but I also have to go by my mother's for some reason. It would not be wise to have you meet her as well."

Timothy put his hands up as a sign of submission, "Fine. No problem. I just felt some animosity coming from you, but if that is not the case, let us proceed to this strange event." He slammed the passenger door of the jeep. "Would you mind if I followed you or you could follow me or we could at least pretend to be with one another on the open road in case something would happen?" He walked around Sophia's vehicle, patting the hood he asked, "How old is this war horse?"

Sophia opened the passenger door to toss in her backpack. She had already put her water bottles in the holders in the front of the dash. There were two blankets rolled on the backseat and her tent and sleeping bag were rolled together and stacked beside the blankets. "This vehicle is close to forty-two years old and has never missed a day's work, if you must know. This vehicle has withstood many a trauma and like it, we have both weathered life well." She laughed as she pointed to his jeep, "Your jeep appears to be doing well in the mud."

"A muddy jeep is a happy jeep, that's my motto." Timothy jumped in the driver's seat of his jeep.

The two dogs barked at the closed gate, hoping to go for a long walk. Sophia walked to the gate, knelt to pet them, "I'll see you two, in a couple of hours. Perhaps a day or two, so be good, love life and again, do not eat any books." She stood up to walk around Timothy's jeep. "I'll follow you, Timothy, since you know where we are going once on the road to Colorado. Although, you will have to follow me to my mother's."

The two vehicles stayed close together as Sophia turned off of I-25 onto the frontage road leading to Calavera. Sophia noticed that Timothy

47

was thoughtful enough to stay way behind her, giving her space and not eating her back bumper. Parking in front of her mother's falling down mud wall, Sophia quickly jumped out of her vehicle to go through the wrought iron gate. It stuck fast.

Timothy was soon beside her, "Here, let me help." He lifted the wrought iron gate over the stone path. The top hinge came completely unhooked and fell forward. He held it open for Sophia to squeeze through as he attempted to replace the hinge.

The backdoor was locked. Sophia banged on the door, calling out, "Margaret! Margaret, your daughter is here! Please, open the door!" Sophia heard the metal walker scraping towards the back door as it was shoved along on the brick floor. Her mother suddenly appeared coming through the kitchen. The walker was shoved into the kitchen table where it promptly fell over. Margaret gasped as she leaned on the doorknob of the backdoor to open it. "Thank God, it's you! That visiting nurse keeps trying to get into the house. I will not have strangers coming into this house! Sophia, I forbid her to enter!" Margaret pulled out a kitchen chair and fell into it.

Coming in right behind Sophia was Timothy. He smiled as he asked, "Is it all right if I come inside? I fixed your front wrought iron gate. You need to repair the hinges, they're too low and hit the stone path." He put out his hand, "Hi, I'm Timothy Turpin. Sophia's friend. We're going to my uncle's wedding in Colorado. Too bad you can't come with us since your Sophia's mom."

Glaring eyes focused on Timothy, "I am no one's MOM! I am Margaret and you shall refer to me as Margaret, do you understand!" Margaret did not take his hand but continued to glare. Timothy backed out of the door and stood outside. Margaret lifted herself to stand by placing her hands on the kitchen table for purchase. "Sophia, I have the perfect dress for you to wear at this wedding. Come with me."

Sophia lifted the walker and handed it to her mother Margaret. "Here, do you want this?" Margaret huffed, "You can let that young man in if you want to, but let him know in no uncertain terms that my name is Margaret." Under her breath, Sophia responded, "I think he knows that now."

They left Timothy to stand outside. Margaret huffed and puffed her way back down the hall to her bedroom. The room smelled of feces and wet paper. Not choosing to say anything, Sophia watched her mother

48

pull out a lower drawer from her heavy dark wooden bureau. Wrapped in tissue paper, leaden with mothballs was a baby blue dress with a lace collar and lace sleeves. It appeared to be cotton with silk trim around the lace neckline. "Here, take this. You'll be the beauty at the wedding." Waving her hand, she continued, "I know, I know, she is getting married on a mountain, but you could wear this over your long johns." Flinging the dress at Sophia, mothballs scattered across the floor as the tissue paper tore. "This has been in here too long. Here, Sophia, take it, wear it and enjoy looking nice for once in your life!" Margaret's face puckered in an attempted smile, which turned into a grimace. "I'm sure it will fit you if you suck in your tummy. I wore this dress in my youth when I met your father."

Sophia took the dress cautiously, as her mothered moaned, "You are always wearing jeans and sweaters. Don't you have anything decent to wear? You'd think I raised you in a barn!" Sniggering she added, "You look like an old man in those clothes. No one can tell if you even have a figure."

Shoving the walker in front of her, Margaret moved to the bed. The sheets and blankets were pulled back as if she had just risen from the bed. Plopping down firmly on the mattress, Margaret again waved at Sophia, "Go, go, just go! Leave me alone. What am I supposed to do if I have an emergency? Huh, what am I to do? You obviously don't care, so go, just go, go away." Margaret sighed as she leaned back on her pillows, lifting her feet out of her slippers to put them under the sheet and blankets.

Sophia helped her with the quilt, "Margaret, you have Sybil's phone number right there next to your clock. Sybil knows about my leaving, she knows she is on call and she can be here in twenty minutes if you need her." Sophia folded the dress to hold it against her chest. "I'm not going to be gone for very long and you do have my cell number on speed dial if you need to talk." Carefully, moving to the door, Sophia added, "Also, you have Granger's phone number if you need him. He's not far away, right?"

There was a loud gasp from Margaret, "Sophia, you are so cruel. You know your brother is in Montana with his family! You know this and yet you have to rub it in, always, always, putting your brother down! I'm sick of it. I want to be with Granger!" Sobbing uncontrollably, Margaret

TERESA PIJOAN

fell over on her side with her face against the pillow. Sophia remained by the door, "Margaret, I am going now. Please, calm yourself. If you need to talk call Sybil."

Working her way closer to leaving, Sophia watched her mother reach out for her, "Sophia, Sophia, please don't leave me! Your oldest daughter detests me! I know she hates me! Oh, Sophia, what am I to do without Granger?"

There was not a second thought as Sophia turned, walked down the hall, locked the backdoor knob, shut the door firmly to walk back to the wrought iron gate. Timothy was jerry rigging the gate so that it would open with more ease and not scrape the stone path. Sophia shook her head as she met him, "Timothy, you are a sweetheart to fix this, but we really have to go. We must leave now, pronto." Timothy gave the gate another swing to show how it opened now freely. "Well, at least something positive happened here. I didn't mean to be a snoop but I heard your mother screaming at you. Yes, I agree, it would be best to get on the road." He pointed to Sophia's item, "Looks like a lovely dress. Shame it smells of mothballs." He smiled at her.

"Yes, let's go." In her elderly SUV, Sophia followed Timothy's dirty jeep back to the interstate. They drove one in front of the other all the way to Wagon Mound. There they pulled into the gas station to fill up with gas. Timothy hurried inside to come out with two hot beef burritos and two cups of coffee. He handed one of each to Sophia who was still filling up her vehicle. Smiling, Sophia took the burrito, "You drink the coffee. I'm a tea drinking girl. Besides, I'm all right. Are we making good time?"

Timothy chewed on his burrito, "Yep, we're doing all right. You know, I never thought you'd have short hair and that you were so tall. Robert gave the impression that you were a long-haired beauty. He was most infatuated with you for years and years."

Frowning, Sophia put the nozzle back in the gas hold. "Oh, now I'm not a raving beauty, is that what you're saying?" She touched her lower lip, "You have more burrito on your chin than in your mouth." He laughed, wiping his mouth with a paper napkin, "Not saying that at all. You are younger than I imagined. I thought you were in your sixties, like me, but obviously I was wrong."

"No, you're right. I'm sixty-nine and proud of it! I worked hard to get here as did your uncle. We have fallen off many a cliff, suffered a few serious issues, but hey, we are still going strong." Sophia wiped her hand on her jeans. "So, you're in your sixties as well?"

"Absolutely. Sixty-four and like you, proud of it. I worked hard to get here, although I didn't fall off any cliffs or down any caves. My life has been filled with love, loss and finding out I have a wonderful uncle who still remembers me and wants me back in his life." Timothy gloated as he took another bite. The red chili sauce dripped down his chin, "Damn, this is a messy burrito." Sophia smiled as she jumped onto the driver's seat of her vehicle.

51

# 5

The drive was long and tedious, broken only by the amazing scenery. There were airplanes flying overhead with airplanes stationed in huge lots and signs stating restricted areas all along the main road. The two vehicles pulled into a Marriott hotel off the main road. As Timothy jumped out of the jeep, Robert emerged from a hotel door. He waved at the two of them. Sophia quickly made a call to Sybil letting her know she had arrived safely and to keep aware of Margaret's needs.

Robert all but pulled Sophia out of her vehicle to give her a huge bear hug. "Damn, it's good to see you!" He squashed her between his arms and his body. Sophia pushed him away, "Robert, I need to breathe." As she regained her footing, she studied his face. The man was absolutely beaming with joy.

He took her hand, "Come, come and meet my beautiful bride. We have separate rooms since this is the law of the land on the night before a wedding. I put you in with Karen. Timothy and I will bunk together so we can catch up on our lives." He kept tugging on Sophia, "Do you know Timothy and I have only spoken on the phone? I haven't seen him since he was sixteen years old and was involved with a drug addict. Come, Sophia, move, let me introduce to you the most beautiful woman in the world."

Sophia followed him into a dark room. The curtains were pulled shut on the double front windows. There was only one light on between the twin beds. Standing by the television, which appeared to have been just shut off, was a woman of an age with orange hair that had purple ends. She was wearing a long, tie-dyed dress of many colors. The first impression Sophia had of this woman was her nose. It was a huge bulbous nose. Her eyes were small with her long bangs dripping down almost into her eyes. She appeared to be frozen in place.

TERESA PIJOAN

Standing between the two women, Robert did the introductions, "Karen, this is my longtime friend and associate in many of my adventures and someone who is going to be your matron of honor. Come, meet Sophia!" Robert put his hands out to each of the women, "Come on, meet and greet!" Sophia decided to move forward holding out her hand with a smile on her face, "Hello, Karen. How lovely to meet the woman who has caught this most eligible bachelor!"

There was no movement from Karen, but she did say, "Hello." Robert clapped his hands, "Well, there you go. I'm going to talk to Timothy." He stepped around Sophia to leave the room through the open door. Sophia followed him.

Timothy was unloading his pack and was moving to Sophia's vehicle, "Do you want me to get your pack and bring it inside?" Sophia shook her head. "No, I think I need to talk to Robert first. You do what you do, I'll do my thing once I've spoken to Robert."

The room next door was filled with light. The curtains were open, and all the lights were on inside. One of the beds appeared to have been used. Robert was getting a drink of water at the open bathroom sink. He looked in the mirror as Sophia entered. "I don't know what got into her. We were doing so well and suddenly, she's gone cold. Do you think she wants to cancel the wedding?" His face was red with perspiration. He gulped another glass of water. "Sophia, what if she wants to cancel?"

Moving to him, Sophia put her arms around his waist with her cheek against his back, "No, she's just scared. She'll be fine. I'm sorry. Don't you worry, we'll all get along like a house on fire. Meeting us probably made everything become more real." Sophia gave him another hug. "I'll go talk to her. Listen, Robert, Timothy and I are starving. Do you think we could go and get something to eat? Food is always a good ice breaker. What do you say? Do you know a good place to eat around here?"

Timothy dropped a pack on one of the twin beds. "Yeah, I'm hungry. When do I get to meet this prefect woman?" The water glass was put down. Robert turned to his nephew, "First I need a hug, then let's get Karen and go for a fine fancy wedding dinner."

The restaurant was filled with Air Force personnel. Robert had asked for a table away from the mass of people in uniforms. The four of them sat at a table with a white tablecloth, linen napkins and a menu of two pages. Robert ordered a bottle of champagne, steaks for the four of them with baked potatoes and asparagus. Fresh made bread rolls were placed in the center of the table with sliced butter paddies in four different dishes.

Raising his champagne glass high, Timothy said, "Here's to the loving couple on the night prior to their wedding! Bravo, to you both!" Karen proceeded to empty her glass and ask for more. The dinner conversation was directed to the past. Robert spoke of his life in Ohio and his affection for Timothy's father, his brother.

There were several bottles of champagne emptied thanks to Karen who appeared to appreciate each bottle more than anyone else at the table. As dessert was being served, a thick order of chocolate mousse with a high topping of whipped cream, Karen finally started to speak. She held up her half empty glass of champagne to say, "Thank you all for coming to our wedding. I never thought I would ever get married nor did I believe my nose would make it to the altar! Never once has Robert mentioned my nose and neither one of you." Waving her hands over the table, she declared, "You are truly my friends!" The half empty glass of champagne was drunk with gusto and she asked for more.

55

Robert's hand was put over her glass, "Karen that is enough. Tomorrow, you need to be sober and ready for a most important event. Perhaps it's time for us to head to bed." Spoons were licked clean of the chocolate as everyone jumped into Timothy's jeep. At the hotel, the four were divided into two's. Robert blew his wife-to-be a kiss as he watched Karen and Sophia disappear into their room.

Sophia hung up her mother's blue dress in the closet. She unpacked her toiletry pack and headed to the open bathroom sink. Karen collapsed on the bed closest to the door. She rolled over and started to snore. Sophia brushed her teeth, did her necessaries and tried to wake Karen who only rolled over, grabbing the pillow to hug.

With the cellphone in her hand, Sophia walked outside to the far side of the hotel building. The loud noise of helicopters roared overhead as she punched in Donna's cellphone number. On the third ring, Donna answered. "Hi, Sweetie, its Mom, how're things at the farm?"

"Mom, what's wrong? What's going on? You never call unless somethings up. What's up?" Donna's voice sounded serious and concerned.

"Oh, dear, Donna, the bride may be someone you know. Once you spoke to me about the lovely Edna Sullivan who you were helping to write her memoirs? Do you remember?"

"Of course, Mom, she was such a kind and delicate woman who accomplished so much in her lifetime. Why do you ask?"

"You spoke of her granddaughter. The granddaughter with the large bulbous nose, remember?"

"Yes, of course. The woman was a greedy cad, always coming around begging for money. Her name is Karen Sullivan. Mom, what's going on? Tell me?"

"The woman with the large nose is here. She is to be the bride of Robert's love life. I'm sharing a room with her. She drank three bottles of champagne practically by herself and now she is passed out on her bed fully dressed, snoring away and tomorrow is her wedding day!"

"No, Mom, no. It can't be the same woman. The woman I was talking about had orange mango colored hair with dipped purple ends. She was or is an old hippy, wearing tie-dyed clothes and wore flip flops everywhere even in the winter. This cannot be the same woman." Donna's voice was strong in her belief.

Sophia shook her head as she spoke, "Donna, this is the same woman. Orange hair and all with bare feet passed out on the bed. Do I say anything to Robert or do I just go along with this charade?"

There was a moment of silence, "Mom, I was at the reading of Edna's will. This Karen woman did not get a single dime from Edna. Not a dime. She must be frantic for money for I understood she had debts she couldn't pay."

Donna sneezed, "Evidently, Karen's mother died when she was young and her father couldn't take care of Karen for some reason. He inherited his mother's everything. From what the other's in the room told me later, Karen went to Las Vegas to try to pick up some rich guy. Is Robert wealthy? Because I didn't think he was rolling in dough since he's a professor at the university and their pay is pathetic."

Donna cleared her throat, "Mom, you can't get involved in this. Do not get involved, do you hear me? She was once one of Granger's pupils. This Karen told Edna all about how great Uncle Slime Bucket is and even taunted her with his teas, which may or may not have killed Edna." Donna could be heard pacing, "Mom, do not get involved! According to her grandmother, Karen was a spoiled only child who constantly insisted on getting her way no matter what. Your life could be in jeopardy. Leave this alone."

"Donna, dear, I am the matron of this marriage. I can't just walk away now. Robert wants me to participate. He claims he truly loves her. He holds undeniable love for this woman! I can't walk away from this now that I'm here and Robert is so excited and happy!"

"You have your own vehicle, Mom. Pick up your backpack and drive home now. Please, please, Mom, please, this woman is pure poison."

Turning, Sophia noticed Timothy walking toward her with his cellphone against his ear. "Donna, I must go. I am staying for Robert not for this Karen woman. Thanks for the heads up and I will be careful, seriously careful. Have a good ride tomorrow. I love you!" Sophia closed her cellphone as Timothy walked to her. "Well, well, we have a cold-hearted bride. Were you able to thaw the bride for tomorrow?"

"No. She is passed out on the bed, fully dressed, oblivious to life itself. How are you doing with Robert?" Sophia leaned against the side of the building.

"Robert is truly smitten. Sophia, somehow, I do not feel she is being honest or truthful with Robert. He is truly in love, totally infatuated without a doubt. I wish we could get some warmth from the ice queen in there. She says she loves him and wants to marry him. But, there is this feeling as if something is missing." Timothy leaned against the building's wall next to Sophia, "What about you? What kind of vibe are you getting?"

She turned to look at him, "Nothing, not a thing. If I didn't know better I would think she was dead inside. There is no bounce, no joy, nothing." She continued, "I don't trust her, but we're doing this for Robert, right? This is about his happiness. He must have found some flicker of life in her to want to marry her for he's not an idiot, right?"

They heard someone approaching. Robert peered around the corner, "Hi, you two. Are you having a romantic interlude? Weddings do this to people."

Timothy had his back to Robert, but appeared to feel his coming presence. Quickly speaking, Timothy said, "You know when you and your mother were discussing the dress you should wear tomorrow, I was outside walking around. Over by the ancient wood pile covered with spider webs and sawdust was a large black dog lying in the sun."

57

TERESA PIJOAN

Slowly, turning toward Robert, he continued, "At first, I thought the dog was dead since he didn't move as I came closer. When I knelt to touch him, his tail started to wag. It moved just slightly, enough for me to appreciate he was still alive. Is this dog your mother's?"

Sophia nodded, "Yes. That's Gizzy, my mother's dog. He is a large Rottweiler and is seventeen years old. He has chronic diabetes, heart issues and has cancer of the intestines. My mother refuses to put him down even though he is in pain." Sophia put her fingers through her short hair of curls. "My mother swears that if I put Gizzy down I will put her down next."

Robert moved to stand in front of both of them as they were leaning against the hotel wall. He opened his mouth to speak just as a pair of helicopters hovering close to the ground came flying to the right of them on their way to the base. Once the noise settled, Robert spoke, "Your mother, Sophia, is a serious piece of work. I have met her on several occasions. Her southern background allows her to give you a compliment while stabbing you in the back at the same time."

He put his hand on Timothy's shoulder, "Listen, you two, tomorrow there is a specific agenda. Timothy, you are going to drive me to the second landing of the train. The minister and the guitar player will meet us at the landing dock. We can walk up from the parking lot. This is the halfway landing on the mountain. We will leave two hours prior to Sophia and Karen who will ride on the train. Once we are there, Timothy and myself, we will put up the flowers, the cloth over the trellis and make pretty the wedding area."

Dropping his hand to his side, he continued, "Please bring your nice suit up with you. We will be leaving here, the hotel, at two o'clock in the afternoon. The wedding is to be at five o'clock, just prior to sunset when the sky will be a glorious shade of orange and reds."

Interrupting him, Sophia asked, "Karen and I take the train? Are we to be dressed in our fancy clothes or do we dress up at the landing? Actually, what are we supposed to be wearing?"

Snickering, Timothy added, "Yes, Robert, if we are going to sleep the first night up on the mountain, are we supposed to wear our long johns under our fancy outfits or do we just wear our winter clothes at the wedding?"

"No, bring your winter clothes with you. You know what, let's load up the jeep now with all that you will need for the camping trip."

He looked at Sophia as the sun was almost completely over the horizon, "If you have your tent, rappelling gear, sleeping bag and your pack ready, let's just load up Timothy's jeep now."

The three of them returned to Karen's hotel room. Karen was still unconscious asleep on the bed. She was softly snoring into the pillow. Sophia handed Robert her sleeping bag with her tent rolled up into one bundle. The stakes for the tent were in a plastic bag tied around the whole bundle. Timothy removed the blue dress Margaret had given Sophia, from the closet leaving the hanger. "Here, you can roll this up to put in your pack. What shoes are you planning to wear with this dress?"

The blue dress was taken away as Sophia laughed, "I can't wear this dress. It is too small and there is no way it will even go over my shoulders. My sweet mother is delusional. But, yes, I'll roll it up in the pack." As she rolled it on the bed, she turned to look at Robert, "Are we keeping the hotel rooms or are we checking out in the early afternoon?"

He walked to the hotel door. Closing it, he studied the information paper on the back of it. "Well, if we check out, we need to leave by eleven in the morning." There was a loud sonic boom shaking the hotel. The sound was deafening. Robert put up his hand, waited for the quiet before he continued, "Let's keep one hotel room for another night. Just in case something strange happens. What do you think, Timothy?"

Timothy sat on the foot of Karen's bed, "Why don't we move all of our stuff into your room Robert? That way we will only have to pay for one room. I'm sure Sophia needs to get home and my return airplane ticket is for eight o'clock tomorrow night from Albuquerque."

Glaring at Timothy, she asked, "That jeep isn't yours? Did you rent it and then purposely drive through mud?"

Laughing, Timothy answered, "No, it belongs to a friend's of Roberts'. It's a loaner. Yes, I did drive it through mud just to give it that lived in look."

Robert put his hand over his heart "My dear, dear friends, we're really having a wedding! Shall we keep one room during the day tomorrow just in case or should we give up both rooms? What do you say? Should we keep it simple?"

Sophia agreed, "Yes. Let's keep it simple. In the morning after breakfast, we can firm up all the plans when the bride is awake and move everything into Robert's room. Karen and I can put all our wedding clothes in a bag and take it with us on the train to you both."

TERESA PIJOAN

Pointing to Sophia's hiking boots, Robert asked, "What shoes are you going to wear at the wedding? And are you going to wear a dress? Or something more formal? I did hire a young man to take photos of the wedding for keep sake photos." Grinning at Sophia, he added, "Knowing you as I do, you were probably planning to wear your long johns, your boots and your old hiking parka at the wedding."

Taken aback by his abrasive tone, Sophia stared at Robert. His scraggly beard, his long grey moustache of grey mixed with red, his head was a crown of red hair with a bald head at the top gave him the appearance of an old hermit. The faded blue nylon parka with darker blue patches on the elbows and his grey turtleneck with faded blue jeans did not bring about an air of decorum for a formal wedding. She looked at his feet, "Oh, so you are not going to wear your lucky boots? Hopefully, you did bring a suit and tie, right?"

Interjecting between the two of them, Timothy quipped, "Okay, you two, enough. Let's clear this up right now since I have no idea what I'm supposed to wear as well. Robert, what are you going to wear at your own wedding?"

60

"I brought my university lecture suit with an ascot tie that has no stains. My dress shoes and my black socks will complete my attire. I even brought my new cowboy hat. It is dark and will go nicely with my black and blue herring bone suit. Timothy, what are you wearing to the event?"

Timothy shook his head, "I didn't bring a suit or a tie. I brought my nice pressed dress pants, a starched white shirt and an ascot tie with a paisley print of red and yellow. No hat and I am wearing my dress shoes as they are the only shoes I brought. Sophia, what are you going to be clothed in?"

Both men turned to stare at Sophia, "Believe it or not, I brought a long wool skirt with a heavy blue sweater that comes with a matching wool jacket. I am going to wear heavy tights under the skirt with heavy socks and my boots. So there!" She stuck her tongue out at both of them.

Robert grinned, "I even brought some special herbs to keep me going all night. If you hear a lot of grunting, please ignore it." He walked out the door with Sophia's pack. Timothy mumbled under his breath, "Who would've thought he would need herbs with her." He jutted his chin out to the sleeping Karen.

All night, Sophia lay in the twin bed turning and tossing. As the early morning light filtered through the closed curtains, she finally fell into a deep sleep. A piercing whistle woke her. Sitting up, she tried to locate the location of the horrifying sound. It was coming from the closed bathroom door. Karen's bed was empty.

Someone in the next room of theirs was hitting the wall at the head of her bed. Sophia got up. The room was stifling with heat. Clouds of moisture was billowing out from around the bathroom door. There was a white disc attached to the ceiling over the open sink area. It had a flashing red light and was the source of the noise. Sophia lifted one of her boots off the ground beside the bed and threw it with precision at the white disc stuck on the ceiling. It was a perfect hit. The disc fell to the floor still screaming with the red-light flashing. Hurriedly, Sophia scooped it up, pulled out the battery and left it on the sink's counter.

The bathroom door opened. Karen was swathed in a skimpy bathroom towel. It barely covered her breasts. Her lower extremities were uncovered. Her orange hair with the purple tips dripped around her shoulders as she noticed Sophia, "This hotel is a bust. Just look at this towel. This is supposed to be a bath towel! Can you image a big bubba guy trying to dry off with this?" She reached for a hand towel. Noticing the white disc and the battery on the counter, she smiled, "Hey, swift move. I heard something but had no idea what it was. Bravo!"

Sophia had no response. She quickly moved around Karen to use the facilities in the bathroom. Closing the door behind her, she stepped on the rest of the bath towels that were now on the floor. A soft knock on the door brought her attention. "Yes?"

"Hey, I'm sorry I used all the towels. You weren't going to take a shower were you? I can always call the front desk and have them send more if you want me to, although, I hate calling the front desk and I was sure you weren't going to take a shower, right?" Karen was now standing on the other side of the door stark naked.

Shaking her head, Sophia responded, "Evidently not."

"Then would you hand me my bag by the side of the bathtub? It has my toothbrush and stuff in it." Karen put her hand through the small space of the open door. Sophia reached for the pink plastic bag on the floor by the tub. It was upside down. All the products within it fell out to roll on the wet floor towel. Kneeling, Sophia picked up the bottles and

61

TERESA PIJOAN

the tubes. There was one bottle that appeared to be a prescription bottle with directions on it. Sophia pushed the door closed, Karen pulled her hand out just in time to not get smashed.

"Hey! Would you please hand me my bag! Come on, you don't need to go through everything in it, just hand it to me!" Karen's voice sounded desperate. Sophia was of mixed emotions. She wanted to dump everything that was in the bottle down the bathtub's drain and wash it away with water. There was another knock on the door with a loud, "Hey! Give me my damn bag!"

Opening the door, Sophia tossed the pink plastic bag through it. "Here and I didn't go through your stuff. Everything fell out since you left it upside down on the floor in here." Sophia shut the door.

Breakfast was at the restaurant across the highway from the hotel. The smell of bacon, coffee and hot biscuits permeated the room. The four of them were seated at a table close to the kitchen door. Every time a wait person went in and out the kitchen door, it banged against Timothy's chair. Finally, he moved the chair to be next to Sophia's and with a wink, he said, "There. Now, if I try to eat the food it will actually go into my mouth." Turning to Sophia, he asked, "Did you notice the fancy Mercedes in the parking lot? It shown like the Star of David, all waxed and clean in this completely muddy environment. Must be some high mucky muck in the Air Force. All the other cars, like the jeep, are covered in mud and slush."

Chewing on a piece of bacon, Sophia answered him, "No, I didn't notice. I am so tired. I could not sleep, thinking about the wedding and Robert's happiness. Sleeping beauty Karen had no problem sleeping." Taking a sip of tea, she added, "The champagne last night helped, I'm sure."

The table was covered with plates of pancakes, eggs with hash browns, syrup and one plate stacked high with crisp bacon and sausages. Stabbing his fork into a sausage, Robert said, "There is nothing like a hearty meal on wedding day. Eat up, my hearties."

Karen lifted the top pancake from the stack on a plate in the middle of the table. "I wonder if these are vegan. Do you think they cooked the pancakes and the hash browns in animal fat?"

Immediately, Robert was out of his chair and across the room disappearing into the kitchen. Timothy pushed his fork into the pancake Karen was holding, "I'm hungry and I'm going to eat this." Then out of the side of his mouth, he said, "Karen, I didn't know you were a vegan person? If you marry Robert, you're going to have to deal with meat. He's a hard-core meat eater who loves bacon, steaks and pork chops. How are you going to deal with this once you're married?"

The pancake was ripped into two parts as she pulled it away from Timothy's fork. "We shall cross the bridge when we get to it. Robert knows I don't eat animal parts. I won't drink wine either since it kills so many grapes." Timothy smiled at Karen, "Champagne is made from grapes. Champagne grapes. It appears you put away quite a bit of champagne last night."

Karen crunched on a piece of crispy bacon, "Evidently, I am a lesson in contradictions, huh?" The piece of pancake Karen had pulled away from Timothy was stuffed into Karen's mouth. Her mouth filled with pancake, she continued, "No, it isn't! Champagne is made in a lab. There are no grapes involved. I should know my grandfather was a terrific wine specialist and he gave us champagne when we were small children!" Karen suddenly sat up straight. Her cellphone was pulled from her tie-dyed skirt as she glanced at the two of them. "I have to take this. I'll be outside." Shoving back her chair, it almost fell over backwards if Sophia wouldn't have grabbed it.

Robert returned with a proud grin on his face. "They use peanut oil. It's on the menu so people who are allergic to peanuts know about their oil." He sat down to say, "Where's my lovely wife to be? Did she run off?"

Lifting a glass of water to his lips, Timothy whispered, "You wish." Sophia ignored them both, "Karen received a phone call. She grabbed her phone to disappear out the door."

Again, Timothy held the water glass close to lips as he looked at Sophia, "Let's hope she's gone." There was a loud sobbing coming from the front door of the restaurant. Karen hurried through the main room to go into the women's room. Sophia pushed her chair back, "I better go and see what's happening. You guys go ahead and eat. You have to move our stuff into your room, Robert, before eleven and it's getting close to eleven now."

In the women's room, Karen was in a stall with the door shut and locked. Sophia washed her hands in the sink, studied her reflection to notice she had more wrinkles than yesterday. After a time, she finally called out, "Karen, are you coming out of there? Please, let us know what is going on? Time is moving forward."

TERESA PIJOAN

Her answer was a loud sob and then, "That was my brother. I should have let him know I was here and not in Albuquerque!" Another sob came from the locked bathroom stall with a loud nose blow. "My parents are dead! Sophia! My parents were just killed in a car accident on their way here! Is this bad luck or what!" The bathroom stall door slammed open only to slam shut again right into Karen. The palm of her hand shoved it open, "I don't care! I don't care! I'm going to marry my man!"

She charged passed Sophia, again slamming the bathroom door open. Sophia followed as Karen abruptly sat on her chair. Her bulbous nose was bright red, clashing with her orange hair with purple ends. "I'm hungry, let's eat!"

Robert scooted his chair closer to hers, "My love, what is wrong? What's going on?"

Sniffing into her paper napkin, Karen shook her head, "My parents are dead. There was a horrible car accident south of here early this morning. An eighteen-wheeler slammed into my parent's vehicle and quickly killed them." Again, she blew her nose. There were no tears falling down her cheeks nor were her eyes red. "My brother called me just now to tell me. I told him, I said, I told him to take care of things. This is my wedding day and nothing is going to ruin it!" She slammed the table with the flat of her hand. People at the surrounding tables glared at her. "Damnit, this is my day, and no one is going to take it away from me!"

## 6

In the hotel room, Sophia helped Karen unpack a long carrying case. Karen pulled out a hand-woven wool dress of white. There were leg bloomers, also of white wool. Sophia held up the dress, "Karen, this is gorgeous, and it will be warm for you up on the mountain. Where in the world did you find this beautiful piece of luxury?"

Karen giggled her little girl giggle, "Robert had it made for me. Evidently, many of his students are experts in their own affairs. He has a student who makes or rather weaves clothes from the finest of wool. He paid her for this dress and it even comes with long johns of white. Look at this?"

She pulled out pieces of cloth wrapped in pink tissue paper. Thick heavy long johns came tumbling out with a pair of very white long socks of wool. "See? Isn't he a dear? He wanted me to wear white on my wedding day and he would not settle for anything less than perfection. He had his student measure me, fit it to my shape and even went out of her way to find the correct type of bra to wear so it wouldn't be a glaring red under all this white. Do you really like it?"

Sophia was speechless. Robert certainly was in love and his wallet showed it. The two women carefully gathered the clothing in the order they were to be put on and then wrapped the clothing into a pillowcase Karen had brought with her. This outfit would be put on at the railroad stop. It wouldn't do for Karen to wear her beautiful wedding dress on the dirty old train with snow slush on the floors. Robert and Timothy had already left in Timothy's Jeep Ranger with middle seat empty and the back seat filled with the camping gear. Robert had taken the flowers from the flower store to gently place them carefully on the middle seat floor of the Jeep. Sophia had noticed Roberts's excitement and even Timothy caught the mood.

TERESA PIJOAN

The air outside was freezing cold. Airplanes raced over their heads as Sophia and Karen boarded the train. They noticed it was filled with tourists and locals. Friday was a half price day and many were taking advantage of the price change. People sat in padded parkas with large picnic baskets settled in their laps. There were teenagers wrapped in blankets huddling together, all on one train bench at the back of their train car. The smoke from the train wafted through each train car as it idled at the loading docks near the parking lot. Children were running and screaming up and down the aisle as they waited for the train to start.

Older people were wrapped not only in blankets but wore heavy knitted caps and mittens. Couples held thermos bottles of warm liquid. The noise all around them drowned out the sound of the train's loudspeaker. Karen took hold of Sophia's arm as they waded through the mass of people, searching for seats. There were few seats together, but Karen asked a man if she could sit in his seat. She pointed to the front of the train car. He took the hint and moved.

Karen and Sophia now sat side by side. The bundles of clothes, all wrapped and protected, were held by both across their laps in order to keep them clean. The train jerked forward, children called to sit, and slowly, slowly the train moved forward. Karen leaned over to Sophia, "Soon, oh, so soon, I shall be Mrs. Robert Glacie. This is exciting!" In jerks and starts the train slowly moved to the first platform. It was the halfway point up the mountain. Timothy met them at the deck of the platform of well-worn wood. The building was a dull red and the wooden doors were held open with bricks. Taking Karen's hand, he said, "There is a woman's room down the hall from the ticket office. A woman who works here is holding it for you both. Hurry along for Robert has the wedding area all set up and the minister is here with his bible."

The train's loading and unloading dock was of wet lumber. Sophia held the dress high in the bag as she stumbled over the uneven wood deck. An older woman in a uniform was waiting at the end of the hall. When Karen called out, the woman waved then pushed the door open. Karen and Sophia entered a large room. There were three porta pot toilets sitting openly to the left of the door. A large sink was opposite and a drain in the middle of the room was coated in a slimy green matter. Sophia shook her head, "Wow! This is a petri dish for bacteria. Where do you want to stand?"

Karen turned a full circle, "You know what, let's put my heavy coat down on the floor and I'll stand on it and change. This room is a disaster for a pure white wedding dress!" Sophia couldn't agree more. There was no mirror or towels. A filthy rag was hung by the door on a nail, otherwise this is all one had. Sophia took hold of Karen's arm as she attempted to remove her coat. "No, we are not doing this in here! Your wedding is to be pure and beautiful, not crusty with people's passed smells and body offerings. Let's go outside." Sophia pulled Karen to the door.

The same woman was standing guard outside the woman's bathroom. Sophia smiled at her and asked, "Is there somewhere else my friend would be able to change into her wedding dress? This bathroom is not appropriate for a long flowing white gown." The woman stared at Sophia, "You mean she's going to get married here?"

Karen pushed passed Sophia, "No, not here in the hall, but outside under the trees. Is there somewhere else I could change?"

Shaking her head, the woman stated quite clearly, "No! There is no private place here. This is a train station stop, not a hotel." A man in a long overcoat with his hair pulled back in a ponytail stood aside as Karen and Sophia stepped out of the hall to be back on the deck by the train. Sophia was still holding the clothing bag, "Let's go outside then. I will hold up part of my sleeping bag from the jeep and you can change behind it. There is also a tarp rolled up in Timothy's jeep for Robert's tent. Come on, let's get you prepared in the open air with all the spirits of the mountain watching."

Karen laughed, "I love it! Yes, mountain spirits can watch me change! How wonderful! Sophia, you are my kind of girl!" The tarp was placed on the ground about three hundred feet from the parking lot. Sophia hung up her sleeping bag on the low pine branches, unzipped and fully used as a blind for Karen to change behind. Sophia helped Karen pull off her pants, pull on her heavy wool leggings and then the dress of embroidered crocheted wool. The bottom of the clothing bag had paper flowers slightly crushed, but still useable. Sophia straightened them out, wrapped them in Karen's hair and she was ready.

Stepping out from behind the sleeping bag, Karen appeared as a forest queen. Timothy evidently had been waiting with the photographer. They took several shots of Karen in front of the hanging dark green sleeping bag with the tree branches hanging down in front of it. Karen

TERESA PIJOAN

was more than ready to pose. As Karen moved forward, Timothy and Sophia stayed behind the sleeping bag to roll up her everyday clothes into the bag, Timothy and Sophia lifted the sleeping bag and then folded it with the tarp to return the items to the jeep. Sophia pulled off her old sweatshirt to pull on her fancy green sweater with sparkles on it. Sophia brushed back her short curly hair and joined the wedding group, she had to walk around the tall man in the overcoat who appeared to be watching as the wedding unfolded.

Timothy was quickly at Sophia's side, taking her arm, he led her down the wet dock to an open area. There was a blanket of open netting in the trees. Woven in and out of the netting were beautiful garlands of flowers made into an overhead trellis of flowing flowers. There was a large Navaho blanket on the ground covering the fallen pine needles dotted with snow. Standing to one side of the trellis was Robert. He was dressed in a beautiful suit of deep blue. A yellow daisy was in his lapel and in his arms was a full array of flowers made up of mostly yellow daisies. His crown of grey hair was neatly combed, letting his bald spot on the top of his head shine. Thick bifocal glasses reflected the sun over his broad smile. The paisley ascot tie was a nice added touch lying nicely under his trimmed beard.

68

A young woman sat on a stool playing a guitar. Her long brown hair was pulled back over her shoulder as she played a piece by Beethoven. Her jean fabric was torn over both knees. She wore mittens with the fingertips cut out. Her eyes were down, staring at the frozen ground. Walking quickly up to Robert, Sophia took the bouquet of flowers from Robert, turning to give them to Karen.

Timothy whispered to Sophia, "I'm being the best man and the father of the bride at the same time. You're lucky, you just have one role to play in this event." He winked at her.

The minister was a young man who appeared to be no more than twenty years old. He too, was wearing jeans with many torn holes going down each leg. His parka was open, showing a thick black sweater over a turtleneck. Long brown hair was tied back in a ponytail at the nap of his neck. Holding the Bible in his ungloved hand, he was turning the pages with his brown gloved hand. Watching him, Sophia wondered if he was even qualitied, but then thinking of the internet, just about anyone could get a minster's license these days.

The guitar played the wedding march as Timothy hurried back

to Karen. Once Karen was positioned next to Robert, Timothy pivoted to stand beside Robert. Sophia stood beside Karen ready to take the bouquet of flowers when the time came. The young minister asked them if they took one another for better or worse, in sickness and in health and then declared them married. The ceremony was almost over before it began.

Timothy handed Robert a small envelope when the minister asked for the ring. Robert took the envelope, kissed it and then gave it to Karen. Sophia jerked her chin toward Timothy to ask, "Where was the ring?" Timothy shook his head and frowned. The music picked up with a fast waltz as the married couple turned from the minister and walked back through the snowy sludge to the train dock. The minister smiled as he zipped up his parka and walked down the slope to the train decking. Karen ran ahead, bumping into the man in the overcoat.

Sophia caught up with Timothy, "What was the envelope about? What about the ring?" Timothy put his hand on Sophia's arm, "Listen, none of this is what I would call a typical wedding. Right now, I have to open the jeep for the guitar player. The minister and the guitar player are an item, and I let them put their stuff in the jeep. Let me open it for them and then we can talk." Left on her own, Sophia carefully lifted the beautiful Navajo rug, shook out the debris stuck to the underside of it and folded it in her arms. As she stood on the train deck looking down to the parking lot, she watched Timothy hand the guitar player her guitar case, the minister a flute case from the backseat of the jeep. Robert was standing in front of the jeep kissing Karen.

Traipsing down to the parking lot was dangerously slick from the melting snow. The weather was unusually warm for November on this south side of the mountain. Watching where she put her footing, Sophia finally stepped on the tarmac of the parking lot. Robert was handing a white envelope to the guitar woman and another to the minister with the flute case. "Thank you both for coming. This was as perfect as it could be. Thank you, thank you." The young woman slipped her hand into the arm of the minister's as they walked to the wooden steps going to the lower parking lot.

Timothy met Sophia, taking the Navaho rug from her, he explained, "Karen didn't want a ring. She wanted the money rather than what the ring would cost. Evidently, she has bills to pay and the money was more important to her." Timothy gave Sophia a fleeting look, "Listen, I'm not sure that young fellow was even a minister. I asked him for his credentials and he said he'd left them in his car. Robert paid everyone so the minister and the guitar player could have a quick getaway."

Nodding to Sophia, he added, "This has been one of the strangest days of my life, let me tell you. So now, we are going in the jeep up the mountain to set up camp and they can change their clothes."

Smiling, Timothy took Sophia's arm, "By the way, you like nice. Karen's costume was beautiful. You did a good job getting her fixed up. I hardly noticed her bulbous nose." They hurried to catch up with Robert and Karen who were leaning against the jeep in a warm hug. The jeep's keys were pulled from Timothy's pocket, doors were opened, and the men sat in the front seats and the women in the middle seats.

Sophia complained, "Shouldn't the wedding couple sit back here, and I could sit up front with Timothy, giving you both some privacy?" The back of the jeep was cleverly stacked with the tents, the sleeping bags, a cook stove with pots and pans and an ice chest filled with food and drink. Robert waved his hand, "No, I have the directions, besides we shall have time to get cozy later."

70

## 7

While Timothy was waiting for the traffic to clear so he could turn up the muddy track to the mountain road, Karen was pulling off her dress, her leggings and her shoes. She reached for her backpack and pulled on her regular hiking clothes for the cold winter weather. Sophia tried to help but was hit with a sharp elbow. As they drove higher on the mountain the snow became deeper and the road sludge became iced over. There were two signs ahead. Robert called out, "There, Timothy, there! We're camping at fifty-seven. See the sign there?"

Indeed, Timothy did see the sign. He put on his blinker to laugh, "There isn't another sane person around for miles, but it is best to be careful. I would hate to get a ticket!" The icy road moved around huge boulders, over a stream that was frozen over and finally they came to a flat plateau. A faded wooden sign had the numbers fifty-seven hammered to a fat cottonwood tree. Timothy drove around the tree and parked in a clearing. "Here we are, the love nest in the freezing cold Colorado winter."

Jumping out with a resounding howl, Robert opened the middle door for his bride. He scooped her up in his arms, twirled her around as he kissed her over and over again. Setting her down, he called out to the wilderness, "I am the happiest man on the planet!"

Two and a half hours later as the sun was beginning to set, the tents were up, the sleeping bags were in place and the fire pit was roaring strong with one of Robert's homemade stews boiling away in a camping pot. A bottle of wine was opened, plastic cups filled as the four sat on rolled logs around the fire. Robert's eyes sparkled in the firelight. Karen's face was frozen in a warm smile. Sophia stirred the stew as Timothy filled the plastic cups with more wine. Sophia's homemade bread was wrapped in foil sitting beside the fire. Somewhere nearby,

TERESA PIJOAN

high up in a tree an owl hooted repeatedly. It almost sounded like a laugh coming from the dark sky filled with twinkling stars. The moon hid behind thick dark grey clouds. A gentle breeze kept the air cold with some of the tree branches creaking. The smell of the wood fire and the cooking stew kept everyone in a somber mood.

The quiet of the night was broken with a loud, "Here's to us, Karen! We did it with the help of Sophia and Timothy!" Robert held his cup high as he downed the full amount of wine. "We may be crazy, but we are certainly happy!"

Another round of wine was poured into plastic cups as plastic bowls were filled with stew. The loaf of bread was passed around to be torn off in chunks and the cold night wrapped around them. Timothy kept pouring his wine from his cup into Robert's cup. No one appeared to notice accept Sophia. She sipped her wine for she knew only too well what alcohol can do to a person in freezing weather.

Standing next to the big tent, Karen raised her arms up to the sky. Her hands were open as she called out, "Oh, Universe, bless us one and all! Take my parents into your warm embrace and keep them safe!" She then let out a howl. Robert burst out laughing. He lifted his cup high as he sat on the round rock by the fire pit, "Yes, may we all be blessed this night for life is fleeting." Turning to Karen, he added, "Here's to the love of my life, how I dearly love you, Sweet Girl."

Timothy scraped the stew pot clean only to wash it out with the powdered snow. Shaking the pot, he grabbed a cloth from the cooking box to dry it. "This has been quite a day, hasn't it?" He turned to Sophia, "Tomorrow we are going to teach Karen how to rappel in this cold? You know the forecast has the temperature at minus four in the morning. Somehow, up here in the freezing cold, with the powdered snow, well, I don't know, this doesn't seem wise at least to me. What do you think Sophia?"

Holding a broken tree branch, Sophia was moving the hot coals from the middle of the fire pit to the sides where she was smashing them down to cool. "Timothy has a point, Robert. What if we hike the area and avoid the cliffs? We aren't in the know as to how deep the snow is at the edges or if it would hold our pitons." She stomped on a hot coal near her boot, "It is beautiful here. We could have a hiking adventure. Karen, what do you think? Would you like just to explore and avoid the danger of rappelling?"

72

Sticking out her chin, Karen pouted, "Robert, you promised! You promised you were going to show me how to rappel! This was part of our marriage pact, remember?" Walking over to him, she put her arms around his waist. He kissed her gently on the cheek, "What my lady wants, my lady gets."

Timothy took the broken branch from Sophia's hand. He banged on the bottom of the pot, "Hear ye, hear ye, tomorrow we shall rappel." The pot was dropped upside down in the snow near the fire pit. Then he kicked snow over the hot stones around the fire pit, "There! Now, it's time for slumber, so sayeth the scribe."

They took turns going into the woods for a final day's constitution. Timothy's last walk out and back brought him limping into camp. He swore under his breath, "Damn, why didn't I think to bring my boots?"

As he climbed into his tent, Sophia followed him. "What's going on with your feet?"

"My feet hurt. These shoes are soaking wet as are my socks. I never thought to bring boots out here to Colorado. Of course, I knew we would be hiking, but for some reason, I spaced out wearing boots!" He winced as he sat down abruptly on his sleeping bag.

Sophia lifted his foot. She pulled off his soggy leather shoes, 73 carefully removed his wet socks to study his feet. "Damn, Timothy, this looks like frost bite." She patted his feet, "Stay just as you are. I have some heat warmers in my backpack. These will help warm up your feet, but seriously you need dry boots and dry socks." She came back out of his tent only to return minutes later with two packs. She twisted the packs, smacked them on her thigh and then placed one around each foot. Timothy jerked his feet away, "Sophia, hot, hot, hot! You should have warned me!"

"Now keep still. They're not that hot, it's just your feet are that cold. Do you have dry clean socks with you?"

He opened his backpack, dug around for a time to finally hand her a pair of dry dress socks. They were thin nylon socks. Sophia studied them, "These will not do you any good tomorrow, but tonight I'll put the packs inside the socks and the socks over your feet. Hold still and stop complaining." Once the packs and the socks were in place, Sophia patted his feet. "There you go, now leave these on and we might save your poor frozen piglets." Timothy stared at her, "What if I have to visit a tree in the night?"

TERESA PIJOAN

"Then put on your wet shoes. Tomorrow, we'll get you a clean thick pair of socks from Robert's stash." The shoes were placed upside down near the head of his sleeping bag. "These shoes are not going to do you much good in the morning. Timothy, really! You certainly did not think ahead, did you?"

Zipping up his tent, she added, "Now get some sleep. It's been a very busy day. Good night, sleep tight, and don't let the wolves eat you tonight." Timothy's tent was beside Sophia's while Karen and Robert had the big tent on the other side of the fire pit. Each took turns saying good night, until all was quiet. Sophia texted her daughters about the day's events only to fall asleep quickly as her head hit the pillow. The ground was cold, but the sleeping bag was nice and warm.

At the first light of dawn, Sophia's arthritic shoulder really hurt. Osteoarthritis was claiming victory. Slowly, Sophia let out a sigh to attempt to lie on her back. She groaned, for now she was sure her feet were no longer in the thermal socks they were put into last night. "Damn." She moaned.

Timothy's voice called out from the next tent, "Cold enough for you, Sophia? I hear your discomfort and raise you ten. Has anyone heard from Robert or Karen?"

"I'm here." Robert's deep voice came from the tent on the other side of Sophia. "Karen was up before light. She wanted to say morning prayers up on the cliff side." A startling laugh came from Robert's tent. "I have now been married for almost sixteen hours! How wonderful is life. Huh? How absolutely wonderful! Karen is the best person in the whole wide world!" He howled like a crazy dog. "Sophia, I may be four years older than your sixty-nine years, but today I feel about thirty! Karen is a lover of nature like me and here we are with you two wonderful people."

Timothy clapped his hands, "Hey, Uncle Robert, that makes you eleven years older than me. What a strange world we live in. Why aren't you with your lovely bride? After my debacle yesterday, I would think you would want to take good care of her?"

Quickly, Sophia sat up to grab her heavy blue sweater out of her backpack. Sliding her thermal socks back over her bare feet, she added, "She shouldn't go up there by herself at least not in the dark. The crevices are difficult to find even in the daylight because of the blinding snow drifts."

"Hey, my wife has her own mind. Since her parents died on the way to our wedding, she was more decided than ever to come up here and send them prayers. I thought if she wanted to do something in mourning for her loss, it was up to her." Robert could be heard unzipping his tent. "All I need are my boots and I'll go get her. She wouldn't go far."

Sophia met him by the cold fire pit they had built the night before to cook dinner. Sunlight bounced off the snow, blinding the campers. Wind had blown the powdered snow into ridges all around their camp. Still in his tent, Timothy moaned, "You two go. I'll get my act together and build up the fire to fix some hot food and drink. My feet are still numb from the frost bite yesterday."

Pulling back the flap to Timothy's tent, Sophia peered in, "You know you should really put on a double pair of socks. Those toes were bad last night and they won't get better if you get them wet again today." Dropping the tent flap closed, Robert added, "Wearing leather walking shoes for a hiking expedition wasn't your smartest move, my lad."

There was no comment from Timothy. Sophia knelt to tie the laces around her high hiking boots. Her winter green parka was nice and warm. Her green gloves were pulled over cold fingers, she shoved on her wool cap to put the visor on last. "Let's go find your beautiful wife, Robert. She's new to the terrain and hasn't camped before. To be perfectly honest, I am worried for her."

Robert growled, "She's a grown woman, Sophia. She wouldn't have wanted to come here for our honeymoon if she was scared of adventure." He glared at her.

"Robert, don't people usually go on their honeymoon alone with one another?" Putting her hand on his shoulder, she moved to stand in front of him, "You know this is crazy, right? Here we are in the middle of Colorado, on a mountain covered with snow, in freezing weather, sleeping in tents and this is your honeymoon with your retired research writer and your elderly nephew!"

He pushed her hand off his shoulder, "Ours is not to reason why, ours is but to do or die. I love this woman. This is what she wants. Yes, I am an old fart, but she's filled with youth and love. Why would I deny her this?"

Grabbing his walking stick, he stabbed it into the crusty snow. Robert broke into stride. "She's a tough cookie my Karen. Being raised on a farm up north, she knows about snow and cold. Somehow, I think she feels closer to her parents out here than she did back in the city."

TERESA PIJOAN

Their footsteps crunched loudly as they walked on the frozen layer of snow under the powder. Robert chuckled, "Feels like I'm walking on graham crackers." Karen's footprints were still noticeable in the snow. She had walked with a stick and took her normal steps. As they came to the first crevice the footprints disappeared. Robert knelt to study the snow. Sophia called out, "Karen! Karen! Can you hear me?" There was no answer. Robert jumped over the narrow crevice to kneel and stared down into the deep tear in the mountainous icy wound. Shaking his head, he stood, "No. No one down there. Let's go on ahead, maybe she went around." They both walked on, each of them on either side of the crevice. Robert was now frowning. His eyes searching. Sophia was bent, looking for footprints. "Robert, can I ask you another question?"

"Certainly, Sophia, we've been friends a long time. Ever since the great drop at the Grand Canyon in ninety-seven where we fell into the abyss. So, shoot, what do you need to know?"

"How about why are we here? Your marriage in Colorado Springs was beautiful even though sad due to Karen's parents' bad accident. Well, fatal accident. I mean, why did she want to go ahead with all of the grief around this celebration of marriage? Shouldn't she be busy with the funeral?" Sophia caught her breath, "Robert, why did she want to come way the hell up here? Why did she want Timothy and me along on your honeymoon?" Sophia put her hand out to stop Robert from walking ahead, "Robert, isn't this all rather strange to you?"

Robert shook his head as he turned to face Sophia, "When a person is in love, they do whatever it takes to please their new partner. I love Karen. Her choices are mine and I chose to follow her choices. Certainly, we had long talks about all of this with tears of sadness and tears of joy. Karen loves the snow and for her own reasons she wanted you both along for the ride. As for her parents' untimely death, her brother Franklin is dealing with the legal issues. We plan to have the memorial service for them at the end of the month." Wiping his moustache with his gloved hand, he continued, "I can see how you and Timothy would find all of this strange, but I chose Karen and with her comes her choices."

Squinting through the glare of the sun shining off of the snow, Sophia trudged on ahead of Robert. "So, the two of you met five weeks ago and just decided to get married? Just like that?"

Drifts of snow blew up into their faces as gusts of wind swirled around them. Robert grunted, "Yes, yes, we did. Just like that."

"Hey! Hey!" A woman's voice called out ahead of them. Robert took off running. Sophia called after him, "Robert! Robert! Watch your step! Watch where you're going! They're more cuts in the mountain up where you are!" Robert did not stop. He plunged his walking stick firmly into the frozen ground as he rushed ahead. Suddenly, his stick disappeared from his hand as he fell forward barely hanging onto a scrawny Juniper tree branch. Sophia let out a yell, "Stay! Stay! Do not move, Robert!"

Sophia cautiously moved to the edge of the narrow crevice. She jumped over the crevice only to slide on her left side to lie beside Robert. His face was red, tears were flowing down his red cheeks. "Help," he whispered. Sophia remained lying beside him. Carefully, she rolled over to grab the back of Robert's red parka. As she pulled on the parka, it tugged on his neck. The snow covering his bushy grey eyebrows and his trimmed grey moustache gave him a haunting appearance.

Frustrated with the loose-fitting parka, Sophia softly said "Robert, I need to grab your arm. Not your hand, but your arm or your wrist. Do not let go of the tree. I'm going to reach over you to take hold of your arm as firmly as I can since the parka just slides around." Robert stared up into Sophia's face. She was biting her lower lip. Her short curly brown hair was sticking out of her wool cap. Suddenly, he felt her body move closer to the edge, nearer to him.

Her hand reached out to take his bare wrist between the glove and his parka sleeve. She held onto it with both hands. As she pulled, she felt her body sliding closer to the opening. Slowly, she moved her leg. Now her right foot was caught in place around the juniper tree's thin trunk. Her chin was in the snow, her mouth was set as she yanked with all of her might to pull on Robert's wrist. He flung his leg to almost hit her in the shoulder. His leg remained closer to Sophia. Now, she carefully let go of his wrist and with her left hand grabbed his ankle. "Pull yourself up with this leg. Can you just lift your body with your hands and your leg?"

Growling, Robert rolled over to have his right side almost on top of Sophia. She hugged his body to scoot back, pulling him up and out of the hole. Robert burst into tears. "Thank you, thank you, thank God you came with me!" Suddenly, he hugged her with all his might. "Sophia, I was not ready to die! Seriously, I was not ready!" Sophia let him hold her. She could feel his shaking body through his heavy parka. His wool mittens were caked with snow, his nose bright red in the cold. Then they heard the cry again, "Help! Help! Somebody, Help!"

Robert wiped his face with the back of his wet mitten, leaving a wet line across his cheeks and nose. "That's Karen! Karen's down there!" Both of them were lying on their bellies as they peered down into the icy crack in the mountain. Karen was sitting on a small ledge deep in the earth's cracked fault line. She had snow on her pink hat. She was shaking and screaming, "Robert, you asshole, get me out of here!"

Sophia burst out laughing, "She's got your number, Robert. Think we need ropes and tools. I'll go back and get Timothy. We'll bring supplies to get her out. Please, stay here! Do not go down after her, right?" Standing, Sophia added, "Tell her not to yell. The vibration may loosen the ledge that's holding her."

"Right." Robert gave Sophia a weak smile. "There's some of your brother's tea in my tent. Karen brought it along in case we needed first aid." Shaking her head, Sophia said, "Hell, no. Granger's teas kill people. No tea for thee, my friend." Jumping over the opening, Sophia walked back to camp. Timothy, true to his word, had a roaring fire going with water boiling in a tin pan. He met Sophia as she walked to him, "So, where's Robert? Where's Karen?"

"She fell into a deep crevice," Sophia shook her head, "We need the ropes, some gear and the cleats." Sophia pulled open the back of the four wheeled jeep. The ropes were the first items she pulled out. "Oh, and bring goggles. Karen fell into a deep narrow slice of iced earth. Robert is talking to her as she is cussing him out. If she moves too much, I'm afraid she will drop all the way down into the mountain." Sophia slid on the boot cleats, grabbing an extra pair for Karen, she dropped those into a small green canvas bag. The extra halter was clipped to the ties of the bag. The bag was tied around her waist over her parka. "Let's go." Timothy carried the emergency gear in a backpack while Sophia carried two blankets. When they met up with Robert, he was sitting against the juniper tree trunk singing. They could hear Karen singing with him from below.

Robert jumped up when he saw them. "Let's get a helicopter to come. They can lower a rope and get her out of there faster than we can, right?"

"No." Timothy dropped the bag, "A helicopter will cause friction with the loud noise of the propellers. The vibration would cause the ice

78

to shake and who knows where Karen would end up? Maybe in China! We need to stay calm, do what we do and if this doesn't work, then we can call in search and rescue. Right now time is of the essence."

Robert shook his head, "Really, do you think we can get her out? Just the three of us? The helicopter would be better." Robert's beard now had icicles on it.

"Uncle, you're a geologist, certainly you must know about vibrations and the earth's fragility." Timothy put his hand on his Uncle Robert's shoulder.

"Oh, and you do? You who are an accountant! You know about these things?" Robert pointed at Sophia, "She's an ethnologist, why don't you ask her? She must know everything!" Robert walked away, shaking his head.

Sophia pulled the ropes off her shoulder, "Enough of this squabbling, you men are acting like school children. Our first point of interest is Karen. Once she is out, you two can get into it if you want to, but right now we need Karen out of the hole in the earth."

Timothy called down, "Help is here. Do not move under any circumstances!" There was no answer. Robert quickly stood to peer down. "Good, you're still there." There was a snort and then a remark, "Where would I go. I need to be with my knight in shining armor." Timothy tied the rope around a thick cottonwood tree trunk that was about ten feet from the crevice. Bare branches were raised skyward not moving in the soft breeze. The chalk blue sky held only one small cloud on the horizon. Sophia shook her head, "Only one cloud. Not good for us. A clear sky means cold, icy cold air for there's not a cloud to keep the heat close to the earth." Still shaking her head, she peered down into the crevice.

Timothy walked ten feet from the first tree to a tall aspen tree. His wet leather shoe soles squeaked in the snow. He waylaid the rope to tie it with two more rappelling ropes. Sophia nodded to Timothy as he tied a halter around her, "Sophia, you are the lightest of us. Yes, you're the best to go down first and get her. Although, I'm not sure the pitons will hammer into the frozen ice wall. What do you think?" His forehead was wrinkled with worry. Wrapping the long rope around his right arm, then across his shoulder, he pointed to the trees behind him. "The ropes are tied to the cottonwood tree and the aspen over there. Give the pitons a try. Take maybe six with you and if they don't work, well, we have the trees to slowly lower and pull you both back up topside. We can pull you up, so you won't need the zips. Yesterday, they didn't work so they may not work today, but you have manpower. I'll watch Robert, don't worry." He patted Sophia on the shoulder. "Remember, don't risk both of your lives. If she gets antsy, let go."

Sophia reached for the other halter, "No, we are going to be haltered together. You men will have to put muscle into it. Both of us are coming out." Sophia leaned over to give Robert a hug, "Hey, big man, you're going to have to pull us both up! So, stand and be strong, you hear?" Robert nodded. "Bring my woman back to me, please." Sophia kissed his cheek as she pulled down her goggles. There was an extra pair of goggles on her wrist, tied with a strip. "Karen, I'm coming down. Stay put, please, don't move until I get you into a halter, okay?"

A weak, "Yes" drifted up. Sophia kept talking, "The ridge that you are sitting on may break off, as they do, and this would not be good for it is a long way down. I'm bringing you a halter, a safety rope and a pair of goggles. You can tell your grandchildren about your bravery."

Slowly, the two men lowered Sophia as she held the rope in one hand to walk down into the crevice. Her back was against the far wall of sheer ice and her feet were against the opposite wall. She pulled a piton from her front pocket and the hammer from the other pocket. Holding the small hammer firmly she attempted to hammer in the piton. It went in so far and then twisted to fall. Slamming her boot cleats into the frozen crevice wall was the best she was able to do.

"Damn! The pitons are not working. I'll walk it down. Slowly, lower the rope." She was given some slack as she moved carefully down into the dark air. As she was lowered, step by step her goggles clouded up with the moisture in the crevice. Slowly, getting closer to Karen, she felt the air turn colder. The crevice narrowed, pushing her knees close to her chest. Using her shoulder, she pushed the goggles up onto her forehead. Thick air made breathing difficult. Her eyes teared as her nose began to run.

Sunlight diminished as she descended. Her body was now almost completely folded into itself. There was no way she could straighten in such a tight space. Her body was sandwiched between the walls of ice. The air burned her lungs as she breathed. Her eyes watered as she was lowered into the dark hole. Her body was blocking the light below her, making it difficult to see when she turned to find Karen.

"Sophia, you're almost on top of me. Can you push your body sideways?" Karen's voice was a soft whisper. Quickly, Sophia reached between her thighs and her chest to pull the extra halter from inside her jacket. It was warm from her body heat. Sophia's breathing was labored due to the lack of space. Lowering her right hand, Sophia spoke softly, "Here, now let me do this. Karen, do not move your legs or try to help me. Okay, here's one leg, here's the other. No, no, don't move a muscle. Any minute you could go."

As Sophia lifted Karen's arms to pull the halter tight around Karen's waist, a muscle spasm burned in Sophia's arm. "Oh, damn. Karen, you're going to have to help me with the rope loop." Sophia held her rope tightly in her right hand. Her left hand carefully dropped the other rope down. Sophia felt the ice wall behind her melting with her body heat. It was dripping water down her parka and soaking it. "Karen, I'm slowly moving down." Hurriedly, she added, "Push it through the loop that's in the front of the halter. If I crash into you at least both of us are tied to a rope." Sophia's right arm was now spasming, causing her hand holding the rope to shake. Glancing down, she told Karen, "Make sure the rope is taught and then take the carabineer and hook it around the rope loop on the other side."

Quietly, Karen whispered, "Done." Sophia tugged on both ropes as she slid down to be even with Karen, "There. Now, I want you to reach out and hug me."

Karen let out a blood piercing scream, "I can't! What if I fall and you can't catch me! I can't. I won't let go of this ledge! Please, please, just leave me here, I am safe here!" Karen's voice pleaded as tears fell from her eyes.

Sophia whispered firmly, "Karen, staying here is not an option. Come on lean forward and hug me."

Her hands to her eyes, Karen whispered, "No. No. No. I can't do it. I won't do it." Karen shook in fear, "Don't make me, please, don't make me."

Sophia bit her lower lip, "Okay, if you want to stay here that's fine. This is fine with me. All I have to do is jerk the rope and I will be out of here and you will freeze. Your new husband, who dearly loves you and wants to have a life with you, would wish you with him. But if you prefer to stay here, that is your prerogative." When Sophia reached higher on the rope, Karen lunged off the ledge to grab Sophia. The ledge she had been sitting on cracked to fall hundreds of feet below them.

TERESA PIJOAN

At the sound, Karen started to scream, "I had no idea! I thought I was safe! I was going to try to stand and jump up when I heard your voices, but someone whispered for me to stay still!" She leaned her head against Sophia's shoulder. "I have never been so glad to see someone ever! Ever!" Sobbing against Sophia's shoulder, she whispered, "You know, I thought I was going to die, to be with my parents. The voice I heard telling me to stay still and be quiet sounded like my mother's voice."

Sophia gave the rope another jerk. The rope went taught, jerking them up inch by inch. Suddenly it stopped and went slack. The two women dropped about five feet. Sophia lifted her legs to dig the boot cleats into the ice wall in front of her. Karen was beside her, clinging to Sophia's neck. Twisting, Sophia grunted, "Karen, let go of my neck. I can't breathe. You have a rope to hold you. Let go of my neck, please, let go." Karen loosened her grip around Sophia's neck to grab her upper right arm. "Karen, lift your left foot. The one nearest to me. I'm going to slide boot cleats onto your boots. There, now lift your right foot over your left leg. Here you go, now if your arms get tired you can hold the rope tight and try to walk out using the cleats. Understand?"

82

Karen gave Sophia a half smile as she nodded her head in agreement, "I had no idea this was going to be so dangerous. Somehow, I was more afraid in the city, but not out here, not out in the country. Even at my age there is much to learn. Sophia, thank you for coming down here. Somehow, I will find a way to apologize to you after calling you a jerk. Please, forgive me."

Timothy called down, "We have a problem with the ropes. They got tangled up here. It's no one's fault. Just hang on, we're figuring it out." Quickly, the women felt the ropes go completely loose. Sophia jabbed her cleated boots firmly into the ice wall. The back of her wet parka was causing them to slip further down with Karen holding on to her. "Hey, you strong men, we're sliding down! Do you think you are able to pull us up? Or at least pull one of us up at a time?"

Karen's rope went taut, jerking her up and away from Sophia. As she was lifted, Sophia patted Karen's butt, "There you go, lovely lady, keep hold of the rope until you are completely on firm ground." Karen called down, "See you later!" The crevice darkened as Karen was lifted, blocking out the sunlight. Strong hands grabbed Karen's wrists and pulled her out of Sophia's sight. Karen's voice called down, "I'm on the ground with my husband! You're next!"

Keeping hold of the rope as she slammed her cleats on her way up and out, both of Sophia's arm muscles burned. Once she was close to the top, she wrapped the rope under her arms and around her body to shake out her arms. Suddenly, her body dropped as she yelled, "No! No!"

Sliding down, back into the crevice, Sophia closed her eyes and held her breath. "Damn." The rope jerked as she free fell past where Karen had been sitting on the ledge. Shaking her head, she whispered to the ice mountain, "At least there are three of them up there to pull me up." Now her back hurt where the halter had jerked when the rope went taut. Holding the rope with both hands, Sophia whispered, "Thank you rope and trees for keeping me alive."

Using her gloved hands to lift herself with the rope now taut, she stabbed her cleated boots into the ice. Inch by inch she pulled on the rope while stabbing her cleated boots into the opposite side of the crevice. Muscles burned. Her lower back was in tight spasm. Tears welled in her eyes causing the googles to cloud up as she slowly, slowly moved towards the light above her head. The rope coiled in her lap. Her leg calves froze up in pain. It took all her strength to lift and stab her feet into the ice that was in front of her body. "I am not going to die!" She screamed loudly again, "I am not going to die! No! No! Hey, you guys, I am not going to die in this ice box!" Her legs burned in pain, lifting, and stabbing her boot cleats again and again. Using deep breaths to monitor her oxygen now made her throat dry and hurt with the freezing cold air. She closed one eye as she put all her energy into moving upward.

Slowly, slowly, inch by inch Sophia elevated her cold, wet body up the frozen mountain. Her right arm and hand were numb but held firmly to the rope. Every now and again, she could feel someone jerking the rope but not pulling her upward. As she came closer to the top, she called out, "Hey, Timothy, what's going on up there? Where are the men who are to pull me out?"

There was no reply. Taking the last bit of energy, she had, she grabbed at the rope closest to the crevice opening. Yanking hard, her body was now half in and half out of the crevice, Sophia let out a loud sigh, "Damn, that was close."

Dragging her exhausted body out of the hole, she slid onto the flat surface of snow. Every muscle started to shake. The sweat inside her clothes was drying, cooling her aches and spasms. Sophia laid flat on the snow. Her body was spent as she rolled over on her back. Pushing up her goggles, she was finally able to focus.

Quietly, Karen knelt beside her. "We're both out. We made it! Now come on, let's get away from here!" Karen took hold of the halter around Sophia's waist to drag her away from the crevice. "No more falling today! I want to go home where it's warm and cozy!"

Crab walking to the tall cottonwood tree, Sophia used her hands against the tree trunk to finally stand upright. She took notice of the empty area around Karen. "Where are the men? Where are our heroes?" Sophia turned to lean her back straight against the tree trunk, feeling her spine slowly fall into place. Her arms were now burning as the muscle spasms tried to relax.

Karen took hold of Sophia's right arm, "Here, let me help you. That was some feat getting yourself out of there! Let me tell you, I'm impressed!" Sophia stared at Karen, "Hey, let go of my arm. I can stand on my own. Karen, where are the men?"

Shaking her head, Karen let out a soft giggle, "Oh, I told them you wanted to come out on your own. They're back at camp fixing us a nice breakfast. They're so sweet."

Struggling to move on her tired legs, Sophia bent over to swing her arms loose from muscle cramps. "You told them I could climb out on my own?" Disbelief dripping from the tone in her voice.

Karen shrugged, "Well, you're strong. Robert told us you rappel all the time that you're an Olympic rappel monster. Hey, you did it. See you're okay." Lifting a coiled rope beside the cottonwood tree trunk, Karen tried to untie the knot. "You did good, really good." She nodded to Sophia, "Hey, can you untie this knot? I tired, but I think it's too tight."

Sophia glared at her, "You tried to untie the knot? When was this? Was it when I was down there?" She pointed to the crevice.

Karen shrugged, "No, it was just now." She pouted as she watched Sophia flip the rope over, loosened the rope's knot and pulled it free from the tree trunk. "There you go!" Karen wrapped the rope around her hand and elbow as she started walking back to camp. Everything else appeared to have been removed from the drop site. Sophia attempted to stand upright. Her thighs burned, her legs shook, and her back was wet from the ice and perspiration. Rubbing her upper arms, Sophia attempted to keep up with Karen's fast walk back to camp. Under her breath, Sophia muttered, "Well, God bless me."

84

# 8

The two women were silent as they walked. Karen strode confidently ahead of Sophia who continually rubbed her arms and thighs. Her legs were still burning from the effort of getting out of the crevice. Sophia watched Karen as she gleefully swayed her body while humming her tune.

When Sophia entered the camp area, Robert burst out, "Hurrah! I have my wife back in my arms!" He danced with her around the smoking campfire. Timothy gave Sophia a thumbs up and then he hugged her. "Well, girl, you did it! You saved my feet yesterday and today you saved Karen. May your mother know how great you are?" A frown graced Sophia's face. "Doubt she would care, actually."

In a businesslike manner, Sophia slid off her halter, dropping it at her feet, "I don't know about you guys, but I need something hot to drink." The campfire was built up into a roaring blaze. Sophia stared at the others, "I'm going into my tent for a pain pill. Hope you men know that what I did was damn hard work. It would've been nice to have had your help." Robert grabbed Karen to hold her tightly against him, "You told us she wanted to take the challenge and come up by herself. Was that wrong?"

She pushed away from him, "Oh, so now you doubt me?" Pointing at Sophia, she added, "She told me as much. Sophia said she wanted to challenge herself. Do you think I lied?" Her face was red as she spit out, "Some marriage! Here we are on our honeymoon and you're calling me a liar!"

Robert's famous loud guttural laugh echoed through the bare trees, "Hah! Oh, my love, how happy you make me! Never in a thousand years would I call you a liar! Never, never!" He leaned her back in his arms to give her a big sloppy kiss. "There, see, you are loved beyond compare!" Smiling now, she ruffled his gray hair. "Oh, you!"

Sophia flipped her tent flap up as she returned to the fireside rubbing her hands. Timothy poured a hot substance from the boiling pan over the fire.

Tin cups were handed to each person. "Here's a toast to life!" He lifted his tin mug to knock it against Robert's, Karen's and Sophia's. Before Sophia took a sip, she asked, "What is in this concoction?" Timothy swallowed to say, "This is Robert's special brew from the golden sealed tea."

As fast as she could, Sophia knocked the tin cups from each person's hands. "No, this tea is poison! Is this Granger's tea? Oh, no, we just saved Karen and now you may all be poisoned!" The three of them stared at her.

Robert smiled, "We have drunk this tea before and nothing happened. It tastes like chestnuts that's all. Really, Karen and I have had this tea before, and we did all right. Sophia, you really need to let go of your brother's antics. This tea is fine."

A smile lit up Robert's face as he took Karen's hand and retreated into their tent. He closed the tent flap and zipped it shut, yelling "Stay out!"

Timothy refilled his tin cup with the hot tea, "Sophia, don't you think you overreacted a bit?" He reached for her tin cup that was dangling from her hand. "If you want coffee or cocoa there's some in the food box behind my tent. Help yourself." He blew on the hot tea as he sipped it. Sophia went to the food box. "I don't trust Granger. That's a fact. He's a dangerous brother. I'm not taking a chance."

There was a loud scream from Robert's tent. Timothy was the first one there, unzipping the flap. "What, what?" Sophia pushed him aside to see Robert foaming at the mouth as he flailed about, slapping his body on the sleeping bag. His eyes were huge and red. His nose was running when suddenly his body stopped only to jerk and twitch. Sophia knelt beside him. She lifted his head. Putting her finger in his mouth she let him gag fluid all over his sleeping bag.

Timothy pulled Karen away, "Did you drink any tea? Did you drink it?" Karen shook her head, "No, but you did. Didn't you? Are you all right?" Sophia focused on the green slime drooling from Robert's lips. She turned him on his side to let him regurgitate more of the foamy green slime onto the tent's floor.

Reaching behind Robert with her one free hand, Sophia pulled out

86

a white bag with the famous gold seal on it. "What's this?" She lifted out capsules filled with green herblike substances. "Karen, what is this?"

Karen knelt, "Sophia, Granger gave those to Robert to help with his erections. Those were a wedding present." Grabbing the bag out of Sophia's hand, Karen whispered, "Your brother is a nice man. He heals people. These were a gift."

Sophia lifted Robert's head to study his eyes, "Have you taken these before? Have you?" Robert shook his head and then vomited again. Green slime flew out of his mouth. His shaking became worse. Timothy whispered, "We need to get him to a hospital or to a road where we can get an ambulance. Let's move."

Karen was grabbing things to throw in duffel bags. Timothy helped Robert to stand, walking him slowly to the jeep. Leaning against the side of the jeep, Robert vomited again. Holding Robert's shoulder firmly against the Jeep, Timothy dumped out the coffee can and handed it to him. "Here, throw up in this. Come on, let's get you in the front seat."

Robert stepped forward limply as Timothy tried to get the front passenger door open. "Sophia, can you help? Robert is a limp noodle right now and I can't move him without him falling." Sophia ran to his side. Holding Robert's body upright, Timothy pushed the front passenger door open as far as it would go. Then the front passenger seat was laid back to be even with the backseat. The two of them rolled Robert's body along the side of the jeep until he was next to the door's opening. The two of them, without a sound, placed Robert in the front seat, seat belt attached and his body was turned to the side so he wouldn't aspirate.

Karen placed all the necessary items inside the hold at the back of the jeep. Sophia watched her as she continued to cry and wipe her nose on her parka sleeve. Karen still had snow in her faded blonde hair with matted mud on her mittens. Sophia shook her head as she whispered to Timothy, "We saved one only to lose the other!"

Timothy pushed back his baseball cap to respond, "We should not say this out loud, even though I agree with you. Let's get all those items stuffed into the back and get him to an E.R."

Sophia and Karen rolled the tents as tightly as possible since they were in a hurry. These were shoved behind the back seats into the back of the jeep. The small butane cooking stove was dumped out and snapped shut. The cooking and eating utensils were placed on top of the folded tents with the pillows and extra blankets layered on top. Finally, the tent poles were wrapped with twine and dumped on top of the whole as they bungee corded the back of the jeep shut. Karen and Sophia jumped onto the back seats with Karen holding Robert's head to the side. "We did the clear out in record time! How's Robert doing?" Sophia pulled off her parka and threw it in the back of the jeep.

The jeep skidded and roared through the melting puddles. Sophia stared out the window as Karen held Robert's head to the side. The two women were all but sitting on top of one another in the backseat. Suddenly, the jeep lurched into the air only to come down hard. Timothy called back, "This road is truly difficult. The large rocks or small boulders have appeared out of nowhere! Karen, hold Robert's body to the seat. Here we go over another boulder!" This time the jeep went airborne to come down hard with a loud rattle coming from the back. The inside of the jeep oozed with a nasty thick smell. Karen put her hand on Sophia's knee and tilted her head. "Look, Robert has foam coming out of his mouth and his left leg is jerking up and down. What do you think we should do? Should we stop?" The smell of rancid stomach fluid acid filled the jeep.

88          Shaking her head, Sophia removed the scarf around her neck and handed it to Karen, "Put this under his chin. He doesn't need that foam on his clothes or parka. Poor guy, what men go through for us women." Quietly, Karen tried to contain herself as tears fell down her cheeks. Timothy glanced over at Robert. Shaking his head, he twisted the jeep's steering wheel sharply to the right. The left side of the jeep scraped against a black lava basalt boulder. "Don't worry, the highway is right down there. This old jeep now has a scrape story to share in the future." Timothy smiled at Karen who was holding Robert firmly.

Timothy evidently decided speed was of the essence. He wasted no time barreling down the mountain to the main road. Pine trees flew past them, rocky cliffs barely touched the side of the jeep as Timothy hurdled the vehicle around the curves, over shallow streams and flew over the corrugated ridges in the dirt road. They got onto the interstate with a leap from the higher dirt road. Flashers were turned on as he honked the horn at the slow drivers in the fast lanes of the interstate.

A siren sounded, lights flashed as a dark car raced around them to come to a stop ten feet in front of the jeep. Timothy slowed to a stop only to jump out of the driver's door. He ran to the slow-moving sheriff who was lifting out of his vehicle. The passengers in the jeep watched as Timothy waved his hands, raised his voice to hurry back and jump into the jeep. "He's going to escort us to Colorado Springs, to the main hospital." Once again, they were off at full speed. Sophia closed her eyes and prayed they would all live as the jeep raced in and out of traffic following the siren in front of them.

At the emergency doors of the hospital, Sophia pushed her way out of the backseat, raced through the automatic doors to the front desk, calling out, "We have a man at death's door and need help right now! Please, now!" Two men in green scrubs raced from a side door pulling a gurney. Timothy grabbed the white bag with Granger's gold logo on it to hand to the nurse. "This is what he ingested, this might be of some help."

Karen slowly walked behind the gurney as Robert was wheeled into the bowels of the hospital. A tall female nurse put out her hand, "Only, legal family is allowed back here. The rest of you please take a seat in the waiting room." Pushing back her tangled hair, Karen spoke up, "I am his wife. These are our dear friends."

"Then just you, no dear friends." The nurse led Karen into the back as the heavy double doors closed, leaving Sophia and Timothy in the hall. Following the orange stripe on the hall floor, the two found the waiting room. Timothy gently removed his right shoe. His sock was filled with pus. "Do you think someone would be able to help my foot?" Sophia smiled, "Yes, go to the desk over there and show them your foot. It does stink as well. Go, go, go away." She pushed Timothy away as he moaned, "Wow, you're all heart and your father was a doctor."

Timothy limped to the desk across from where they had been sitting. The woman took one look at his foot, got on the phone and a man came from the back with a wheelchair. Timothy turned to Sophia and gave her a thumbs up as he was shoved into the wheelchair.

Sophia leaned back in the plastic chair to rest her back, "Damn, I am exhausted! What a day and it isn't even noon!"

After a few minutes, Karen joined Sophia in the waiting room. They sat drinking hot coffee from Styrofoam cups. Then Karen started to cry. "This is all my fault. I should have waited for all of you to go with me this morning. Oh, Robert is so generous and proud."

Sophia put her hand on Karen's arm, "You can't blame yourself. We have to be brave. After all Timothy's in there with his frostbit toes. At least we women came away unscathed, right?"

TERESA PIJOAN

Wiping her nose on the back of her shirt sleeve, Karen nodded. "Do you know how crazy this week has been?" She stared straight ahead, "My parents died from a car accident on their way here to my wedding. I was married without my father, which was his dream and mine as well. Then Robert surprised me with a new house. He wanted us to start our lives together in a house that belonged to both of us. How I wish my grandmother would've been able to attend. She loved the mountains and the snow."

Wiping the tears from her cheeks, she went on, "Then I met you, Robert's best friend and research writer. You both taught at UNM and loved it there. Do you know at first I was jealous of you? I thought you must be in love with Robert since he is such a fine man and has worked with you for years. Then he tells me his nephew was coming to the wedding." She shook her head, "Robert asked me what I wanted for a wedding present. I told him I had always wanted to climb to the top of Pike's Peak." Karen pulled off her pink parka to place it onto her lap. "Timothy reminds me of what a younger Robert must have been like. Both are good looking, kind and generous. Oh, Sophia, what will I do if we lose Robert?" She doubled over in tears.

Sophia moved closer to Karen, "Listen, Robert is a tough old coot. He's made of strong stuff. Let's not worry until we hear from the doctor. At least Timothy is getting his toes cared for by good looking nurses. Certainly, this must be his idea of heaven. Although, they are studying his feet not his face." They both smiled. "Karen, now is the time for you to be strong. We don't know what those pills have in them or what they will do. The team here will find out. This is the time to think good thoughts, okay?"

"No! Not okay!" Karen twisted in the chair to stare at Sophia, "Your brother killed your father and then tried to kill numerous other people. Sophia, I read the newspapers! I saw what Granger did to those poor people! How can you be so calm when Robert will probably die thanks to your brother! Oh, my God, what if Robert dies!" Karen stood, pointing her index finger at Sophia, "Do you know right now I hate you! I really hate you!" Karen gritted her teeth, "You may have saved my life, but, but, oh, God, you may have killed my husband!"

Sophia stood to back away from Karen, "Hey, you're exhausted, you have been through hell earlier this morning. Robert had a personal choice to take those pills. The choice was his, not mine, not yours, but his. And unfortunately not even Granger's choice. Sure he gave them to Robert, but Robert chose to take them." Pulling off her wool hat, Sophia let her short curls be free. "Yes, Granger is my brother and there is nothing I can do about it, but I don't have to defend him and I won't defend him. He's a bastard and I try to stay away from him!"

Karen doubled over as she sat on a plastic chair, "Damn it to hell! I would've loved Robert whether he could get it up or not! Sophia, I'm angry at the world right now! I would really like to kick something hard!" Karen's long fingers combed through her shoulder length hair. It was dyed a mango color of orange. Sitting beside her, Sophia closed her eyes. She was exhausted and hungry.

It was only ten o'clock in the morning and the day had already been stressful both on the mountain and off. Pulling out her cellphone, Sophia studied it. There was a chance for snow this evening although the weather was to remain warm. No messages from her daughters and nothing from her mother. This was excellent.

Heavy footsteps echoed on the hospital's linoleum floor. An older man with grey hair approached them. Both the women stood. The tall man stood in front of Karen, "I believe you are the wife? I am Dr. Jorge, you husband's doctor. Perhaps we should all sit down." He gestured to the plastic chairs. They sat as he rubbed his hands, "The news is not good. Your husband is stable, but he is in the ICU. The type of poison he ingested is extremely toxic. This type of poison comes from a local plant, Datura. The leaves were ground down and mixed with caster bean and Wolfsbane. The true deadly poison mixed in his rhubarb leaf. Not only is rhubarb poisonous, but it causes extreme abdominal spasms and regurgitation. Anyone who has ever grown rhubarb is warned of the extreme danger of ingesting the leaves."

The doctor put his hand on Karen's knee, "Someone with expertise in the field of poisons knew how to clinically harvest and pack this poison into capsules." Dr. Jorge shook his head, "As I said, your husband is not out of the woods yet, but we have stabilized him somewhat and he is in the ICU."

Standing, the doctor looked at Sophia, "As for your friend with the toes, he should be out soon. He's enchanting my nurses with his adventure stories. His toes will heal and there was no serious damage." Turning, he added, "He should be out soon."

Karen started to cry. "We don't appear to get a break. First, I fall down a hole and almost die and now this! What next?" Sophia pulled Karen to her and let her cry on her shoulder, "Hush, now, hush, you can only go up from here. Hush. Let's find out if you can go in and see Robert. Come on, let's find a nurse. They know everything."

As they stood, Timothy limped around the corner into the main hall. They stared at him. His hair was standing upright on his head. His trimmed beard had pieces of mud in it and his clothes were covered in something unrecognizable. "Hey, look, I have a new shoe." Using one crutch, he lifted his right foot. On it was a flat open shoe held on with blue Velcro straps. His big toe and second toe were wrapped in blue gauze. His left foot was back in his shoe with a sock.

Sophia knelt to study the strange shoe, "Wow, you really do rate. Karen, look. The outer part of this shoe has at least five women's signatures on it." Karen gave Timothy a weak smile, "Good for you. Your Uncle is in the ICU. We're off to find him. Want to come?"

Hobbling over to the plastic chairs, Timothy sat down abruptly. "No, I'll stay here. You girls go. I'm knackered."

The two women found a map at the end of the hall, which showed the ICU to be on the next floor up by the surgical center. A large professional sign was attached to the door. 'FAMILY ONLY. NO VISITORS. ONE PERSON AT A TIME.' To the side of the metal doors was a box with a speaker. Karen pushed the button beside it. After a few seconds a woman answered. Karen explained Robert was her husband. The heavy doors clicked.

Sophia put out her hand, "Please, don't be upset, but I really feel like I need to go home. Can you call me later and let me know how Robert is?"

After a good hug, Sophia returned to the waiting room. Timothy was slumped over in his chair sound asleep. Tapping him gently on the shoulder, he slowly opened his eyes, "Oh, I dreamt I lost my feet. Glad to see they're still at the end of my leg." Smiling, Sophia sat down next to him, "Do you think you can drive with that funky shoe?"

The gallant Timothy cracked a grin, "But of course! I shall drive you wherever you wish to go. Let's go." Hobbling on the crutches to the sliding hospital doors, he stopped to catch his breath. He leaned the crutches against the inside wall of the hospital to pull of his parka. "Too many clothes, too bulky with these crutches."

Sophia lifted the jeep's keys from Timothy's hand, "I'm driving,

92

thank you. Your right foot is in a strange shoe. I'm driving and there is no discussion about this."

The sky had darkened as they headed to the Jeep. Opening the door, Sophia was hit by the acidic smell of Robert's vomit. She grabbed a towel from the back and tossed it to Timothy. "Here sit on this. That green gook still looks wet." Timothy winced, "Well, this old jeep is going to need a major cleaning once I get home." Another towel was placed on the driver's seat. Sophia hit the automatic window buttons to lower all the windows in the jeep. The wind picked up blowing the cold mountain air into the jeep.

"Say, what would you think to a nice hearty breakfast?" Timothy clapped his hands, "Don't know about you, but I'm starving. Are you in a hurry to get back south?"

Sophia laughed, "A nice breakfast would be lovely. Where do think we should go?" She looked down at her right pant leg, "Timothy, we must smell pretty ripe. Do you think a restaurant would let us inside?"

"Hey, Sophia, we have money. Money talks. We can ask to be seated away from the other customers so as not to distract them from their food." Timothy pointed to a small café on the corner of the street. "This looks like a nice place and it isn't crowded, which would be good. We wouldn't want to gross out too many people." The back of the jeep was opened as Sophia reached inside to find her backpack. "Hey, do you have a change of clothes back here? I'm going to grab a different pair of jeans to put on in their bathroom. Where's your backpack?"

Pushing aside the rolled tents and blankets, Timothy grabbed a dark purple backpack. "Here, let's both clean up before we order." His crutches were laid stiffly on top of the debris in the back of the Jeep. "I'm not going to use those. I can walk on my foot." He closed the back of the jeep with a bang.

Timothy held the café door open for Sophia. The small café was dark. It took a few minutes for them to adjust their vision to the quaint small room. Most of the customers were sitting at large wooden tables. Lights hung down from round wagon wheels attached to the ceiling. The chairs were made of curved branch limbs with quilted seat pillows. The room smelled of cooked bacon and hot coffee. Large plate glass windows set in the outer walls gave the panoramic view of snow topped mountains and tall pine trees. A 'Please wait to be seated' sign was set inside the café proper.

A tall woman with six-inch heeled cowboy boots and drawn on eyebrows hurried over to them. "Two? Would you like a booth or a table?" Sophia held up two fingers, "Just us two, but do you have a restroom where we could freshen up? We have had quite a journey to get here and need to clean up some." The tall woman pointed with her two-inch bright pink fingernail to the back of the café, "Over there. Women's is on the right, men's is on the left."

Dark clouds moved across the sky as they walked to the back of the café. A crack of thunder shook the small building. Rain could be heard pelting against the walls and windows. The bathroom was empty when Sophia entered. Heavy boots were unlaced and kicked off, landing on the floor with a thud. As she sat on the toilet, she pulled off her thermal pants. They were crusted with Robert's vomit. Her thighs felt as if they were rubber. Digging into her backpack, she found her jeans and a clean pair of socks. Hobbling to the sink, she placed the backpack on the counter. The scratchy brown paper towels were wetted and used to wash off her thighs and feet. The socks were pulled on and then the jeans. Sophia sighed, she was beginning to feel clean and whole again.

94

The heavy sweater stank as well. Carefully she lifted it over her head. Staring into the mirror, Sophia frowned. Her hair was stuck to her head from sweating as she had lifted her body out of the ice hole. Her wool cap was still in the jeep. Muttering to herself, she said, "The people at the hospital must have wondered about us." Another scratchy paper towel was used to wash off her arms, her neck and finally she tossed the soggy paper into the trash can. She dried using her turtleneck sleeve. Then she dunked her head under the running warm water. "Oh, yes, that feels so good!" Taking a clean shirt from her backpack she dried her hair and face with it. "Damn, now I am human!" Her brush fluffed up her short curls. "Wow, look at all the gray hair!" Sliding the brush into her pack, she turned away from the mirror, zipped up her backpack, turned off the bathroom light and stepped into the corridor.

Sophia hurriedly joined Timothy at the wood table. Timothy had changed as well. His thinning brown hair was combed back from his high forehead. The gray beard was clean. The plaid yellow and gray wool shirt complimented his deep blue eyes. He patted the wooden chair seat next to him, "Have a seat. We made perfect time avoiding the rainstorm." Sophia pulled out the chair and sat down, "Did you order for us?" Lifting his glass of water, he held it up to Sophia, "Absolutely.

French toast, bacon, hash browns and hot tea. Here's to your health." He clicked glasses with Sophia.

The room was fairly quiet. There were four other tables with patrons on the other side of the room. Mexican serapes hung on the walls at odd angles. Soft cowboy music came from speakers at each side of the main room.

Turning to Timothy, Sophia asked, "So, tell me all the hot gossip about Karen and Robert. I haven't seen or heard from Robert for over a year and then out of the blue he calls me to attend his wedding and then we go camping with them. In November! All this smacks of strange, although I did appreciate being asked. What's going on with those two?"

"Oh," Timothy took a drink of his water, carefully placing it on the wooden table, "When Robert semi-retired from the research group, he decided he wanted to go to Las Vegas, Nevada, and shoot the craps. His tenure at the university doesn't pay much, but you probably know all about the university's pathetic pay. Robert wanted excitement, a thrill. This was something he had never done before. I think he was bored with life as a single man and wanted some excitement."

The food was brought and placed in front of them with a small pitcher of syrup and a bottle of ketchup. A glass pitcher of water with ice was placed in the middle of the table. "Would this be all?" The eyebrows asked. Sophia smiled, "This is fine for now, thank you." Once the woman had departed, Sophia said, "Yes, and then what happened."

Timothy waved his fork in front of his face, "Give me a minute, oh, this is so good." He swallowed and put more syrup on his French toast. "Robert has never been a good gambler. Taking advice from others, he left his credit cards in the hotel room and took only fifty dollars down into the casino area. There should be a law against him entering any gambling joint in the world. Poor fellow he lost his shirt." Wiping his mouth he continued, "By the way, the hotel rooms in Las Vegas are extremely expensive. Everything in Las Vegas is big bucks, bigger bucks than what my Uncle Robert has or had." Timothy picked up a piece of bacon and bit it in half, "Robert decided he was done with gambling. He told me it was a depressing hobby."

He bit off more bacon, "With what little money he had left, about eight dollars cash, he went to the bar. Now you know the drinks run for about twenty to thirty dollars for even a cheap beer. Robert had ordered a tall scotch and soda with the request for the bar guy to run a tab."

95

Sophia groaned, "Oh, no, what did he do?"

Lifting another piece of bacon to his mouth, Timothy continued, "As Robert tells it, 'This tall, gorgeous woman approached him for a dollar. Robert had evidently felt no pain in giving her one of his dollars, leaving him with only seven one-dollar bills. Then he watched her walk away only to return a few minutes later to sit next to him. It was no other than Karen, his now wife."

"How did this come to pass?" Sophia put a piece of her bacon on Timothy's plate. "Did she adopt him? What happened?"

"Oh, almost. They had a few more drinks with a lot of sharing. He told her about his troubles, and she told him about hers. She was trying to pick up men for money. She had no money and no credit cards. She was trying to ask for drinks, looking for a man who appeared rich, who would take her up to a room, seduce her and then she would leave his room with his wallet. A type of sting if you will."

Timothy took a drink of his water. "For some reason, Karen latched onto him. She asked him about his job, his life here in New Mexico, who he knew, what he knew.... a veritable inquisition. Then she fell for him lock, stock and barrel. That was that."

Licking syrup off her fingers, Sophia shook her head, "Seriously, with that nose Robert was the only man she hit on and he took the bait? And now, they're married! How is this possible?"

Snickering, Timothy went on, "They had known one another for only six hours when he proposed. She accepted and supposedly called her parents." Wiping his mouth he continued, "Now, Robert never got to speak to her parents or ask her parents for permission to marry Karen. This made him somewhat suspicious, but he was in love. Karen requested that the parents come to the wedding, and he could meet them there."

Sophia put her fork down on her empty plate. "That was delicious! But Karen's parents were supposedly killed in a car crash on the way here to the wedding, right?" Sophia smiled, "Timothy, according to my daughter, who I trust, Karen's mother died ages ago and when Karen's grandmother passed away, everything was given to her father who is evidently still alive. Why would she lie?"

"Damn, straight. No one knew about Karen. As a matter of fact, you were the first one she told about her parents' demise. Evidently, the cops called her from the accident sight. This is all according to Karen, the cops told her to go ahead with the marriage. How the cops knew about the marriage is beyond me, or anyone else. When Robert arrived, Karen stopped crying as you know."

Sophia wiped her chin with a napkin, "When you told me about all of this, my first concern was does she really have parents? Were they really coming to the wedding as she said? Has anyone tried to find out what really happened?" Staring at Timothy, "Does anyone know anything more about Karen?"

The empty plate was pushed to the front of the table. Sophia shook her head, "Was there an agreement made or a will written with a lawyer or something notarized?" The tall woman with the eyebrows arrived with the bill. She placed it next to Timothy's water glass. Nodding, he took out his wallet to place his credit card on top of the bill. He put the wallet on the table in front of him, "Sophia, why did you want us to leave you alone in the crevice? I was prepared to pull you out? What was all that about?"

Reaching into her backpack, Sophia pulled out a five-dollar bill and placed it under her water glass. "Karen sent you away. I needed help! Honestly, I don't know. The terror of being left behind in that frozen ice coffin was sheer survival mode. I was terrified." Shaking her head, Sophia added, "All I knew was I was not going to be left in that death hole. I was going to get myself out no matter what." She rubbed her thighs, "When Karen told me that you had all returned to camp and left me there to climb out by myself, I was so exhausted I couldn't get angry. Then when Robert started convulsing, I just let it go."

Eyebrows returned with the charge slip for Timothy to sign. He signed it and returned it to her. While he was putting his credit card back in his wallet, he shook his head, "Damn, neither Robert nor I wanted to leave you there. Karen was emphatic that we leave you alone to climb out of the hole by yourself. She didn't want to argue about it. She claimed you seriously told her to order us back to camp. Thank God, you were able to get out of there!" He put his hand on hers, "Perhaps we should google Karen's name, find out if she is a mass murderer." He gave a cautious smile. "Let's sit here a minute and try to find out more about Karen Sullivan."

Sophia's cellphone chirped in her pocket. Looking at the caller, she said, "Speaking of the devil, it's the hospital." Lifting it up to her ear, she said, "This is Sophia Pino." Timothy watched Sophia's facial expressions. Sophia shook her head, "Dr. Jorge, this is awful. Do you want us to come to the hospital? What are you going to do now?"

Timothy stared at her. Sophia put the cellphone back in her jacket pocket. "Well, Robert is not dead. Perhaps it is worse though, he is in a coma. The pills he took were filled with five different types of herbs all poisonous. The doctor said they tried to call Karen with the phone number she left at the desk. The number is no longer in service."

Sophia took a sip of her water, "Evidently, Robert had my phone number in his wallet for emergencies. Robert is nonresponsive and the doctor needs to know what course of action they should take since Robert had a Do Not Resuscitate card in his wallet as well."

Timothy grabbed his backpack. Rummaging through his clothes he pulled out his cellphone. He put his finger up as he pushed a button. The ringing from his cellphone soon changed to a female's voice, "The number you have dialed is no longer in service. Please, check the number and try again." Dial tone. He put the cellphone face down on the table, "That was fast. What do you suppose Karen is up to? How are we supposed to find her now?"

The waitress arrived to remove the plates and water pitcher from their table. Both Timothy and Sophia watched her walk across the café. Sophia was the first to speak, "We should go to the hospital. We need to see Robert and speak with the doctor." As she stood up, Sophia added, "You're his next of kin as far as family goes, right? You're his nephew." Timothy nodded, hurrying out of the café's front door, "What the hell is Karen playing at? Do you think she's on her way to Albuquerque to get his house, his bank accounts, his everything?"

# 9

Opening the passenger door, Timothy threw his backpack onto the backseat, "Her stuff is still here in the Jeep. Won't there need to be a reading of the will or something?"

Sophia put the key into the ignition. "Can you call somebody and find out while I drive us to the hospital?" Timothy leaned back to pull his cellphone from his front pant pocket. "Yes, go, go. Let's figure this out. I'm going to call the University. Certainly, someone might know about his life. Maybe his teacher aid?"

Watching the oncoming traffic as Sophia put on the jeep's blinker to turn into the hospital parking lot, she asked, "How did they get the herbs from Granger? The last I heard from my brother he was living in Montana with his wife and two kids." Finally, there was a break in the traffic and Sophia raced into the parking lot.

Timothy was studying his cellphone. "Now, this is news. Karen Sullivan is seventy-four years old and lives in Oregon. She is married to an engineer and has five adult children, six grandchildren and has retired from teaching secondary school."

He showed the cellphone to Sophia, "Look, she is seriously overweight and does not have colored hair. This is the only Karen Sullivan found on my search engine."

Sophia clicked on her seatbelt. "Well, this is certainly news. What did our Karen tell Robert she did for a living beside work at a casino?"

Timothy's cellphone was shoved in his front jean picket, "That's about it. Evidently, Robert and Karen didn't do much talking." Slamming the jeep's driver door, Sophia met up with Timothy at the back of the jeep, "He must not have needed the herbs Granger gave him when he was at the hotel with her in Las Vegas, right? Why did he take them today?"

She stood in the middle of the parking lot, "Unless, unless Robert had other pills he took prior to the herbs. Do you think he was using a different type of pill and ran out? Maybe we should check out his backpack?" She tossed the jeep's keys to Timothy.

An elderly woman stood behind the front desk of the large reception room. She wore a pink loose jacket over her white blouse. Sophia and Timothy walked up to her. Sophia asked, "Can you call Dr. Jorge for us? He asked us to come to the hospital regarding our friend who is in the ICU."

They found the plastic chairs in the main waiting room, but instead of sitting they stood staring out of the large plate glass windows. Pike's Peak was clearly visible. Pointing his finger, Timothy noted, "That's our peak. Right up there. All of this seems ethereal right now."

Heavy footsteps echoed on the linoleum floor as Dr. Jorge approached them. "Thank you for coming. We have a legal obligation to notify his next of kin regarding his choices. Please, let's sit."

The clipboard in Dr. Jorge's hand was opened. "Here is a copy of Robert Glacie's Do Not Resuscitate legal paper. As his condition is now, he is in a coma with a breathing tube. He needs the breathing tube, or he will stop living." Dr. Jorge's voice softened, "Do you know his next of kin? Please, tell me you do."

Sophia turned to Timothy. Timothy stared at his hands, "I am his remaining family. His parents passed years ago. He has no living siblings. My father was his brother. My father died years ago doing research in India. My mother passed when I was eighteen. I'm it."

Dr. Jorge studied Timothy, "Then you are the one to tell us what to do."

Shaking his head, Timothy asked, "What are you asking me to do? If you're asking me to kill him, I can't do it. Robert was a father to me. He was my best friend when I was growing up. Killing him is not an option with me."

Timothy shook his head as he rubbed his hands together. "No, no, no, Robert is a part of me, of my life. No, I cannot hurt him!" Timothy quickly stood up to walk to the wide window. "Robert is a man who is loved by his students, his friends, and his new wife and especially loved by me. No!" He turned face Sophia, "There is no way, no!"

Sophia put her arm around his shoulders, "Do you want to see Robert before making a decision? Would that help you to decide?

Because what the doctor is saying is that right now Robert is a vegetable and cannot survive without a breathing tube. Do you want to see him first? I'll go with you, if it's allowed?"

Timothy didn't move. Sophia put her hand on his arm, "Do you want me to come with you or would it be better if I stayed here? Tell me, Timothy, what are you thinking?"

Dr. Jorge put his tablet under his arm, "Listen, I have to go. There is an emergency in another part of the hospital. Why don't you two figure out what you want to do and have a nurse page me? I can meet you at the ICU."

An empty gurney was pushed by them with an orderly studying his cellphone. Timothy leaned against the wall. "Sophia, I don't think I can do this. Two years ago, my wife was diagnosed with cervical cancer. She refused treatment. I sat with her watching her die. Nightmares flooded my life. Only lately have I been able to put her pain filled face out of my nights. Seeing Robert, watching him die will only make my life more miserable. Shouldn't we try harder to find Karen? After all, she is his wife now?"

Shaking her head, Sophia walked away from him down the hall. "Damn, Timothy, damn, damn! Certainly, let's try and find Karen. Somewhere, someone must know more about her. If she had Granger's bag, she must have known Granger." Her cellphone was pulled out, "I hate doing this. I really, really hate doing this, but I can't think of any other way to find out about her. I will go straight to the source."

Punching numbers onto the cellphone, she put it up to her ear. "Hey, Granger, guess who this is?" Sophia shook her head as she marched back and forth up and down the hall. "Is that right? How wonderful for you and the family. It must be lovely in California this time of year." She stopped in the middle of the hall to stare up at the ceiling, "Certainly. Yes, it is important for the kids to learn to swim and see the ocean. Listen, I have a question for you." Shaking her head, she paused then said, "Do you know a woman by the name of Karen Sullivan? Am I saying that right?"

Timothy walked over to Sophia. He smiled at her. His eyes filled with hope. Sophia motioned to him for a pencil and paper, "Yes, I'm getting something to write with, hold on." Timothy pulled a broken pencil and wrinkled paper to hand her. She walked behind Timothy to place the wrinkled paper on his back. Studying the broken pencil, she

101

said, "Yes, I'm ready. Go ahead. So, the woman you think I am talking about has the name of Karen Gilbert. Why?"

Her hand rested on Timothy's back, "Oh, her grandmother and grandfather loved musicals and Gilbert and Sullivan were writers of musicals. Okay, I guess probably. Do you know how we can get ahold of her? Is she in Colorado or New Mexico?" Sophia started writing on the paper while Timothy smiled at a nurse that was walking by them.

Sophia stopped for a moment, "Do you know how she would get some of your herbs for erectile dysfunction?" Quickly, she added, "No, I don't need them. No, I don't know anyone who may need them. Come on, Granger, this is a simple question." She wrote something down on the paper.

The paper was handed to Timothy from over his shoulder along with the pencil. "Granger, did you know my boss at the research center by the name of Robert?" Sophia whispered, "Damn! He hung up on me. I guess he does know Robert and he had Karen Gilbert as a student in one of his herbal workshops. Granger said she put her address down as Reno, Nevada when she took his class. As far as Robert is concerned, he hung up on me."

Timothy whipped out his cellphone, "Let's find Karen Gilbert. But first let me ask you this, did you believe Karen really loved Robert? I mean did you think all her crying and holding him was real while he was throwing up in the jeep, did you believe any of that? Or was it a show?"

"Yes, I believed her. Although I was so exhausted I would believe just about anything. The important issue here is did Robert believe her. Did they make love before this incident? You know we need her backpack. Let's go back to the jeep and get her backpack before we make any decisions." Sophia started walking quickly to the hospital's main door. Timothy was right behind her. "What if she was play acting out of some sort of vengeance? Did you know her from somewhere before?"

Waving her hand in the air as she pointed to the jeep, she called out, "No, I didn't trust her either. Come on!"

Karen's backpack was zipped shut as Sophia dropped it on the ground by her feet. "We can go through this inside the Hospital. Come on." Timothy bent over the folded tents to push them onto the back seat. He was shoving items around until he found Robert's backpack. Continuing his search, while whistling he tugged on a leather strap.

A pouch suddenly flew up, almost hitting him on the forehead. It was leather with a large hummingbird drawn on with pastels. Fringe hung off the bottom of it and feathers were tied to the side of the pouch. "Do you have any idea what this is?"

Sophia reached out to take it from his hands. "Ah-ha, this is her purse or her personal bag." Leaning against the side of the muddy jeep, Timothy asked, "Do you think we should get a hotel room and go through this stuff in our own privacy?"

Glaring at him, Sophia answered, "Hell, no! These hotel rooms cost an arm and a leg. We can do this in the hospital. Robert didn't give me enough time to even buy them a wedding present." She paused to shake her head, "Wonder where all of the wedding gifts are now?" Above them the clouds covered the sun with rumbling thunder echoing across the land. Sophia picked up the backpack from the ground, "Do you have any idea how expensive a hotel room is here in Colorado Springs?"

"Okay, then where are we going to examine this stuff? In the men's room or in the women's room? How about on the floor in the waiting room? Come on, Sophia, where are we going to snoop through her stuff that isn't public or sterile?"

Sophia turned around, "Here, right here at the jeep. Come on, let's sit and go through this sitting on the front seats."

Timothy stared at her, "Here? Really, here in the wind with people walking around us in the parking lot? Oh, and the smell!" She turned, looking around outside of the hospital. "There is a waiting room by the ICU. Certainly, we could go through some of this stuff there. At least it will be warm and out of the wind. Also, we won't have to listen to all the airplanes, jets and helicopters."

Following the stripes on the floor of the hospital, they found the ICU waiting room. The room was empty aside from six chairs, a small table with a black phone and a sign stating No Food Allowed. Karen's backpack was placed on Sophia's lap as she unzipped the top of it. Timothy sat beside her. In Karen's pack all they found were some letters addressed to Karen Gilbert. There was a notebook with a handwritten name inside, claiming ownership to Karen Sullivan. Taped inside the notebook was a house key wrapped in tissue paper. Sophia shuffled through the pages, realizing it was an address book. Sure, enough there was Granger Pino's phone number and address. There was also an

103

address for a woman marked 'Grandma Edna.' Sophia read it to Timothy who put forth the call.

He shook his head, "No answer. Is there another number?" Sophia thumbed through the little notebook page by page. "Oh, here. This is a phone number for a lawyer here in Colorado Springs and a number for Albuquerque. Let's try the Colorado Spring's number."

Timothy punched the number into his cellphone. A secretary answered and then put him through to the lawyer. Timothy gave Sophia the thumbs up sign. After a brief conversation, he clicked his phone shut. "Well, here is the development. Karen's grandmother passed away six weeks ago under mysterious circumstances. Karen was at first considered a person of suspicion, but then she was back East at the time of her grandmother's death. Her last name is Gilbert-Sullivan. Her main address is in Las Vegas, Nevada. The lawyer did not know of her marriage to Robert and has no knowledge of where she may be now."

Opening every small container in Karen's pack, Sophia asked, "Did she inherit a lot of money? Because if she did why would she marry Robert? Right?" Four small capsules fell out of one of the small envelopes found in a hidden pocket of the backpack. "Hey, what do you suppose these are?" She handed them to Timothy.

He answered her first question, "Evidently, she did not inherit anything. There was, however, a young woman by the name of Donna Pino McGuire who was left a substantial amount of money due to her helping Miss Edna with her memoirs. Would this Donna be your daughter?"

Sophia's mouth fell open, "What? My Donna helping someone with the written word? Couldn't be."

Glaring at her, Timothy lifted his cellphone, "What's Donna's phone number?" Sophia rattled off the number. As the phone rang, he handed it to Sophia. "You better ask her. She doesn't who I am."

"Hey, Donna, it's your mom. How are you, Sweetheart? Oh, that's good. Say listen, do you know a Miss Edna who passed away recently?" Sophia smiled, "Yes, how kind of you. Do you know her granddaughter by any chance? Her name would be Karen." Sophia pulled a pen from the pile of items in front of her and a torn piece of paper. "When did she say this? Where her parents there as well?" Sophia frantically scribbled onto the paper. "Right, right, well, I will let you go. Thank you, Sweetheart. Know that I love you!"

Sophia handed Timothy the pencil, "Well, Timothy, Donna met the famous Karen at the reading of Edna's will. Karen's mother had passed away when she was a young child. No one wanted to take care of child Karen due to her bad temper and selfish ways. Edna and her husband took her in and raised her as their own. Karen's father deserted both Karen and her mother when she was three. Evidently, the father could not deal with their issues, whatever they were. He was at the reading of the will. The lawyer had a detective locate him, cleaning him up somewhat to have him presentable at the reading of the will. He is Edna's son."

Studying the pills in his hand, Timothy mentioned, "Wow, and I thought my family was messed up, for sure you only have to look at others' to realize how normal your own family is." He rolled the pills in his palm, "Do you think we should take one and find out what they do?"

Quickly, Sophia removed the pills from his hand. "These are decomposing aspirin tablets. There's an A on each one."

Thunder rattled the sides of the hospital. The wind could be heard blowing against the walls. A siren screamed on the highway. Timothy took a silver tube from the front pocket of Robert's backpack. Whispering under his breath, Timothy stated, "Do you know I cannot pull this tube top off, I can't? Sophia, why don't you do it? You are a strong woman." Timothy sniffed, "I remember when my wife died. I didn't believe I would ever feel whole again. What are we to do if Robert dies?"

Holding the tube in her hand, Sophia pulled off the top of it to find it empty. There was nothing inside. Sophia glared at him, "We have had enough, just enough negative stuff going on around here, Timothy!" Sophia slapped her leg, "This morning Karen fell into an ice crevice, you guys pulled her out and then you left me to die in that ice box of hell!"

Pointing her finger at him, "My legs hurt, my arms are sore and here we are inside a hospital, sitting while going through all these dirty backpacks that don't even belong to us, searching for answers. Timothy, let's deal with this stuff first. Karen is the next of kin. She should be the one to be with Robert!" Giving him a stern stare, Sophia went on, "Seriously, let's not think about ourselves while Robert is in there fighting for his life and Karen is out there trying to poison the world!" She threw a white sock at him, "Come on! Get with the program! You are here now, and we have an emergency that we can solve. Pull yourself together, man!"

Timothy glared at her. His face was wet with tears. "You are cruel! Do you know how cruel you are?"

Sophia lifted the backpack, "Please, let's deal with this and try to find some positive action for a change." She brushed his long bangs from his face. "You need to shave once we find what we are looking for here. I'm sure we are both a mess. First things first. Here, look in this stuff." She handed him Robert's pack.

Gritting his teeth, Timothy shook his head. "All right. Here goes." He unzipped Robert's pack to dump it upside down on the floor in front of him. There were small notebooks, maps, a survival handbook and a round pill bottle with writing on it. Timothy pulled his reading glasses from his shirt pocket. "This is Karen's handwriting. It's not typed by a pharmacist. Here, see if you can read it."

Taking the bottle from Timothy, Sophia held out her hand for Timothy's glasses. He handed them to her. "Well, it is a type of medical mixture. Not sure of these words. Hold on to them." The two of them stuffed the items back into the packs. Timothy pulled out a pair of Robert's jeans and a shirt. "I'm going to the bathroom and clean up. These clothes might be big, but they're clean!" He disappeared down the hall.

Sophia returned to the front desk to ask the pink lady to page Dr. Jorge. The woman told her, "It will be a while. He is in conference. Please, have a seat and he should be with you soon." Sophia ran out to the jeep, opened the back and dumped the packs. Locking the jeep, the sky darkened with the rolling sound of thunder. Lightning struck across the sky. Birds flew against the wind as leaves blew through the parking lot. The tall pine trees danced while smaller branches creaked, cracking and falling on the far side of the forest by the hospital.

The sky opened with rain falling hard, slapping against the parking lot pavement. People were running to their cars or running into the hospital. The air smelled fresh, pure, as Sophia stood letting the rain wash over her. Her hands were open with her palms cupped to catch the rainwater.

She heard her name being called. Turning to face the hospital there was Timothy waving. Her walk to him was delightfully wet. He grabbed her arm to pull her into the main room. "Are you crazy? You're soaking wet! Dr. Jorge's tech is here to speak to us. Come on, let's hear what she has to say."

Returning to the front room of the hospital brought the pungent odor of Lysol with an undertone smell of antiseptic. The overhead speaker repeated a doctor's name over and over again. Sophia blinked several times to adjust her vision in the stark, bright light of the hospital's hallways. A middle-aged woman met them at the front desk. She was dressed in faded green scrubs. Her brown hair was rolled up on top of her head, tied with a bright red ribbon. She pushed her thick glasses up her freckled nose as she waved them to walk with her. "These herbs you brought in, Timothy, we will evaluate. Right now, there is not much we can do to help your uncle. His body is shutting down. His lungs need help to breathe with incubation." She turned down another hall, leading them to closed heavy metal doors. "This is the ICU. If you wish to visit him, now would be the best time."

Sophia leaned back against the cold wall, watching Timothy. His eyes wandered from the floor to the double doors. The woman was patient as she stood stoic beside him. Finally, Timothy nodded, "All right, I'll go in and see him. Don't ask me to make any decisions though, but I'll see him." Turning to Sophia, he said, "Alone."

The woman held up a plastic card attached to her wrist bracelet. The double doors swung in as she nodded for Timothy to precede her. Sophia did not move, nor did she make eye contact with Timothy. She continued to lean against the wall. An orderly pushing a gurney out of the double doors, stopped, "Miss, you cannot be here. Please, go back to the front and wait for your party there. Thank you." He pushed his gurney down the hall.

Following the pink stripe on the hospital's floor, Sophia returned to the front of the hospital. The plastic chairs were even less inviting than they were when they first arrived. As Sophia turned to sit, a yellow cab pulled up in front. Amazed at what she saw, Sophia moved to the sliding doors. Karen walked in with a frown upon her face. She hurried to Sophia, "Is he dead yet? Oh, Sophia, he never signed the marriage forms! Sophia, I need him to sign these." A handful of legal papers were thrust into Sophia's face.

"Where is he? He's not dead yet! Please! Please, don't let him be dead yet!" The screech of her voice turned the heads of those walking down the halls. Quietly, Sophia asked, "Karen, Karen, slow down.

TERESA PIJOAN

Where have you been? What is going on with your cellphone?"

"Sophia, I can't talk right now! Where is Robert?"

"Where have you been and why is your phone off? We have been trying to get ahold of you for hours. What's going on with you and Robert?" Sophia stood squarely in front of Karen.

"My cellphone is off because I can't pay my bill! I have no money! Robert promised me money! I was back at the hotel, taking a shower to get the stink off me! I had to change my clothes and pack up my things, okay?" Her voice gained in volume, "Now, where is Robert, he has to sign these papers or our marriage is null and void! Do you understand? I need to find Robert!"

Stepping aside, Sophia answered, "He's in the ICU. Follow the pink stripe on the floor and you will get to the ICU. Go! Just go!" Sophia pointed to the pink stripe.

Karen walked around Sophia to spit words at her, "Did you know the envelope he gave me was empty? Empty! It was empty!" She raced down the hall. Sophia shook her head, with her cellphone in her hand, she texted Timothy, 'I'm going home.'

A group of young men dressed in SWAT gear came rushing into the hospital. They quickly asked the Pink Lady about the ICU. The men hurried off, following the pink stripe on the floor. Sophia and the Pink Lady watched and then returned to face one another. A tired Sophia asked, "Excuse me, but would you be able to tell me how to get to the Marriot hotel from here? I need to retrieve my vehicle."

The woman sat back on her high secretary chair to think, "I do believe the hotel is just three blocks down from here. If you turn right, as you go out of the parking lot, you should be able to see the high sign of the hotel. It isn't that far, but aren't you with the other man? Wouldn't he be able to drive you there? The wind and the rain have seriously picked up, you will be soaked by the time you walk there."

Studying the weather by looking out the tall windows of the hospital, Sophia had to agree. Trees were dancing back and forth as the rain plummeted the ground, bouncing off the asphalt. The sound of heavy footfall brought her attention back to the hall. The SWAT team was pushing Karen in front of them. She was in handcuffs with tears streaming down her face. Jerking away from their strong hold, she yelled at Sophia, "Call Bethany! Please, Sophia, call Bethany! She's at the hotel waiting for me! Tell her, please, tell her!"

Her voice faded as she was pushed out of the hospital's front double doors into the pouring rain. Following them slowly, came Timothy. His face was wet with tears. Sophia reached out to him as he fell into her open arms. "Damn bitch, she admitted it. She admitted it all. She was frantic about getting him to sign her blasted pieces of paper. All the time yelling at him that he shouldn't die until he signed the papers."

Quietly, he spoke as he hugged Sophia, "Robert is dead. He died on his own. I pray he was not able to hear her screaming at him." He pushed away from her, "Let's go home. I think I'm done for today. The doc signed the papers for Robert's body to be released to me. I can deal with all of this later. Let's go home."

The two of them sat in Timothy's jeep. There was no discussion, no movement, just the sound of the rain hitting the roof of the jeep. The two of them watched the trees, the airplanes flying overhead, it was only one o'clock in the afternoon. Timothy started the jeep, the traffic was busy as usual. At the hotel, they found the guitar player sitting on the side of one of the twin beds. She was puffing on a joint. Neither Timothy nor Sophia said anything. Clothes were gathered into two piles. Sophia loaded up her items into her ancient SUV, gave Timothy a tender hug, and drove off through the rain.

109

As she turned onto the main road going south, her cellphone chirped. Sighing, Sophia pulled off onto the shoulder of the highway. Leaning back in the driver's seat, she held her cellphone, "Yes?"

"Mom, it's me Sybil. Something is up with grandma. You know how she does that thing when she calls you and asks if you're busy and if you say 'yes you're busy,' she says never mind? Then you know she's in trouble, right? I asked her if she wanted me to come and help her, but she just hung up."

Sighing, Sophia asked, "Well, what did you tell her when she asked?" Sybil spoke clearly, "I said, Ethan and I are grocery shopping. I told her that. She just hung up on me, so something's going on with her. Should I go over there, or should I just ignore her call?"

Sophia stared at the thick pine forest surrounding the highway. Closing her eyes, she answered, "I'm on my way home. Let me stop by and talk to her. She's feeling fragile because Granger and his family are on holiday and he's not there to care for her."

"Mom, you must be exhausted. You sound tired. Why don't Ethan and I go and see her? You just come home. Take care of yourself first."

"No, that's all right. I'll visit Mom. You and Ethan haven't had a day off for a while. It is Saturday. You two do your chores and I'll check in with you once I'm home. Thank you for letting me know. I love you, Sweetheart. Just enjoy your day."

Watching the oncoming cars, Sophia carefully returned to the highway. She looked for Timothy's jeep behind her, but didn't see it anywhere. Perhaps he needed to rest first and decided to stay at the hotel. Slowly, Sophia's right leg started to shake. Her thigh muscles were still sore from the climb out of the crevice. There on the side of the highway were two young people with their thumbs out. Not thinking of anything but resting, Sophia pulled over.

The two young people raced to the SUV. The young man appeared to be in his twenties. His prep-school hair cut was dripping from the rain. He was taller than the young woman. Both had rain slickers, but their backpacks appeared to be soaked. The young woman and young man were about the same age. As the young man pulled open the passenger door, he asked, "Are you going to New Mexico? We're trying to get to Negara. Do you know where that is?"

"Yes, I certainly do. My sister-in-law once lived in Negara. But listen, before you get in, I have a question for you both."

The two stopped and stared at her. Rain dripped from their packs. Cautiously, Sophia asked, "Do either of you have a driver's license?"

The young man put out his hand, "Yes, I do. Do you want to see it? My name is Matt Aragon, and this is my cousin Collette. We were ditched at a gig in Colorado Springs. We were left stranded. This would be great if you could give us a lift." He pulled out his wallet and handed her his University I.D. and his New Mexico driver's license. It was valid and everything was in order.

Sophia took a photo of his driver's license with her cellphone. Her seatbelt was unstrapped as she asked, "Would you mind driving, Matt? I am exhausted from a rather strenuous morning. Would it be too much to ask for you to drive?"

Collette giggled, "Wow, lady, you're a blessing! Where do you want us to sit? Where should we put our things so they're not in your way?"

The young woman pushed back her long brown hair. Her green eyes shone with her eagerness to please. The sharp cold air mixed with the smell of fresh rain entered the SUV as the doors were opened.

Sophia walked around to the passenger side of the vehicle. "Put your packs in the back, or better yet, put them in the middle seat. I'm going to lie down on the back seat. Matt, you can drive and Collette you can ride shotgun. Let me know when we get to Wagon Mound because we will need to fill up there."

The quiet sound of the tires on the road rocked Sophia into a deep sleep on the backseat. There was a loud ringing that woke her. Matt's voice was heard, "Bethany, what do you want now?" Sophia sat up at the sound of that name.

Collette took the cellphone from Matt, "Listen, Bethany, we are done with you and Karen. You got this gig. You promised to pay us out of your money and then you ditched us. We won't have anything further to do with you! Oh, and tell your friend Karen, she's a bitch who deserves her place in hell for marrying that man."

Sophia watched the two up front. Matt and Collette high fived as Matt said, "That's telling her. What did she want anyway?"

Collette, smirked, "She wanted to know if we could get her a ride back to town. Her lover friend Karen was arrested for murder."

Matt let out a quiet laugh, "Serves them both right. What a nasty duo. Next time, let's do our own thing. At least we trust one another." 111

Curious as to the conversation going on up front, Sophia moved to the middle seat, pushing the backpacks to the side. "You two know Karen Gilbert-Sullivan? What can you tell me about her? Robert was my friend, a colleague from our work. What do you know about all of this?"

Turning in the front passenger seat to face Sophia, Collette said, "Bethany is a member of our performing group. She plays the guitar, Matt here plays the mandolin and I play the flute. We were told to play at this wedding at Pike's Peak. Karen told us where to meet. She talked her fiancé into giving her money for renting a car. We drove up here with Bethany and her brother J.J."

Matt interrupted, "Yeah, J.J. isn't really a minister. He just says he is and gets paid to do the deed. He's a real jerk. He'd steal the shirt right off your body. He takes the test to be a minster, gets this phony license, asks for a fortune, has the people sign the forms and when the married couple take the forms to the courthouse, they're told the forms are illegal. He's a slimy bastard."

It was Collette's turn to interrupt, "Yeah, well, Bethany said we would be paid a hundred dollars each to perform. That is big money for us university kids. So, we get up there and Karen is nowhere to be found. Then we find out the service was done, and we weren't told anything." She turned forward to look at the highway ahead, then continued, "Karen told Bethany that she was going to give her fiancé some drugs to do him in or something like that and take his money because she was poor and in debt."

A tall sign came up by the side of the highway. Matt pointed to it, "Here we are at Wagon Mound. Shall we stop and get gas and maybe some food? I don't know about you girls, but I'm starving." He pulled into the gas station to stop at the one free pump. Sophia reached into her purse, handed Matt twenty-five dollars and told him to get some food for himself and Collette. She'd fill up her vehicle.

The little gas station still had the burritos for sale. Collette and Matt walked out with a burrito in each hand, a bag of chips under their arms and cold drinks. Sophia topped off the gas, paid with her credit card and jumped back into the SUV. Collette asked, "Don't you want something to eat? You must be hungry, too? Here's your change. All this cost more than we expected, but thanks!"

112    Once back on the road, the food eaten, Matt picked up on the previous conversation. "Bethany and Karen were or are a pair. They hooked up after Karen's grandmother died. Bethany said it was love at first sight, but Karen insisted she had to play this charade with this old man if she was going to have any future at all."

Nodding in agreement, Collette added, "It was sick, sick. The whole thing was sick. Anyway, I guess the deal is done if Bethany said Karen was arrested. Some guy came back to the hotel, kicked Bethany out, and told her if she didn't get lost, he was going to call the cops on her. There was no money left at the hotel. Bethany must be in serious trouble, especially if Karen sings like a canary."

Sophia leaned forward to better hear the two young people, "Was Bethany involved in the killing of Robert, too?"

An eighteen-wheeler raced past them as they turned to go down into a canyon. The sky was still gray with heavy clouds. The highway was wet from the rain. Ravens flew overhead as the wind began to pick up again. Matt shook his head, "Who knows what Bethany did? We know Karen had pills made up by some doctor of herbs or something. She had used them before, so she knew they worked."

Twisting to look directly at Sophia, Collette added, "We didn't know anything about all of this until we got to Colorado Springs. J.J. and Bethany were toking on some strong weed and they spilled the beans, laughing about it all the time. Bethany almost peed in her pants she thought it was so funny. J.J. is a real doper."

Agreeing, Matt spoke, "Yeah, we don't do dope. That's not our thing. We both are on scholarships and don't want to screw things up for our families."

Sophia sat back, watching the trees go by. Karen had scammed everyone. Poor Robert was used, completely used. He had been ever so happy. Joy had radiated from him at the wedding, at the campground and then to have been used, and killed. Lifting her cellphone from her lap, she tried to call Timothy. There was no service in the canyon. She rolled onto her side, on the seat, letting her head rest on one of the backpacks. What a tragedy.

113

# 10

She felt someone shaking her knee. "Miss, ah, Miss? Matt, what's her name? Did she tell us her name?" The vehicle came to a stop. Matt walked around to the side of the sliding door. He opened it to pat Sophia on the back, "Miss? We're here. Are you okay? Miss?"

Sophia slowly became conscious. "Yes, oh, yes, are we here already? That was fast." Rubbing her eyes, she sat up and looked around. There was a tall cottonwood tree, a tractor and an old adobe house on her left. "Oh, yes, we certainly are here. Where are we exactly?"

Collette burst out laughing, "Wow! You really gave me a scare what with all this talk about killing people. Miss, we're here at Matt's family home. My home is down the road. I can walk over there. Wow, you really gave us a fright!"

Sophia stepped out of the vehicle. The air was fresh, warm and the sky was clear blue. Matt put out his arm, "Would you like to come in and meet my parents? I'm sure they would like to thank you for saving us." He patted the hood of the SUV, "You know this old girl really has charm. She got us here with no problem and you still have a quarter of a tank of gas."

Two people walked to the van. Matt glowed, "Mom, Dad, this is the woman who gave us a ride home. Well, she let me drive her ancient SUV, but she got us here. No problem."

Smiling, he added, "This is my father Carl Aragon and my mom Dion." Matt turned to Sophia, "Do you know, you never told us your name?"

Sophia put out her hand, "Hi, I'm Sophia Pino from the South Valley, way down south from here. Your son and niece were nice enough to drive down here from Colorado Springs. They were pleasant enough to let me sleep in the back."

Carl Aragon smiled, "I remember you and your family from long, long ago. I was one of the sheriffs who came to your mother's farmhouse the day your father died. That was in Calavera, right?"

Walking with them toward the adobe house, Sophia nodded, "Oh, my goodness that was a while ago. What a mess that day was with people coming and going and all of us in such shock."

Carl shook his head, "Well, no, some of you were not in shock." He turned to point to the left, "As a matter of fact, your brother and his wife bought some land just north of us here. He divorced her, didn't he?"

Dion interjected as she opened the screen door to the front room, "If I remember right, your sister-in-law Emily still has the house here although her daughter Shirley is married and lives in Arizona. We ran into one another in the post office last Christmas when Shirley was visiting her mother. Shirley is the proud mother of two little girls who are just darling."

Then as she walked ahead of Sophia into kitchen, she added, "Emily rarely is home now a days. She's working for the Forest Service, and they have her traveling all over the United States. Have you spoken to her lately?"

Matt, Collette and Carl followed the two women into the kitchen. Matt went directly to the cupboard to pull out a large bag of potato chips, "Mom, we're starving. Can we take these outside to munch on while you guys talk?"

Dion reached over and took the bag away from him, "No, you may not. It is getting late. Why don't you take your cousin home to her house while I fix dinner?" She patted him on the back, "Go on. Take Collette home. Her parents must be eager to hear about her adventures."

This time Collette spoke up as she sat down on a kitchen chair, "Aunt Dion, the trip north was a bust. We were supposed to have a gig with Bethany and J.J., but they dumped us. When Matt and I went to use the bathroom, the two of them took off in the old truck of J.J.'s. They went ahead and did the wedding without us while we were stranded."

Carrying their packs into the kitchen, Matt agreed, "Yeah, this was supposed to be big bucks for each of us. J.J.'s history teacher was getting married, and he promised to pay us one hundred dollars each. What a waste of time." He frowned.

Collette studied her cousin, "Yeah, what was that all about

anyway? Bethany and Karen—Karen was the supposed bride—they were supposed to be lovers, right? I mean how was that supposed to work?"

Carl cut some slices of cheese. Crackers were added to the plate as he placed it on the kitchen table, "When last I spoke to J.J. and his father, J.J. had failed his history exam and was losing his scholarship. J.J.'s father explained to me that J.J. had blown off studying and somehow blamed his professor for failing. J.J. was angry because now he must go to work with his father's roofing company, which he hates."

Agreeing with his dad, Matt explained, "J.J.'s family doesn't have the money for college. His family is from Mexico and they're here illegally. The whole family is working under the radar although J.J. did get a scholarship because of his soccer scores."

Dion sat down next to Sophia, "Families. They are so complicated, aren't they? I'm still working, or we wouldn't be able to pay for what we need. Matt outgrows his clothes faster than we can buy them and he's twenty-four!" Turning her attention to Matt, she asked, "I thought you and Bethany were an item. What about Bethany and Karen? Karen is the one with the strange hair, right?"

Matt made a horrible face, "Me and Bethany? Mom, you must   117 be crazy! I can't stand that bitch! She's a nasty piece of work! She's in with the holistic crowd of Buddhists who are vindictive, cruel and backhanded. No! I don't have anything going with Bethany!"

He stood up with his backpack to walk out of the kitchen while munching on crackers and cheese. "Come on, Collette, let me take you home. We'll go in my truck. Bethany and me! Damn!"

Collette followed him out of the kitchen. The backdoor slammed shut behind them. Sophia stood, "Thank you for the pleasure of meeting your family. Those two really helped me out today! Please, let's stay in touch?" Dion hurried to the counter, "Here, let me give you our phone number and please, please, if you come this way again, stop by and say hello?"

Sophia took the paper from Dion, "You know, Dion, I feel as if we have met before, but I can't think where?"

"Ah, yes, most people don't recognize me out of my scrubs. I work at the hospital. I do believe we have met several times while I was taking care of your mother. Your brother Granger is well known to us at the hospital. My husband here," She put her hand on Carl's arm,

"He now works with Waste Management. He's the main manager for our county." She smiled, letting wrinkles form around her mouth, "He's known to many as the good guy to call when there's a problem."

Carl reached over to kiss his wife on her cheek, "She also works part time at the main optometrist's office. My lovely wife is determined to get Matt through college. Maybe you've seen her at the eye clinic?"

The three walked out to Sophia's vehicle. Birds were chirping in the trees beside the house. Dion answered, "Yes, it was last spring when you took your granddaughter to the clinic, right?" Sophia smiled, "You have a good memory!"

Dion gave Sophia a hug, as she said, "Yes, the world is a small place, isn't it? We helped you get the discount for your granddaughter's spectacles."

Carl burst out laughing, "Spectacles? I haven't heard that word in a long time!" He came forward to give Sophia a hug as well, "Do keep in touch and if you need any help, please, do not hesitate to ask."

Driving out of Negara, Sophia had to focus on where she was. This day felt years old. It seemed ages ago when she was stuck in an ice-cold freezing crevice, trying to save Karen only for Karen to turn around and murder an old friend. She pulled over to the side of the dirt road that lead to the interstate. An old cottonwood tree gave her shade as she took out her cellphone. Standing next to the tree, she stretched her legs and watched a sparrow fly in and out of a chamisa bush.

The cellphone rang several times before she heard Timothy's voice. "Yeah?"

"Timothy, it's Sophia. Where are you?"

"I'm going into the canyon south of Springer. Where are you?"

Sophia leaned against the side of her vehicle, "I'm almost home, well, I have to stop at my mother's first. Can you talk now?"

There was a long pause. Sophia could hear the sound of the jeep's tires. "Well, I don't want to talk about anything right now, if that's all right with you. I'm dead tired. I need to return this jeep and catch a flight home. Perhaps we can share our thoughts tomorrow. I'm dead tired." There was a sigh, "Sorry, a poor choice of words. Let's talk tomorrow." The phone went quiet.

The traffic was heavy as Sophia drove through town. Turning off onto the old road to Calavera helped her come back into focus. The last twenty-four hours had been a whirlwind of bizarre personalities mixed with death. The cows were wandering toward Mr. Chavez's barn. A dog was running down the road ahead of her, probably heading home as well. Tall cranes stood in open pastures with fat bottomed geese. The smell of fireplace smoke wafted through the air.

Margaret's front wall appeared worse in its falling appearance than two days ago. The tall cottonwood trees were stoic and still lacking wind or breeze. As she parked her SUV under a leafless cottonwood tree, she noticed so many of the trees around her mother's property were dead or dying. Not good to have them looming over the roofs of Margaret's property. She slammed the vehicle door hard, hard enough to be heard inside the old adobe house. Evidently, it was loud enough for old Gizzie to waddle and stand at the wrought iron gate.

The gate pushed in gracefully, now that Timothy had repaired it. Sophia bent down and scratched Gizzie behind his ears. "Hey, old fellow, how you doing in this crazy world? Hope you know it is safer to stay inside the wall then outside where all the boogie men are." He wagged his tail and peered up at her with his brown cataract eyes. "Let's go find your Mama, okay?" Gizzie followed her to the back door.

The door was locked, of course. Sophia pounded on the wooden door until she heard the scraping of the metal walker against the brick floor. Peering through the glass in the door, Sophia saw her mother raise her hands, gesticulating wildly. Finally, Margaret made it to the door as she tossed the metal walker against the dining room table. Gasping as she opened the door, she said, "Well, Sophia, it took you long enough to get here!"

Sophia squeezed through the small space between the door frame and her mother to get into the house. Gizzie, evidently, chose to stay outside. The door banged shut with Margaret's weight on it. "Where have you been? I was worried sick! I couldn't get ahold of you and there was no recording when I called! What happened, what's going on?"

"Margaret, you do know I was in Colorado Springs for a wedding? Oh, by the way, here is the dress you loaned me. It was lovely and, yes, I did wear it over my sweatpants and sweatshirt, but it was a hit. Thank you for the dress. Do you want me to hang it up, or put it in the wash or wrap it back up in paper and put it in your bureau?"

"What's this? I have never seen this dress before in my life. Put it away. It's probably something you found at a junk store. Just put it away. Now tell me about the wedding. Were there a lot of single men?

Older, rich single men who were looking for you?" Margaret pulled out a dining room chair to plop herself on it. "Tell all."

Folding the dress on the dining room table, Sophia pulled out a chair to sit facing her mother. "Yes, it was a beautiful wedding. I couldn't take any pictures since I was the Maid of Honor. It was cold, freezing in fact, but a good time was had by all." Sophia stood, "Margaret, would you like a cup of tea? I'm really parched. Would you mind if I fixed myself a cup of tea?"

"Oh, go ahead. I'll have a cup, too. Your brother Granger brought some delicious tea, it's in the box by the sink. I think it's your typical English tea, nothing terrific." Sophia noticed the box with Granger's seal on it. Carefully, she opened the box, turned it upside down over the waste basket and emptied out the contents. She put the box back by the sink with the seal pushed firmly into place.

The old copper kettle was filled with water and placed on the electric stove with the temperature on high. Reaching up over the stove, Sophia found a box of lemon ginger tea. She took out the tea bag and placed it in the white china tea pot. Under the top cupboard was a box marked with ginger snaps. Sophia knew the mice did not like ginger and therefore there might be a good chance of a cookie or two still in the box. The box was full.

The copper kettle whistled on the stove. Hot water was poured into the china tea pot to let the tea steep. The ginger snaps were placed on a white plate. Walking back and forth, Sophia placed all the items on the dining room table. "Here, let's have a treat." Margaret glared at Sophia, "Well, make yourself at home! Do you want to pay my property taxes, too?"

Being tired, Sophia bent over and kissed her mother on the top of her head. "You know, Margaret, I dearly love you. Let's enjoy our tea party, because I have to go home soon. You are important to me. Today has been a crazy difficult day and I wanted to see you and be with you. Is that all right?"

"I don't know what you're talking about. You go to the University; you teach a bunch of stuff that you really know nothing about and somehow you are exhausted. I truly do not understand. If you are so tired, perhaps you should go home now!"

Margaret stood up, pushed the teacup away from her, grabbed two cookies to stuff into her pant pocket and turned with her walker to leave the room. Sophia sighed. She drank her tea, ate four cookies, put the china tea pot by the sink and left the blue dress folded on the table. Gizzie was lying upside down right outside the back door. Sophia scratched his tummy and departed.

# 11

Sophia drove home with the tumbleweeds smacking into the van. As soon as she stopped in front of the garage, she heard her dogs barking. Her eyes teared up as she whispered, "There's no place like home!" Next to the garage was parked a red truck with bumper stickers covering the back tailgate all about saving animals. Speaking under her breath, "Oh, no, please I don't need any company!" On the far side of the farmhouse was Donna's little Toyota car. The dent on the side was earned when her granddaughter Fleur was learning to drive years ago.

The tired SUV came to a stop inside the garage. The garage door closed as Sophia pushed the automatic button on her dashboard. The side door was pushed open and two large dogs raced to the driver's side door. One dog was white with brown spots, his tongue was hanging out and his tail was wagging furiously. The other dog followed. She was brown and more hesitant, but when she noticed Sophia, she sat to let out a long howl.

Barely tapping the horn, Sophia called out of the window, "Hey, guys, Mama's home!" She jumped out of the driver's door to hug her dogs. "Wow, wow, how I missed you both! You two are my rocks, my sanity! How I love you both, love, love, love!" The dogs ran into her arms as she knelt to hold them.

Donna, Sophia's youngest daughter of thirty-six years, came striding through the side door to her. "Mom! Finally, you're home!" She knelt next to her mother to pet the pups. "They seriously missed you! Believe it or not this plump bundle of love Sassy would hardly eat. She kept searching for you. This big fellow Tucker slept most of the time." Donna swiveled to hug her mother, "So, are you home to stay or are you going out again?"

TERESA PIJOAN

Sophia kissed her daughter's cheek, "I am home to stay this time. Donna, I dearly love you! Do know your Mama dearly loves you?" Donna laughed, "Yes, Mom, I got that part."

Sophia stood realizing her legs were stiff and sore. She took Donna's hands in hers, "Thank you, for your help with the crazy Karen ordeal. Poor Timothy is still driving back here from Colorado Springs. He did not do well dealing with his dead uncle."

"He died?" Donna put her hand on her chest, "Oh, Mama, wasn't he your boss and friend?" Donna studied her mother's face, "Is that why you were asking questions about that Karen woman?" The dogs were doing zombies all around them. Sophia handed Donna her backpack and bedroll, Sophia lifted the tent with the spikes wrapped around with rope to hang on a pole in the garage. "Let's go inside. How I have missed my home, my bed, my family and of course my critters!"

As they walked toward the front door, Sophia asked, "I noticed a red truck in front, hopefully, we don't have a lot of company for I am ever so tired and filthy. I just would like a hot cup of tea a warm shower and my cozy bed filled with cats."

124 "Oh, Mom, some of your friends are here not only to welcome you home but also to get the horses ready for the big move tomorrow." Putting the backpack down inside the front door, Donna spoke quietly, "They won't stay long. I can push them along if you don't feel like a big gathering."

Shaking her head, Sophia turned to Donna, "I completely forgot about the horses being moved! These last two days have been a complete disaster and then on top of all of this the horses! What time are the guys coming to move them?"

"It's all right. Sybil and Ethan are coming in the morning with Ethan's buddy who is buying the horses. Just remember, Mom, the horses are going to be only an hour drive south of here and you can visit them whenever you want."

The dogs pushed their way between Sophia's legs to get into the living room. "Mom, just take one thing at a time. I knew that woman Karen was bad news. You should have just left when you found out who she really was." Donna picked up the backpack to hold it at arm's length, "Mom, this really stinks. It smells of vomit and some strange herb. Are you sure you want this in the house?"

Sophia took the pack from Donna, "You know what? Let's leave it in the garage. Come on, let's go inside. I hope you fixed something for dinner because I'm starving!"

"Grandma just called to say she wanted you to come by her place right away. Evidently, she has issues with Marcus. You do know he was given orders by his father to check on Grandma while Granger and family are in California."

"Oh. No, I just came from Grandma's house. She's on her own with him. I have so much to share with you!" Sophia clapped her hands for the dogs to follow as she walked into the main hall. She came to a dead stop as she peered into the living room, "Donna! The house is beautiful! The wood floors absolutely shine, and you put the couch back in its original place!" Sophia turned to her daughter, "Did you do all of this yourself? I've only been gone two days!"

A voice called out from the kitchen, "Hell, no! I helped, too. Come in here, stranger, and say hello." Sophia quickly kicked off her boots by the front door. "Oh, my goodness. I know that voice. Is it? No, it couldn't be. Clementine?"

Laughing as she entered the kitchen, Sophia put her arms out, "Clementine, I thought you were in Australia? What are you doing in my kitchen of all places?"

125

Clementine hugged Sophia as she said, "I fell in love with New Mexico and the women in Australia hardly have any rights especially in law enforcement." A delicious odor wafted up from the stove. Clementine hurried to the pot on the stove to stir it with the wooden spoon in her hand, "Donna and I decided to welcome you home with some posole. She even soaked the beans and marinated the pork. This should be enough for a couple of weeks."

There was a bowl on the counter with a dish towel covering it. Smiling at Donna, Sophia asked, "So, not only posole, but it looks like sopapillas as well, huh?"

Donna lifted the towel, "Yes, we felt that you would probably like to help though, since you are the sopapilla maker in the family."

Pushing her fingers through her short curly hair, Sophia shook her head, "I seriously need to take a shower first and change out of these disgusting clothes. Clementine, I need your help in solving a murder and it is very nasty." Turning to walk down the hall, Sophia called out, "First, cleanliness then food!

Standing under the shower with the warm water washing away the last two days events, Sophia sighed, "Life is fragile. One day Robert was fully alive, enjoying being in love and today he is quite and completely dead." Tears flowed down her cheeks as the water washed them away. She just stood there under the hot water, remembering the freezing cold of the ice crevice, the wild ride to the hospital and the sadness in Timothy's face as he walked to see his Uncle in the ICU.

The clothes of the day were rolled up in the moist towel and thrown out into the hall. Sophia pulled on her clean sweats, slid on her cozy slippers and attempted to put on a happy face. She brushed her curly hair until it was lying flat against her scalp. There was a soft knock on the bathroom door and then her daughter said, "Mom, dinner is ready. Are you ready?"

After dropping her clothes into the washing machine, Sophia walked arm in arm with her daughter down the hall and into the kitchen. The table was beautifully set with the red checkered tablecloth, red linen napkins and one single candle lit in the middle. Donna led Sophia to her chair, "The one candle is for Robert. He will be remembered for his kindness and caring. Most of his students respected his tough grading for it made them try harder, learn more and become better at being students."

Under her breath, Sophia said, "Amen." Clementine sat opposite Sophia at the table. Next to Clementine there was a setting, but the chair was empty. Donna busied herself with the bringing of the posole in its large pot to the table, the fluffy hot sopapillas were wrapped in a linen cloth placed in a basket. Honey was already on the table along with glasses filled with water.

Clementine lifted her left hand, "Sophia, I have some exciting news. As one part of our lives changes, another part of our lives grow. I am ever so sorry about your friend. But would you look at this before we say prayer? We are still waiting for someone else, too."

There on Clementine's finger was a gorgeous ruby stone with a gold setting. Stuttering, Sophia asked, "What? What does this mean? Are you thinking of getting married or becoming a jewelry saleswoman?"

Smiling with bright eyes, Clementine whispered, "I'm getting married! Really, I'm going to take the plunge with someone who loves me as much as I love him." Sophia held Clementine's hand to study the ring better, "And just who is this person? Would I know him or her?"

The back door was pushed open. A tall man with a formidable

126

moustache and beard walked into the kitchen holding a tiny kitten. "Here she is. I found her high up in a tree behind the barn. I think Oscar showed her how to climb and then he ran off." The kitten was handed to Donna as the man put out his hand to Sophia, "Hello, you must be the intrepid Sophia? I happen to be Ignacio Cruz's middle brother, and the husband-to-be of this beautiful woman named Clementine."

Donna put the cat down on the kitchen floor. Sophia stared at Clementine and then at the man, "And I am sure you have a name to go with this great introduction?" She reached back to shake his hand. Clementine pulled out the chair beside her, "This fine fellow is named Perfecto. Isn't that a fine name?"

Sophia shook her head, "No, no, what is your name really?"

Pulling out his wallet from his back pant pocket, the man opened it to hand Sophia his driver's license. There it was in black and white, his name being Perfecto Cruz. She handed the driver's license back to him. "Well, I certainly hope you have lived up to such a name. Your mother had high hopes for you at birth. What did your father think of this?"

Perfecto laughed, "My father was the one who choose the name. He had been told that his wife would not be able to have another child after Ignacio. Yet, amazing grace, I came along sandwiched between Ignacio and my little brother Milagro. Hey, we're a very special family."

Clementine lifted his hand and kissed it, "He is indeed a special fellow."

Donna spooned the pasole into everyone's bowl. Once the bowls were filled, prayer was said and the four were quiet as they ate. As Sophia reached for a sopapilla, she asked Perfecto, "How is your brother the honorable Sheriff Ignacio? He was so helpful to us when we lived up north and bordered horses. He is a marvelous fellow."

Perfecto handed Sophia the honey jar, "My brother is a grandfather now. Unlike his riding along buddy A.J. who has retired, Ignacio is still strong and feels his purpose is to remain a sheriff. Although most weekends when it is quiet the two of them spend their days fishing up by Taos. You wouldn't recognize him with his pot belly and gray hair. He still has a wonderful sense of humor, though. You should look him up sometime."

The dinner conversation was pleasant and peaceful. Perfecto left soon after dinner saying that he would return in the morning to help move the horses with Ethan, who is Sybil's husband. Clementine

TERESA PIJOAN

listened to Sophia as she spoke of her day and all the adventures that had befallen her. At one point, Clementine started taking notes. When Donna had finished washing the dishes, she asked Clementine to please go home and let her mother rest.

Clementine stood with her hands on her hips, "Donna, you have become rather pushy in your old age, did you know this?"

Turning to her mom, Donna said, "Hey, Mom, you're exhausted and once you start talking to Clementine it's as if you are unable to stop. No one knows what happened to Robert and Karen. I wish you would just leave it well enough alone." Donna pulled her mother to stand from the easy chair in the living room. "You seriously need to go to bed and rest your body. I cannot believe you crawled out of the ice crevice with no help from anyone! I would've been pissed as hell!"

As her guests left, lights were turned off and doors were locked. Sophia was glad to be able to fall back onto her bed and turn off the bedside light. The window was opened about an inch, just wide enough for her to hear the horses walking around in the barnyard. A heavy weight tugged on the side of the bed as her fat cat Oscar walked up her legs to her shoulder. He began kneading her arm. Sophia closed her eyes and fell into a blissful sleep.

128

# 12

The wind plummeted against the side of the building as Charlotte and Margaret bent walking into it. Trees danced along the side of the parking lot as birds tried to fly against the harsh blowing air. Fat clouds floated overhead to disappear behind the Sandia Mountains. Dust devils whirled about smashing dirt particles against the building and the cars in the parking lot of the old church with its thick adobe walls. The meeting had been a celebration for Margaret and her husband Mark Pino who had brought the old church back to life with their donations of money, hard work and expert advice. Over fifty people wearing formal attire had attended.

Refreshments of home baked goods were served after the celebration. The award given to Mrs. Mark Pino and family was a beautifully carved pine bench placed outside the parish priest's house with the name 'Pino' inscribed on the bench's seat back. Margaret blushed and gratefully thanked the people of the village for their appreciative gift.

Eighty-two-year-old, Margaret pulled the passenger's car door shut with all her force. The wind blew hard against the shut door. Margaret turned to face her longtime friend and neighbor Charlotte. "There, the door is closed. Lunch is done and we can go home! At last!" She reached for her seatbelt and clicked it in place. Her arthritic hands grasped her leather purse in her lap. "I am more than anxious to get out of these clothes! When was the last time I wore pumps? My feet were certainly smaller years ago than they are now." She took the shoe off her left foot to rub her ankle.

Charlotte cleaned her sunglasses on the cuff of her shirt, "That wasn't so bad, now, was it?" Ignoring Margaret's shoe statement, she went on to say, "You know there are times when a person feels all alone

129

in the world and then we have a celebration for them. All those people really appreciated what you and Mark did for the church. There were so many new faces who want to join committees now. Gives you a warm feeling all over, doesn't it?" She patted Margaret's left arm.

Charlotte placed her sunglasses over her cataract glasses with the tortoise shell frames. Her white hair was braided around her head with a pink ribbon, matching her pink sweater.

Margaret scrunched up her face, "Well, it might have been worse if you had decided not to come. Thank you, for being my chauffeur and for holding my hand, so to speak, through all of this." Margaret pulled her gray wool skirt over her knees.

Charlotte laughed, "These people appreciate you and what you have done for the community. Before you and Mark arrived, this place was a hippie haven for druggies and thieves. Once Mark met with all the other farmers and spoke to them about turning this village into a true farming community, this place thrived. Yes, they appreciate you and what you and Mark have done over the last twenty or so years." Her hand reached down to shift gears as she drove onto the highway. The vehicle shot forward with a jerk.

130      Margaret fluffed up her thick salt and pepper hair with her fingers. Her wrinkled face was pale, with sharp cheek bones. There were corrugated deep wrinkles around her mouth, eyes and chin. "Someone would have come forward eventually. Actually the Ortega's and the Trujillo's were working with the county. We just gave everyone a shove." She pulled the sun visor down to block the bright sun's rays shining straight into her chalk blue eyes.

Turning her head to watch for traffic, Charlotte exited the main highway and onto the two-lane road. "Personally, I believe it was Mark's European charisma that captivated everyone. His ascot ties, his suave manner and his slight Italian accent. Also, Margaret, you are a classy woman educated back East and always wearing high English riding boots."

The wind blew hard against the side of Charlotte's small Honda sedan. The two women were quiet as they watched the road. Tumbleweeds rolled frantically across their path as the trees danced wildly on either side of them. Charlotte pulled into Margaret's driveway to stop by the wrought iron gate. "Well, finally, we are here. For a moment I believed we would blow away into Oklahoma."

Margaret sat still staring at the cracked adobe wall surrounding her home. Chunks of adobe had fallen, crushing the withered brown cactus dying on the ground. The large wooden beams framing the wrought iron gate were listing to the inside, pushing the gate down onto the bricks leading to the front door. As she sat in the car, she noticed the house roof was peeling. The cottonwood tree she had planted with her husband had branches scraping across the roof, tearing away at the tar paper material.

"Oh, God, Charlotte, this house looks as old as I feel. It is truly falling apart. What am I going to do?" She turned to her friend, "Mark has been dead now for twenty-two years this February. There is hardly any money left. Granger has Mr. Gonzales leasing the lower field for his steers to bring in one hundred dollars a month." Pointing with her index finger at the house, she went on, "The roof is falling in, look at that! The wall is pathetic and now I no longer have a horse, the barn is a hollow shell of empty. Oh, Charlotte, what am I to do?"

Unclicking her seatbelt, Charlotte took her friend's hand, "First, you must stop giving all of you money to Granger. Mark left you with a surplus of funds to keep this place up, but you gave it all away to Granger." Speaking more firmly, she added, "Margaret, enough of him. He hasn't done anything for you but take and take. Why don't you move in with Sophia? She has a lovely home with animals, bedrooms, and two bathrooms. Plus, she loves you and cares for you."

Shaking her head, Margaret explained, "You know I do believe Sophia is more like Mark than she is like me. Sophia makes friends easily and is outgoing. Mark was charismatic and loved everyone." She sniffed as she watched the wind blow sand across the field in front of them. "When I was in college, back East, we were told to go out our junior year and get a job in our field of study. Mine was in early education and I applied for a job on the Navajo reservation."

Charlotte turned on the car's engine to put on the heater. "Go on, the wind is getting colder. Please, tell me about your job." She put her arthritic hands on the steering wheel. Margaret gave her a demure smile, "Do you want to come inside? Don't think it's much warmer in the house?"

Shaking her head, Charlotte said, "No, no, please, continue. I'm fine here, if you are?" Charlotte patted the braids that were wrapped around her head.

Opening her leather purse, Margaret took out a tissue to wipe her

131

nose. "There was another student who was going with me. Her name was Georgia and she was from Maine. We were told to bring only long skirts or long dresses since the Navajo women didn't wear pants or jeans. We packed our belongings in duffel bags. Well, she had one and I had one. Both duffel bags had our initials stenciled on them." Margaret blew her nose, "Excuse me." She put the tissue back into her purse. "Do you know I can remember all of this as clear as day, yet I can't remember what I did yesterday?"

Margaret bent down to put her shoe back on her foot, "We took a bus to Chicago to board a train going to Verde, New Mexico. The train trip took eight hours for it had several stops along the way." Margaret dug into her purse to pull out a roll of lifesavers. "Would you like one?" Charlotte put her hand palm up to receive a yellow lifesaver. Margaret popped a green one into her mouth. "When we arrived in Verde, there were trains everywhere. All we knew was a fellow called Juan Yazzi was to gather us up and drive us halfway to our boarding school assignment."

Crunching the lifesaver, Margaret continued, "As we disembarked from the train, I noticed Georgia was shivering. It was August and quite warm in New Mexico. I wasn't sure what was going on with her, but I took her arm, and we maneuvered our way to the station house. There were many Navajo people there. At the back, was a man holding up a flimsy cardboard sign with our names printed on it with crayon."

Margaret smiled, "He was tall about six two and had a Stetson hat with a flat rim. As we walked to him, he appeared as unsure of us as we were of him. He took our duffel bags. We followed him out into the busy parking lot filled with a lot of horses and trailers with cattle and sheep. He stopped at a small red truck that had certainly seen better days."

She wiped her nose with the tissue, "Just thinking about the ride reminds me of how very young we were. Only nineteen years old and here we were out in the Wild West surrounded by Native Americans. My grandmother would've been shocked."

Giggling she continued, "The front of the truck was small as I said. I sat in the middle, while Georgia sat next to the passenger door. My feet were under hers and Mr. Yazzi was kind enough to shift gears to avoid my knees. As we drove, we noticed a busy town of people, animals, and vehicles. Once away from the small town, we came to desolation. There were no buildings and very few vehicles on the road. Georgia started to shake. Tears were falling from her eyes and her breathing was labored."

Charlotte nodded her head, "Oh, dear, she was agoraphobic! Poor girl. What happened with her?"

Margaret nodded, "The farther we moved away from the train station the more serious her mood became. I wasn't sure what to do since I was young myself, but this was something I always wanted to do. The Native American experience had been my dream since I was a child. Georgia had appeared excited to come with me and teach, but now I just didn't know. At one point I fell asleep with my head on her shoulder. The sound of barking dogs woke me."

The lifesavers were shared once again. This time Charlotte took an orange one. Margaret popped a red one into her mouth. "Yes, the rez dogs. A whole pack of mutts met us as Mr. Yazzi pulled into a yard with a hogan in the center. He jumped out to calm the dogs, walking around to the passenger door. One hand opened the door, the other hand grabbed our duffel bags.

"Georgia didn't move. She appeared frozen to the seat. I couldn't get out nor could I get around her. Finally, I gave her a strong nudge. Turning her head, she said firmly, NO. Mr. Yazzi stood there holding the door open for her."

Charlotte put the heater fan on high to ask, "What could you have done? The poor girl sounds frightened out of her wits."

"Well, yes, she was. Both of us were hungry, thirsty and had to go to the bathroom. A wide, wizened woman appeared through the blanketed doorway of the hogan. She waddled over to us. Standing in front of Georgia, she put her arms out wide and said something in Navajo. Georgia hurried to the woman and hugged her crying.

"I followed Mr. Yazzi into the hogan. Mr. Yazzi put our duffel bags beside two pallets, excusing himself to disappear outside. Now I really had to go to the bathroom. There was no bathroom, just an eight-sided huge room.

"Soon, Georgia came in with the woman and she showed us the outhouses. There were two. One for guests and one for the family. Who would have thought, right? We spent the night sleeping on pallets with many blankets under us and many over us. When I woke up in the morning, there was no one else in the hogan. Later, I found out Mr. Yazzi had taken Georgia to his neighbor's hogan for the neighbor was going to drive Georgia back to the train to go back East."

Charlotte clicked her tongue, "She deserted you? Were you scared?

What happened then?"

Margaret pointed to the tall cottonwood tree next to her toolshed. "Look at that branch. Do you think it's going to fall?"

Charlotte leaned forward to study the branch, "No, looks sturdy. Go on, what happened?"

"That afternoon a woman from the boarding school arrived to pick me up and we drove to Navajo Mountain's boarding school. Oh, how I loved it there. The students were creative, accepting and for once I felt I was truly at home. Then winter arrived. One of the coldest winters in history. Students were coughing up blood. Sickness was everywhere. Our principal called the BIA, and they said someone would be coming directly to help. Hopefully, it would be a medical doctor.

"There were eight of us teachers. We were up all night and day with warm blankets, hot water and doing laundry, because every kid was sick. We had one hundred and eighteen students, and we fought to keep each one of them alive. It was around eight thirty in the morning when we heard the helicopter. It landed on the roof of the lunchroom. A tall, dark, handsome man appeared with a black bag. After he alighted from the helicopter, large, belted bags dropped from the sky after him onto the roof.

"Oh, Charlotte, my heart stopped when I saw Dr. Mark Pino. He immediately went into action. We were given orders to make charts for each student. Take temperatures, weigh the students, put those at high risk in one area, others in a different area. Students who were not sick were to work in the lunchroom making special meals."

Clapping her hands, Charlotte laughed, "That's where you met your Mark? During a blizzard at Navajo Mountain? How romantic!"

Margaret lifted her chin, "Ah, yes, the magic man appeared as a Savior to our beloved students. I was so cold running back and forth from one building to another with wet boots that Mark pulled me aside. He gave me his extra pair of boots, which were huge on my feet, but wonderfully warm and waterproof. Then he gave me his thermal underwear. Two years later I married him."

Margaret wiped a tear from her cheek, "Now, he's gone. My dear friend and buddy is gone! Our home is falling to pieces around me. Oh, God, Charlotte, what am I to do? I need Granger's help, I need Granger." Margaret gave a sigh as she wiped her tears.

Handing Margaret another tissue, Charlotte spoke softly,

"Margaret, you have Sophia. She dearly loves you and she will help you. Just because she's female doesn't mean she can't help you. Her home is beautiful. She keeps wanting you to move in with her. Why do you fight her with this? Granger is taking all of your money, and he only gives you grief. Margaret, get smart! Let Sophia help you!"

Frowning, Margaret pushed her hand away, "No! You have it all wrong! Sophia only cares for herself. She comes over here to earn points so I will leave her everything. She's greedy, thoughtless and uncaring. Granger is here for me! Charlotte, you have no idea how wonderful Granger is to me!"

Margaret pushed her long bangs back from her forehead. "Besides, Sophia needs to find a husband who will support her. As her mother, that is not my job! She needs a man to care for her, to provide for her not me!" Hugging her purse to her chest, Margaret attempted to smile at her friend, "Thank you for your company and thank you for picking me up. Please, do be safe going home in this wind." She opened the door, pursed her lips into a slight smile and slammed the door shut.

Shaking her head, Charlotte watched her friend scrape open the wrought iron gate to get inside her property. Under her breath she whispered, "Ah, yes, dementia keeps the memories of the past strong and the idiocy of the present cloudy. Granger will be the death of you, dear Margaret, just you wait and see." She turned on the radio to drown out the sound of the hard blowing wind as she drove down the road.

Gizzie, her elderly Rottweiler, met Margaret at the back door. Once inside her bedroom, Margaret slumped on her bed. Her shoes hurt her swollen feet, the pantyhose was tight across her belly and the white ironed shirt rubbed at her neck. Slowly, she disrobed to reach for her black socks, jeans and soft cotton shirt wrinkled from the latest wash. The old boots could use a polish but why bother when she would only get them scuffed again. Gizzie ambled into her bedroom to collapse on the rug at her feet.

Leaning down she rubbed behind his ears. His large brown eyes stared up at her in gratitude. Smiling, she said, "You know, Gizzie, you are my best friend in the whole world. You and me against the world, that's what it feels like most days, right?" He thumped his gray tail. "Gizzie, you know I dearly love you!"

She ran her fingers through her shoulder length hair to stand. "We best go check on the steer in the lower pasture." As she walked through the long living room her attention was taken by the geraniums in the window seats. "Ganger's son Marcus will come and check on us, Gizzie. You just watch and see." She patted her dog on the head. "I do wonder how Granger moved those steers here on my property. My Granger can do miracles."

Noticing the geraniums, she added, "Best water these first, everything is looking a little dry what with this wind." Gizzie followed her into the kitchen where he rolled over for a tummy rub. "No, no, it's time to water the flowerpots. You stay here on the cool bricks, but your Mama has things to do." A tall pitcher was filled with water and the flowers were watered. Between two of the pots on the window seat in the living room was a framed photo of Mark and Margaret taken on one of their horseback riding adventures.

Held in her shaking hands, Margaret stroked the photo. "How I loved that man, yet he jumped into bed with anything in a skirt or jeans or nothing at all." The photo was put back, "No matter how I tried to please him, it was never enough. Unlike Granger, who is devoted to me and is loyal to his wives." She giggled, "Oh, dear, perhaps he is like Mark, although Granger is my perfect boy."

136   Picking a dead leaf from one of the geranium plants, she added, "Sophia on the other hand is not interested in anything but herself, humph." Crumbling up the dried leaf, she dropped the debris in the flowerpot. "Granger and I had no choice, but to drop Mark's hospital bed and let him aspirate." She bent to scratch Gizzie's head. "Mark was going to drain our money dry with his nurse's fees, the medicine costs and on top of all of this he had put in place a hold on any money he had in stock until his death."

Straightening, she groaned, "Oh, my back is still hurting! I'm so tired of back pain, Gizzie. Besides, Granger wanted his Mercedes, and it was going to cost more than what he had in his account. Then he was put in prison and we had to buy it all over again."

Lifting the empty pitcher, she turned on her heel to return to the kitchen. "Adult children are nothing more than demanding infants in big bodies. Sophia claims to have her own money, but every time she comes over here, I know, just know she is about to ask for some. I stop her before she can ask. I'm getting good at deflecting her. Granger is the one who needs money now that he has a wife he really loves and three children who are perfect in every way. Well, aside from the youngest girl. She looks like her ugly mother and there isn't a thing we can do about it." The pitcher was placed back under the kitchen sink. Turning her head, she whispered, "Gizzie, listen the cranes are arriving. Fall is finally coming at last!"

The woven straw hat was tied tightly under her chin as Margaret pushed open the back screen door. Gizzie stood in the kitchen and watched her go. His tail wagged, but he didn't follow her out into the hard wind. "That's all right, stay inside, old fella, Mama will be right back. Stay put where it's safe." Margaret grabbed her wooden walking stick as she walked to the barn gate. "I've got to take care of my Granger's steers or bovines. He counts on me. I'm his special friend."

Clouds were forming over the mountain range to the east. The wind was rattling the barn's doors. Swallows were fighting the wind as they tried to fly under the barn's eaves. Dirt blew in spirals in the dry barnyard. Below the barnyard, Margaret could see steers stepping over the barbed wire fence that had fallen into the ditch. Patting her front right jean pocket for her cellphone, Margaret found the pocket empty. She had left it in the bedroom on the bedside table.

Indecision took over her plans. Should she go back for the cellphone or keep going and try to fix the fence before all eighteen of the steers got out of the field? Grimacing against her frailty, she continued, after all who would she call? Her weight was thrown forward onto her left side where she held the walking stick. "I have lived on a farm for most of my life, just because I'm old doesn't mean I'm finished!" Gritting her teeth, she continued, stabbing the ground with the walking stick using it to propel herself forward. The wind continued to toss dirt in spirals all around her. She pushed up the wooden spool on the leather ties holding her straw hat firmly in place. Squinting through the wild dirty air, she only noticed four steers still standing in the barnyard.

The far barnyard gate leaned to the right. The post attached to it was rotten to the core and had fallen to drop the gate into the dry dirt. Staring at it, Margaret realized she would not be able to lift the heavy wooden posts wrapped with barbed wire. Moving closer to the gate and the steers, she knew her chances of stopping the steers were hopeless. If she were ten years younger, she might go over the fence or through the fence, but not now with her bad back, her arthritic knees and weak legs and her arthritic shoulders and hands. The steers were moving onto the road.

TERESA PIJOAN

"Damn, damn, damn, why did I have to become so fragile? Damn!" She tried to lift her right leg to go through the wooden posts of the sagging gate. Her knee would not oblige. Using her hands, Margaret put all her weight against the gate, thinking she could pull it up even if it was stuck in the dirt. The gate gave. It fell forward and with it came Margaret. She landed on top of the collapsed gate with the walking stick stuck between the ground and her hip. Margaret was wedged. She could not rise, roll, or move. She was stuck.

Her left wrist was twisted between the walking stick and a gate post. Tears fell from her blue eyes as the wind blew dust into her face. "Damn! Gizzie! Pup!" Margaret's voice faded away in the wind. Elm trees around her danced, dropping leaves as they swayed into one another. Waves of dirt pummeled her face, drying her cracked lips. Her eyes teared as her hair whirled around her head.

She used her good hand in an attempt to lift her body from the dry earth. The arm was not strong enough. Her boney arm gave way. Her voice was fragile and dry as she attempted to call for help one more time. There was no one to hear her. Especially over the blowing gale. The damn cellphone was comfortable in her bedroom! The wind continued to blow as the sun moved across the sky. Margaret stared at the empty dirt road. It separated her land from the Flood Control Association. Rarely did anyone ever come down that specific road.

Resting her head on the broken gate panel next to her shoulder, Margaret gave up. Eventually someone would have to come by to check on the steers or at least Sophia would come by just to bother her. She closed her eyes to keep the dirt out of them only to find herself slowly falling asleep. Her wrist throbbed with sharp pain. There was nothing she could do about it. The walking stick had gouged into her hip, yet again there was nothing she could do. Letting her body relax appeared to be the best solution because she was definitely stuck. She decided to let her body go limp and sleep.

"Hello, Ma'am, are you all right? Senora, que paso?" An older man's voice woke her from her stupor. There was a grunt as a man knelt in the dirt beside her. His strong hands attempted to lift the fallen gate, but Margaret was on top of it. "Senora, can you hear me? Senora, are you all right?" Gently he pushed her hair from her face. She had dirt in her mouth, her nose and in her eyes. She tried to shake her head, but her neck was stiff.

Smiling at him, she cautiously spoke, "I fell and here I am, can you help me?" He let out a laugh, "Senora, you scared me! Yes, let me go around to the other side and I will lift you off the gate." His age did not stop his chivalry. He went through the fence to come up behind her. "What do you want me to do to get you up?" There was a loud growl behind him. Cautiously he turned. There was Gizzie with his hackles up, his teeth bared and his tail straight out.

"Gizzie, no! It's all right!" Margaret called out. Wagging his tail, the dog sat. Mr. Gonzales slowly tried to lift the gate out from under her, but the weight was too much. Margaret could hear him speaking Spanish on his cellphone. "Senora, I have called my grandson, he is coming, and he is strong. Between the two of us, we can get you and the gate separated. Right now, somehow, you and the stick are all involved with the gate. He is coming right now."

There came the sound of a truck. It parked several feet away from Margaret. "Hey, Gramps, what happened here? Did she try to run away from you?" A young man laughed as the older man growled, "Get over here, Raphael. Your jokes are not needed." The young man carefully stepped over the falling fence. "Grandpa, how did she get into this mess? She's covered in dirt. Why did she let the steers out into the road?" Pushing back his stained cowboy hat, he scratched his head.

"Raphael, I found her like this. You know she speaks English, right?" The older man stepped back, leaving the younger man to observe the situation. "Ma'am, what happened here? Did the steers attack you? What happened?" The young man knelt beside Margaret. His voice was soft and calm. She tried to swallow, but her mouth was filled with dry dirt. She whispered, "I tried to lift the gate, and it fell. It took me with it, and I'm stuck."

"Damn right, you're stuck. We need to turn you onto your side away from the walking stick." Raphael rolled Margaret over onto her left side, noticing the walking stick rammed into her hip, he gently pushed it forward into the dirt horizontally. Margaret sighed with relief.

Mr. Gonzales then placed his hands under her armpits and lifted. Margaret came free to lean back onto Mr. Gonzales' chest. "Oh, dear, I'm sorry, but it seems I cannot stand on my own two feet."

Raphael stood in front of her. His eighteen-year-old face beamed as he said, "Don't worry, Gramps will hold you up." Chuckling, he turned his attention to the broken gate. "Good thing all the steers are out

139

on the road, or you could've been trampled. Do you want me to try to put the gate back up or leave it here on the ground? If you want me to fix it, I can come back later and put it up, but right now we need to round up the steers."

He pointed to the bovines wandering around on the dirt road. "Your son Granger told us the fence was in good condition. Doesn't look like it, does it?" The young man slapped his straw cowboy hat against his right thigh. "We should've checked it first in the daytime, Gramps!" Kicking the dirt he added, "That Granger lied to us. He better give us our two hundred dollars back!"

Mr. Gonzales lifted Margaret's right arm to put it around his neck. "Here, lean on me, let's get you inside where you can wash and relax with your killer dog." He smiled at her as Gizzie trotted ahead of them to the back door. Once inside the house, Margaret was seated on a kitchen chair. "Do you want me to call someone for you?" The elderly Gonzales removed his leather hat to reveal a head absent of hair. His forehead was white where the hairline would have been, but his face was tanned and wrinkled. His warm brown eyes showed concern as he bent down to hear her answer.

140       She shook her head, letting dirt fly around her shoulders. "Would you be so kind as to get my cellphone? It's down the hall, to the right, in my bedroom on the bedside table." Stepping over Gizzie, Mr. Gonzales disappeared down the hall. He returned with the cellphone in one hand and a wet washcloth in the other. "Here you go. If you don't need me for anything else, I will go help my grandson round up the steers."

He started out the backdoor only to turn to her, "We will take the steers back to my farm since the fence is down they'll just wander off again." Margaret nodded in agreement as the wind caught the back door to slam it shut. Margaret looked at her furniture. It was old, ragged and tired. What did Mr. Gonzales think of her pathetic furniture in her run-down house?

Gizzie stared up at her as he sat at her feet. "Yes, boy, I am a mess. Oh, what will the children think of me now? They'll want to put me in an old folk's home without you. Damn!" Margaret let her tears fall as she washed the dirt off her hands, her neck and finally her face. "Damn."

Margaret closed her mouth only to realize her tongue was covered in dirt. Leaning forward, she attempted to stand. Her right leg was not having it. Slowly, she lifted her leg and massaged it. The tingly feeling slowly dissipated. Once more, she rocked forward and with her right hand holding onto the table edge she pulled with all her might and stood upright. "Hurrah! I'm up! Let's go, Gizzie old boy!"

Her hands were placed firmly flat against the white-washed thick adobe walls of the hall, taking some of her weight off her legs. She slid her feet slowly forward on the uneven old-brick floor. Her left shoe was lose but sliding her feet kept the shoe intact. Slowly, slowly, she moved forward, flat hands on the walls keeping her balanced and the feet propelling her slowly forward. At last, she made it to the bedroom door frame. Each flat hand was on the opposite wooden door frames. She reviewed her situation. Estimating her free walk would be about eight to ten feet, she would have to balance with her arms out like a gymnast.

Gizzie pushed against her as he moved into the bedroom. He walked confidently to her side of the bed and collapsed on the rug. Margaret took a deep breath. Every part of her body ached. Every part of her body was covered in dirt. "I wish I could fly. Then there would be no problem with the legs failing. I could be in bed already!" Arms out wide, away from her sides, she slid her feet to skate to the bedroom floor rug. Here, she would need to lift her feet or risk the chance of catching on it and falling.

Taking a deep breath, her weeping eyes wide, her arms out in front of her, she lifted her left foot first, hoping the shoe would not fall. Once her foot was down, having cleared the rug's border, she did the same with her right foot. "Yes! Gizzie, I'm almost there!" Her voice was joyously shouting. Gizzie wagged his tail and watched as she moved directly to him. His head up, his front paws at the ready to move, he watched her almost run straight at him and at the last moment she swerved to fall on the bed. Gizzie woofed.

Now, she was lying on her face. This would not do, because her neck was screaming in pain. Carefully, she pushed onto her right side with her left hand. Barely moving her right foot, she used the toe of her right shoe to push off the left shoe at the heel. The shoe fell on the floor with a 'thump.' Gizzie moved closer to the head of the bed. Slowly, Margaret tried to remove the right shoe with her foot in the sock. Her toes hurt too much. "Oh, well, one shoe off, one shoe on, one shoe down and one to go. At least, the foot that hurt is free."

She wanted to lie back, but her right arm was stuck under her. Her

141

mouth was still filled with grit. Damn, she needed water to rinse out her mouth. There was a plastic yellow cup filled with last night's water on her bedside table, but she was not able to reach it. Pushing her knees up in the fetal position scrunched up the quilt in such a manner that she was more confined than she had been. Tiger cat jumped on the bed to begin rubbing his head against hers, purring and kneading her shoulder. "Oh, Tiger, shoo! Shoo, boy, I'm stuck and need help not someone making me crazy!" She blew on his face, he continued to rub against her shoulder. The right arm that was under her body was beginning to tingle. She needed to move it before it went to sleep and would become useless. Lifting her left arm, she fell forward onto Tiger who hissed and jumped off the bed. "Good boy, go get help! Just not my adult children!" Tears welled in her eyes to fall onto the quilt. "Oh, no, now I need to go to the bathroom!"

Pushing with all her might with her left hand on the bed to move her onto her back, she slowly fell back. Her right arm was now free. She waved it to increase the circulation. Once, her arms were both functioning, she lifted herself to sit upright. Shaking her salt and pepper hair, which was shaped into a bowl cut around her head, dirt flew. Her feet shoved her forward to the head of the bed where she relaxed against the extra-long pillows stuffed into white cotton pillowcases.

Swallowing the cold water with the dirt in her mouth brought relief. Certainly, it would not be good for her expensive front teeth veneers to be filled with dirt. Turning her head, she heard a car door slam in front of the house. Quickly, she grabbed the quilt to fling one half of it over her body, hiding her dirty clothes, her one shoed foot, and all the dirt. Holding her breath, she started to choke. Her hand loosened on the plastic cup and the water poured out as it fell onto Gizzie who stood up promptly staring at her. "Sorry, old boy, but I bet you feel cooler, huh?"

She listened for a door to open, "Gizzie, what if Marcus comes? He's young and young men are stupid. He won't be able to help. Oh, Gizzie, we are in a predicament."

Margaret stared at the empty wall where the oil painting of her husband had hung for over thirty years. "Gizzie, it's just us right now. Granger is off gallivanting around the west coast on my dime while I need him here with me. I need my Granger! Oh, Gizzie, I need Granger! I hurt!" She reached over the side of the bed to pat Gizzie on his wet head, "Well, I guess I must call Sophia who only criticizes and scolds me. Oh, Gizzie, I don't want to die alone, I really don't. You are a dear friend Gizzie, but seriously, you don't bring much comfort."

Grabbing her cellphone from the bedside table, Margaret hit a button on it with her gnarled arthritic index finger. "Damn, I wish those granddaughters of mine were more polite and helpful, but they're female and females are not helpful or polite. Those independent entitled girls don't care about their grandmother and their grandmother isn't going to care about them! Let me tell you, Gizzie, they're not going to get a dime from me!"

There was a squawk coming from the cellphone and then a "hello?" Margaret yelled, "I don't know who this is, and I don't really care. I need to speak with Sophia, and I need to speak with her right now. Get Sophia!"

The soft female voice answered, "Margaret, you have called me, Sybil. Mom just got home last night and she's just getting up. Do you need help? I can come and help you if you need something?"

"No! I do not need your help, Sybil. Go get your mother."

The cellphone went silent. Margaret shut the cellphone, threw it onto the other side of the bed. She fell back against the thick pillows. "Damn."

143

## 13

A soft knock on the bedroom door brought Sophia to answer it. She was fully dressed and had been listening to the men's voices as the horse trailer arrived. "Mom, I thought you would want to say goodbye to the horses before they drive off. Ethan and Sybil are with Craig. All the tack, alfalfa bales and the water troughs with the water buckets are loaded."

Sophia followed Donna through the house to the barnyard. The rich smell of horse mixed with moist warm manure was fresh in the air. River Shore and Smoke were being walked around the horse trailer with their halters and lead ropes. Perfecto's truck was parked beside the horse trailer loaded up with alfalfa and the water trough. Ethan was speaking with a deep voiced man inside the barn.

145

Sophia walked to Sybil who was leading the horses, she called out, "How are my boys?" Sybil laughed, "They're all grown up and leaving home that's how they are." The horses made a straight line to Sophia to nuzzle her hands and her arms. Sybil stroked River Shore's long mane, "He's your baby boy. He's telling you he wants you to come and visit him often."

Sophia rubbed her cheek against River Shore's long nose, "You know I love you, right? Yes, we will need to have a riding date. Sybil, when you are free from your university classes perhaps you could take some time off from work and we could go on a pack trip?"

"Absolutely, Mom. Ethan could take care of our cats, and he could watch your house just to be sure the house is okay. The dogs can come with us. We could have some quiet time on the mountain and away from all the stress."

Ethan walked up to the two women who were with the horses. His friend Craig was opening the back of the horse trailer. The horses smelled the fresh alfalfa in the bins and walked right into the trailer's double hold. Ethan closed one side of the trailer doors while Craig closed the other side. Perfecto came out of the barn holding the long-handled pooper scooper. "Here, you better take this with you." He handed it to Craig.

Standing behind the trailer, Sophia sniffed, "I'm going to miss these guys." Then she straightened to stand tall, "But I will not miss mucking out the stalls in the freezing cold winters or the burning hot summers." She turned to Craig, "Thank you, so much, for buying these two family members. I trust you to take good care of them. I know your horses already know River Shore and Smoke and all should be fine, but still, I'm going to miss them."

Enfolding Sophia into an embrace, Craig whispered into her ear, "They're right down the road. They're still your babies, just now they are in boarding school. Come anytime and visit." He pulled away and held her shoulders to look her in the face, "Thank you, for these two magnificent friends. Thank you, for the good deal. My kids will love them as much as you do."

146

Craig's truck pulled the loaded horse trailer down the drive away from the farmhouse. Perfecto followed with Ethan riding shotgun in the red truck. Sybil, Donna and Sophia watched as the farm became incredibly quiet. Slowly, Donna walked to the end of the barnyard to shut the double gates with a clang. Sybil put her arm through her mother's and led her back to the house. The dogs were sitting under the tall elm trees sunning while cats stalked low flying birds or sat on the backyard picnic table.

"Mom, it's going to be all right. You know you can call on Donna or me if you need help with anything, but and I repeat what I said yesterday, do not get involved with anything to do with Granger!" Sybil pulled open the screen door to the back porch, "Remember, what happened last time? It may have been about what? Forty years ago, but Mom, it was a nasty business. Please, please, let Clementine and the police deal with Granger and the Colorado Springs mess. Please!"

Sybil's cellphone chirped in her pocket. She pulled it out to speak briefly only to put the cellphone back in her pocket, "That was grandma. She needs you. She sounded awful, but then she always sounds awful."

Donna ran into the house behind them, "Hey, guys, I've got to go and pick up Fleur. We're going to do our shopping today and later Fleur evidently has a date with some guy named J.J."

Sophia pulled away from Sybil, "Donna, what did you say?" Turning Donna to face her, Sophia asked, again, "What did you just say?"

Studying her mother's face, Donna repeated, "Fleur and I are going shopping. Fleur has a date tonight with some guy named J.J. when I asked her why he didn't have a real name, she said he does, but everyone calls him J.J."

Sophia took out a kitchen chair to abruptly sit, "No, no, no, J.J. was the name of the young phony minister who affiliated the wedding in Colorado Springs. He worked with Bethany, Matt and Collette. Bethany and J.J. stood up Matt and Collette. Donna, you absolutely cannot let beautiful Fleur get mixed up with him. Please, please, please, keep Fleur home or bring her here."

Donna knelt beside her mother, "Mom, I've met J.J. he works with Fleur. He's a nice kid. What are you going on about?"

Sybil filled the water kettle. "I think we need an explanation. This sounds like a long story. I'll fix the tea."

147

Sitting back on the kitchen chair, Sophia explained in detail what had happened regarding the four youths and the prior day's events. Her eyes were filled with sadness, her hands were shaking as she held her tea mug, "Yesterday, was an ethereal day. Matt and Collette drove me down here, but the other two, oh, Donna, I don't trust them at all."

Staring out the kitchen window, Donna held her empty tea mug in her hand, "Mom, you went through hell. Did you tell all of this to Clementine?"

Sybil put her right hand flat on the kitchen table, "She must have. Perfecto told Ethan and me that Clementine was going to be working all day today even though it's Sunday." Studying her sister's face, Sybil asked Donna, "What are you going to tell Fleur? You must tell her something or she's going to go out with this guy."

The empty mug was placed in the middle of the kitchen table. A fuzzy white and black cat jumped on the table to sniff the mug. Donna watched the cat, "What can I do? Fleur is twenty years old. She's old enough to make her own decisions. We have a pact, I stay out of her personal life and she stays out of mine."

The kitchen chair scraped on the wood floor as Sybil jumped up, "Then I'm going to tell Fleur! She should not get involved in all of this! Donna, remember what happened to us when Granger threatened us with the man...what was his name? Oh, yes, Don Juan Calderon! Donna, tell her or I will!"

Sophia reached out to pet the cat, "Both of you sit down. Donna, let Fleur know what's going on. You don't have to order her to leave J.J. alone. Just lay out what I told you. Fleur is a smart young woman. She's one of us after all. Explain to her the situation." Lifting the cat into her lap, Sophia continued, "We cannot control other people. All three of us know how this ended up badly when we tried to control one another. Just inform her and let her make her own decision."

Sybil's cellphone made a horrible squawking noise.

Smiling, Sophia said, "Is that the noise for my mother?" Sybil nodded. "Well, I best get over there. Life goes on, doesn't it?" The three women stood for a group hug.

The old smelly backpack was replaced with the new one Sophia had received for Christmas. Sybil and Ethan were great gift givers, and they had specifically found the perfect backpack for Sophia. This one was made of heavy brown canvas with a photo of her two dogs silkscreened onto the front.

The wind picked up outside, shaking the dead brown leaves from the stark elm tree branches, Fat geese honked overhead as Sophia quietly drove to Calavera. She was lost in thought as she pulled her old SUV into her mother's driveway.

Sophia parked her SUV under the tall cottonwood tree in front of her mother's old adobe wall. She noticed a faded red truck further down the dirt road that appeared to be herding cattle. As the wind whipped around the old cottonwood tree, she heard a branch crack overhead. It crashed down in front of her, missing the hood of her vehicle by inches. Quickly, Sophia jumped back into the old SUV to back it away from the trees to park by the adobe wall. Tumbleweeds had blown up against the wall to make a tall pile of prickly weeds.

Then she pushed through the wrought iron gate to the back door. It was unlocked but at least shut tightly so as not to bang. Pulling it open she dropped her backpack on the floor of the kitchen. Standing, she kicked the back door shut with the heel of her foot. Her reflection in the glass on the back door caught her attention. Her short curly hair was more gray than brown, the wrinkles around her mouth had grown in number, age and outdoor life appeared to have caught up with her. Sophia tried to push her bangs back on her forehead, but the curls kept bouncing back over her eyebrows.

Sophia called out as she turned into the kitchen, "Margaret? Hey, Margaret, it's your only daughter. Where are you?" The kitchen smelled of burnt toast. There was a pile of dirty dishes in the kitchen sink. Burnt breadcrumbs were scattered over the kitchen counter under the window. Mouse droppings decorated the counter under the long kitchen cupboards. The copper kettle lay on its side on the counter, the bottom of it burned out. Sophia turned her head to listen only to call out again, "Margaret! Where are you?" Her mother's straw hat appeared to be torn as it lay half on the kitchen table and half off.

"Sophia, come to the bedroom. I'm back here with Gizzie. Bring some water with you, please, in a glass not in your hand."

Shaking her head, Sophia smiled, "Duh, why would I carry water in my hand? What's she up to now?" First, washing her hands, she cleaned the burnt breadcrumbs into the sink. Quickly she wiped down the dirty dishes, leaving them to dry on a dish towel on the counter. She reached for one of her mother's tall glasses and filled it with cold water. As she turned to go down the hall, she noticed a trail of dirt on the brick floor. Halfway down the hall, she found a dirty washcloth lying in the middle of the hall. Inside her mother's bedroom, Gizzie came to greet her. The top of his head was soaking wet. "Are you washing the dog or are you thirsty?"

The bedroom was dark. Only the light from outside lit the room. This light came from the shade's broken slat hanging over the window. Cobwebs shivered as the hard wind blew through the cracked window glass. Sophia stepped around Gizzie. She noticed her mother had on only one shoe. It was on the foot sticking out from under the quilt. "Margaret, what do you want me to do with this water?"

Not waiting for any further remarks, Margaret stuck out her left hand, "Please, yes, I'm thirsty. Today has been a trial beyond belief." Taking the water, she asked, "Sophia, tell me about the wedding in Colorado Springs. Was it beautiful? Did you wear the green dress?" Margaret sipped the water to continue her questions, "You have been gone for almost six days, right? Who's looking after your animals at your home? Was it fun?" Margaret took a long drink of the water before turning her attention back to her daughter.

149

Teresa Pijoan

Smiling at her mother, Sophia answered, "Yes, it was a beautiful wedding. Margaret, I was here yesterday and returned the blue dress. Don't you remember? I told you the dress was worn over my sweats and the wedding was outside on this side of Pike's Peak, the mountain not the peak." Sophia pulled the black rocking chair close to the bed, "For their honeymoon, the new wife wanted to hike to the top of Pike's Peak."

The quilt was lifted to put over Margaret's shoeless foot still in the dirty sock. Sophia touched the toe of the shoe, "Now what is going on with you? Your face is dirty, you have leaves in your hair and you are in bed with only one shoe. What's up?" Sophia took the empty water glass from her mother, "Do you want more?"

Waving her hand, Margaret tried to wipe her face with the palm of her right hand. Sophia handed her the washcloth found in the hall, "Here, is this what you were needing? Margaret, what happened?"

"Oh, so you arrive here and the first thing you do is criticize me? Not a 'hello how are you?'" Smirking, Margaret shook her head, "You may have been out in the wild doing god knows what with who knows who and you walk into my home and the first thing you do is complain and criticize me! Some daughter you are!"

Sophia frowned, "I brought you water." She held up the empty glass. "It is important to show concern for I have never seen you so covered in dirt and in such a state. My criticism is concern, that's all." Sophia reached out to brush some leaves off of her mother's sleeve. "Sybil told me that you desperately needed me to come to you. Here I am. Now what is going on?"

Smiling, Margaret confessed, "I had a battle with the barnyard gate and it won. Mr. Gonzales and his grandson came to save me." Margaret tried to smile, but her cracked lips were stiff. Sophia took the washcloth away from her mother, "Here, let me get you a clean cloth. You know what? Let's go into the bathroom and I can help wash you?" Sophia lifted her shaking mother letting her lean against her as they limped to the small bathroom off of the bedroom.

"Hey, let's take off these clothes and get you into the shower to wash off this dirt?" Sophia sat Margaret on the commode as she pulled off her mother's dirty jeans, took off her socks, her shirt and tried to brush her mother's hair. Dirt and leaves fell in quantity around the commode. Sophia turned on the shower, allowing her mother to remove her underwear herself. Pulling her fragile mother upright, she lifted her into the shower. Margaret's feet hit the side of the tub. "Sophia, leave me be" Sophia's hands were smacked. "I can wash my hair and myself by myself. Just leave me be, please." Margaret stood tall in the shower. She pulled the shower curtain closed in Sophia's face. "Go away! I know what you're doing and it won't work."

Sophia retrieved a broom from the cleaning closet in the hall to sweep up all the fauna and flora in her mother's bathroom. She could hear her mother groaning and grunting in the shower. Soon, the steamy bathroom began to cool. Sophia asked, "Do you still have hot water? Are you doing okay in there?"

"Yes, would you help me out? For some reason my legs feel weak, and I think I should sit for a change." Sophia lifted her frail mother over the edge of the tub, sat her on the closed commode and dried her off with a big bath towel. A clean white T-shirt and loose-fitting navy blue sweatpants dressed Margaret.

Sophia studied her mother's face, "Your forehead and cheek are slowly turning a dull color of blue. The scrape on your chin looks deep." She gently touched the cut with the towel. "Think we should put some ointment on it."

151

Margaret swatted her hand away, "Sophia, you are always finding fault with me. No, no ointment. Just get me back in bed. I'm exhausted!" The extra baggy clothes seemed to bring relief to Margaret. As Sophia helped her mother to the bed, she asked, "The beautiful oil painting over your bed, the one with the ballerina dancers on it, where has it gone? Now there is just a space on the wall. Oh, and the large painting of Papa over the dresser, it's gone, but where?"

Huffing and puffing, Margaret slowly lifted her legs up onto the bed as she explained, "Those paintings were not my favorite, and Granger understood this. He couldn't find a job. And so, Granger needed money for his family. He found a man who was interested in buying those paintings for his home, or gallery, or some such. He paid Granger enough money for Granger's down payment on his house down the road." Sniffing through her nose, Margaret smacked Sophia as she tried to dry her mother's hair. "Just leave me alone, why don't you? Just leave my things alone. These are my things, now and I can do what I want with them." Sophia backed away.

Resting in her cozy bed, Margaret appeared to perk right up. "Do you know I am seriously hungry? Are you willing to make us something to eat?" Margaret's hand shook as she tried to hide them under the cover sheet. Sophia noticed that her mother's hands were not only shaking, but they were bruised as well.

Reaching down to take hold of Margaret's hands, Sophia mentioned, "Margaret, you were badly hurt in this fall with the gate. Can't you tell me more of what happened?" The wind picked up outside with the tall cottonwood tree branches scraping against the toolshed roof. The scratching sound echoed in Margaret's bedroom because it was conjoined with the toolshed wall. Margaret bent her chin towards her chest as she peered up at Sophia through her eyebrows, "Please, Sophia, would you fix us some lunch? I'm very hungry."

Sophia smiled, "No problem." When Sophia returned with two plates of hot quesadillas, she was met in the hall next to the linen closet by Gizzie. "Hey, bud, do you know there are villages of mice living in the lower shelf of this linen closet? They have tunnels under the brick floors, which are sitting on sand. The mice have school buses, court houses and a whole interlocking tunnel system just to make you crazy. They tunnel into the kitchen, climb the wall into Mom's cabinets and eat through the cardboard cereal boxes to devour the junk food inside. These rodents live to make your life crazy, right?"

152

Gizzie wagged his tail. He knew this already. He didn't need her to remind him. Nudging the plate in her right hand, she quickly stood to walk into her mother's bedroom. "Here you go, me Lady! One quesadilla with cheese, chili sauce and a slice of ham. Potato chips on the side and two slices of orange to keep you from scurvy. Did I do well, or what?"

Lifting her hand for the plate of food, Margaret shook her head, "Sophia, what are you going on about? Scurvy? There has never been a case of scurvy in this family for generations if ever! Can't you just hand me the food!" Margaret's eyes narrowed as she stared at the food on the plate. "That's not enough potato chips."

Laughing, Sophia smiled, "Well, that's all you have. You received the last of the bag. I'm afraid the mice ate most of them. Perhaps you should put the bags of chips in a metal container." Sophia put her plate of food down on the side of the bed. "Margaret, you hardly have any food. The freezer is empty, and your fridge has only three tortillas left, a jar half filled with salsa and a container of watery milk. Do you need groceries? I could go to the store for you?"

Sophia studied her mother's face. Margaret's cheek and her forehead were turning purple. "You do have some cheese in the drawer, but the lettuce and vegetables in the drawer I had to throw out. They were all rotten. Or are you only interested in feeding the mushy vegetables to the mice?"

"Don't scold me about the mice. They are my friends. We keep each other company." Margaret pointed to the heavy maple desk on the other side of her bedside table. "There are three families living in that desk. Do you know, Sophia, there are people who buy shredders to shred their important papers. Well, I don't need a shredder." Margaret smiled her coy little girl smile. "My mice chew up all my old checks, check books, old letters, junk mail and your father's old prescription tablets. They make glorious nests out of them and raise their families."

Sophia quickly moved around the bed to the old desk. She opened the lowest deep drawer of the desk to find, as her mother had stated, a whole family of mice staring at her. There were tiny, pink-skinned babies with fat adult mice nestled in shredded paper. Not only were the mice in the shredded nests, but also, large quantities of mouse poop and yellow sludge coatings on the rims of the nests and the drawer. The drawer above was found to be the same. The only drawer that was vacant of mice and their excrement was the wide top middle drawer. It was filled with numerous pens, chewed on pencils, paperclips, ink cartridges and empty tape dispensers. There was, also, a pair of her deceased father's eyeglasses beside a round container of the deceased Dr. Mark Pino's false teeth. "Margaret, you do know that mice can carry diseases, right?"

"Sophia, you always think the worst of everything. These are helpless little people stuck in mouse bodies. Everything needs love and care. Those little guys are my friends. Sometimes when it's cold here, they get in bed with me. Gizzie doesn't mind, why should you?"

"These mice weren't here when you had the young cats. Margaret, I do believe we should get you a kitten. Seriously, this isn't healthy."

"No, no kittens. Cats are demanding. My mice lead their own lives and do not, I repeat, they do not bother anyone." Margaret shook her head. "Granger takes me out for meals. That's what he does. I don't need food here because Granger or Marcos takes me out for food. Besides they turned off the electricity to the stove and the oven. They're afraid I'll burn the house down and the house is made of mud!" Giggling,

TERESA PIJOAN

Margaret said, "I found the old toaster to make toast and the microwave still works."

Margaret padded the right side of the bed. "Come over here. Tell me all about the wedding and how beautiful Pike's Peak is. Seems I'm stuck here in isolation and not invited anywhere."

Shaking her head, Sophia asked, "You had the memorial service at the old church, right? Charlotte comes and takes you shopping with her." Sophia sat on the bed next to her mother. Margaret's arthritic fingers smoothed down the quilt beside her. Sophia lifted her legs onto the bed to lean back on the cold adobe wall, "So, how was the memorial at the old church?"

"Well, it was nice. They had fresh zucchini bread and fresh flowers on tables. I think they were from John's garden. You know the man who takes cares of the honeybees when Benjamin is away? They were lovely."

A large pillow was pushed behind Margaret's head as she went onto say, "They had a carpenter make a bench out of white pine in remembrance of your father. The Pino name was engraved on the back part for everyone to see. Actually, it was quite nice. Your father would have been very pleased since he loved working with wood."

Sophia turned on the bed to face her mother, "Where is this bench going to sit? Did you bring it home with you?"

"Oh, no. It is going to be right outside the priest's quarters. The parishioners will see it as they go in and out of the church. I wasn't sure what I was supposed to say or do with the bench, so I just thanked them for it." Margaret fluffed up her hair with her fingers to help it dry. "Charlotte brought three large quiches she had ordered from the Corner Market store. We had a lovely lunch. Don't know about that woman Phyllis, she ate almost one of them by herself and she certainly didn't need to feed that hefty body of hers. Don't know how her husband can stand to have such a fat cow for a wife."

Pushing Margaret's bangs to the side of her forehead, Sophia noticed the extensive bruising on her mother's face. "Your bruises are showing up now. There's a bad one right in the middle of your forehead. Let's check your legs." As Sophia stood, she pulled the top sheet down to the bottom of the bed. Sliding the sweatpants up to her mother's knees, Sophia began rubbing her mother's legs. "You must have hit the gate hard. Bruises are beginning to form. This one on your left leg is dark, it wants to turn purple. Do you think we should wrap it with an ace bandage?"

Margaret jerked her leg away from Sophia. "Just leave my legs and me alone! You constantly find something to pick on when you come over here." She kicked her leg up to hit Sophia in the chin with her toes. Sophia moved back from the bed. "Fine. I don't appreciate people trying to tell me what to do with my body either."

"Do you know what Granger told his wife before they were married?" Margaret wiped the cheese off her chin.

The words spit out of Margaret's mouth, "Well, according to Emily, his ex now, Granger told her that if she became fat he would divorce her. Granger wants a thin wife or no wife." Margaret took a drink of water, "He told me as much when he was between wives. Can you believe that? He told his wife to do exactly what he told me?"

Sophia decided to change the subject and asked, "What happened when you finally made it home from the church? How did you end up entangled in a gate?"

As they sat on the bed, side by side and ate their snack, Margaret explained her day's events. Sophia stood to walk to the window. The wind was blowing hard against the warped pane of glass. 155

When Margaret finished speaking, Sophia turned slowly to face her mother. "There was an incident on the mountain yesterday," Sophia shook her head, "Wow, yesterday morning feels as if it were ages ago."

The rocking chair was pulled back from the foot of the bed to be pushed closer to Margaret. Sophia sat down and rubbed Gizzie's shoulder, "The bride of my boss Robert, gave him some herbs. No, that isn't right. She said that Granger gave Robert some herbs to help with his wedding night love making." Sitting up straight, Sophia watched her mother's face, "The herbs were deadly. Robert became deathly ill..."

Slapping her thigh through the sheet, Margaret glared at Sophia, "NO! No! You are not going to smear your brother's name again! I will not hear it! Sophia, you are constantly trying to destroy your brother with all these fictitious facts. Was Granger at the wedding?"

Shaking her head, Sophia said, "No. But, he..."

Margaret interrupted her, "No! No, he wasn't! No! Leave this alone, Sophia! I swear one of these days your words are going to come back and bite you right in the face!" Margaret pushed the quilt off the bed as she struggled to get up, "Don't you dare say another bad thing about your brother! He walks on water! He has helped me through all the struggles of life and all you do is complain!" She fell back onto the pillows as she reached for the glass of water. Sophia handed the glass to her mother.

Sophia faced her mother, "You do know how deadly Granger can be? You and Granger killed Papa and then killed the nurse because she knew what you did. Margaret, you are not completely innocent in Granger's life."

"Sophia, we didn't kill your father. You know we didn't. We put him out of his misery. He was dying slowly, ever so slowly and there was no hope of any medical miracle. We just put him down like people put down their cats and dogs" Margaret glared at Sophia through her eyebrows with her head down. "Granger is a good boy, he is a love and has a kind soul. Sophia, Granger takes care of me! He loves me and helps me here on the farm. Granger has a soul of godliness."

Suddenly, the back door slammed shut. Gizzie stood to let out a warning bark. His hackles went up, a low growl rumbled out of his mouth as he stared at the open bedroom door. Glancing at her mother, Sophia stood to walk to the far side of the bed. "Margaret, it appears you have a visitor. Perhaps I should go since our conversation is over."

156

"Oh, God, Sophia, I forgot to mention your nephew has come to look after me. This must be him now." Margaret put her hand on Sophia's arm, "Please, do not make a stink. Granger and his family have run out of money. Please, Sophia, Granger has had a difficult time. I gave them some money so they could take the two youngest children to California. Marcus has a job at Charlie's gas station, so he stays here." Shaking her head, she added, "Well, I don't know if he stays here or he is to check on me. I know you hate Granger and live to rub his face in his failures, but please, please, try to be thoughtful and kind to Marcus, please!" Margaret's bony fingers dug into Sophia's hand, giving it a hard squeeze. "Please, please, be nice to your nephew."

His hard leather soles echoed as he walked down the hall into the bedroom, "Ah, my aunt has arrived. Sophia, you left all your stuff right in the middle of the kitchen floor. You wanted me to trip over it, is that it?"

He gave Sophia an evil grin, "What's your plan, Auntie dear?" The nineteen-year-old young man stood tall, erect. His brown hair was cut short in a prep school cut. The thin moustache and goatee on his face was barely visible. His jeans were smudged with grease and oil. His cotton shirt with rolled up sleeves to his elbow, appeared to be immaculate.

Marcus stared at the empty plates on the bed. "Grandma, I thought you invited me here for dinner. Did you already eat?" He shoved Gizzie with his foot, "Get up, old boy, I'm tired and need to sit." Marcus fell more than sat in the black rocking chair. His heavy brown working boots were lifted and placed on Margaret's quilt on the bed.

Margaret put her hands up, "Marcus, your dear Auntie just prepared a snack for us. I've had a very difficult afternoon." Arthritic fingers pushed back her bangs of grey and white. Her furrowed forehead showed concern as she stared at the large boots on her bed. The quilt was pulled away from under the stained boots as she shook her head. The old rocking chair creaked as Marcus rocked it back and forth, not removing his feet from his grandmother's bed.

Sighing, Sophia stood. She removed the empty plates, nodded to her mother and walked to the kitchen. The bricks on the hall floor were uneven, some raised higher than others. The whitewashed interior adobe walls were crumbling to leave piles of dirt where the wall met the floor. Her mother's oil paintings and her father's famous wooden carvings were covered with dust and the cobwebs hung low from the ceiling in each corner of each room. 157

The usual smell of lemon oil was long gone. As she carried the plates through the high adobe door into the kitchen, she heard a scurrying of tiny feet. On the counter, that she had cleaned earlier, were small piles of mouse excrement. Peering into the dining area, which was off the kitchen, she noticed the plate glass windows at the end of the dining room table were cracked. The wind whistled through the large window on the right. Spider webs glistened as they moved in the draft from the windows. The sun was moving low in the sky. To the east there were glorious clouds of bright orange frosted with pink.

# 14

Sophia returned to the sink. The water pouring out of the faucet was brown caramel in color, smelling of rotten eggs. The sink of chipped porcelain slowly filled. The plates were submerging in the putrid water.

Papers on the far counter were laid out in order. Sophia leaned over with the dish cloth in her hand to read. These were real estate contracts. The offer recommended on Margaret's farm was four hundred and forty thousand dollars. Photos of the farm showed only its best side. The uneven brick floors, the piles of dirt on the floors, the large cobwebs and deteriorating conditions of the roof, the crumbling outside walls and the lopsided doors were absent from the vast quantity of photos. The fireplace had been cleaned to show off the Pueblo beehive shape with a deep flat mantel. The photo of the dining room was taken from the living room, illustrating the length and the large area of the dining area. The bedroom photos were a bit blurry, but the barn in its pristine prime condition had an excellent photo. Although, the barn no longer looked like that now because the wooden stall doors were cracked and the stalls were filled with spiders and bee hives. Shaking her head, Sophia whispered, "God help he who enters here." She finished washing the dishes and then put them in her mother's dishwasher. It no longer worked and was used as a dish cupboard.

The cellphone in her pocket gave off its chirping noise. Sophia pulled it out to study it. There was a text from Donna, "Fleur is staying home tonight to help me with the laundry. Will share tomorrow,"

Marcus walked into the kitchen, "You do know, Sophia, that none of us trust you. Papa says you lie, cheat and steal from grandma. We all know it and we all don't like you. Maybe you should just go because I'm staying with grandma, and I'll take care of her. I don't steal her stuff." He stood directly behind her as she finished loading the dishes into the dishwasher. She wiped down the counter beside the papers. Sophia remained quiet.

There was movement behind her and then her backpack was lifted from the floor to hit her hard on her back. "Here, take this with you. We don't need you here. Go, just go!" His hand touched her shoulder. The wet dish cloth smacked his hand on her shoulder.

Sternly, Sophia said, "Do not touch me! Do not tell me what to do." The sink water was turned off. The wet dish cloth was draped over the faucet as Sophia turned to take her backpack. Marcus shook his head, "My Dad hates you. Do you know that? We all hate you, even grandma." He turned on his heel to go back down the hall to his grandmother's room.

Suddenly, he reappeared. Sophia was pulling her car keys from her back pocket. Leaning against the kitchen door frame, he shoved his hands into his jean pockets. "Okay, so why are the Gonzales' taking back their steers? Sophia, what did you do? You have a knack for upsetting people that my Papa has befriended. What happened?" His tone was condescending and forceful. Sophia just stared back at him. Silence filled the room.

There was a low growl behind Marcus who turned to stare at Gizzie. "Get out of here, you dumb dog! I don't like you either!" He lifted his hand to hit the dog when they heard Margaret calling, "Sophia, do not hit my dog. Leave my dog alone!" Gizzie moved to the living room.

Margaret called out to Marcus, "You need to feed the cat and the dog now that you're here! You didn't feed them this morning!"

Under his breath, Marcus mumbled, "There isn't anything here to feed them. What am I supposed to do if they don't have any food?"

The clang of Margaret's metal walker on the brick floor in the hall moved closer to them. Margaret stared at Sophia from around Marcus, "Yes, Sophia, what did you do? Were you the one who knocked over the gate and let the steers out? What did you do?" Margaret pointed at Sophia, "You do know you almost killed me by knocking down the gate? You could've killed me! Was that your purpose to get your money from the will? Sophia?" Margaret glared at Sophia.

Sophia studied her mother. Her gray hair, which was usually coiffed in a bowl cut to her shoulders was now in total disarray. Margaret was

160

bent over the walker showing her fragility. Margaret's thin frame was barely holding up the heavy black sweatpants. The white t-shirt showed off Margaret's sharp ribs and flat chest. The cold blue eyes still sparkled when she eagerly berated her daughter. It was obvious Margaret was enjoying herself as she stood behind Marcus. Spitting out her words, Margaret spoke sharply to Sophia, "Yes, go, go home to your pathetic small farm. Go away and leave!"

Clenching the keys in her right hand, Sophia stared back at her mother, "Now, what?" Sophia moved to the back door, to say, "Margaret, when I arrived you had already fallen onto the gate. What are you doing? What is this all about?"

Pushing Margaret and her walker further behind him, Marcus growled, "You tried to kill her? You are a nasty piece of work!" He moved forward, his index finger was now in Sophia's face, "You lied about traveling and doing research! You lied about publishing books! You lied about going to Colorado Springs for a wedding!" His face was bright red with anger, "My friend at work tracks cellphones. He's a pro! He tracked your cellphone here to Grandma's. You're a horrible, horrible person and a liar!"

Sophia stared at his finger in front of her face, "Kindly remove 161 your finger, Marcus, you are badly misinformed. As to why my own mother is attacking me, I have no idea." Her cellphone was lifted out of her backpack. She studied it for a minute and then handed it to Marcus. "This is my cellphone. This cellphone has been with me in Colorado Springs. Is this the number your friend-the-computer-genius is tracking?"

The phone was observed without picking it off her hand. Marcus shook his head, "This area code has a six one seven number." Rather than saying anything, he turned to lift his grandmother's landline phone, removing it from the kitchen wall. It was an ancient white plastic phone. Margaret bought it fifty years prior. Turning the phone over, ignoring the petrified butter smears on the mouth piece, he studied the area code. "Grandma, this is your phone. Here. Your phone here. Why did you give me this phone number to use? Grams?"

Margaret ripped the phone out of his hand. The coiled cord stretched to fly off the wall. "Give me that! Marcus, I have told you over and over and over again not to call me Grandmother, Grandma, or Grams! I have told you, have I not?"

Marcus nodded. Margaret's voice raised to a high pitch as she added, "Now, if you want my money as I am sure that you do, you will call me Margaret! Is that understood? If you cannot get this through your thick head, you can go and I don't care where you go, understood?" She rolled the coiled cord around the phone. "Now fix this since you broke it." She handed it to him, firmly placing it in the palm of his hand. "Sophia, as far as your trip to Colorado Springs...."

Before she could finish her thought, there was a hefty knock on the front door. This was a door rarely used and was kept locked. Margaret smirked, "I bet that's the police. I called them about Sophia letting all the steers out and throwing me into the fence."

A whisper came from Marcus, "Good, let them arrest her!" The cord was reattached to the wall phone base. Marcus followed his grandmother into the hall, turning where there were floor to ceiling books in wall shelves. Now out of breath, Margaret unlocked the heavy front door to let it swing open. Mr. Gonzales stood with a paper in his hand. His well-worn jeans covered his cracked black leather boots. His chambray shirt was decorated with stains and black animal fur. He said, "Mrs. Pino, I am glad to see you are up and feeling better. Is this your grandson?" Marcus nodded.

Mr. Gonzales went on to say to Marcus, "Your father charged us for putting our steers in your grandmother's field. The fence is no good. It fell with one push from the steers. Your grandmother was trying to lift the gate, and she fell face first into it." He shook his head as he spoke directly to Margaret, "You never should have tried to lift it. It took both myself and my grandson to get it upright."

Sighing, he went onto say, "The gate has different posts bolted to it. Someone put it together with remnants of old rotten posts that have seen better days." Mr. Gonzales shifted his weight to the other foot, "It would be wise to have someone make a better gate for that field, or you could order one from the feed store. They don't cost all that much and it would protect your property and not fall over as easily."

He peered around Margaret and Marcus to see Sophia. "Hi, Sophia, how nice to see you. My wife Rachel loved the zucchini bread you brought over last week. She wanted me to say thank you." He removed his hat with a dark leather band around its center. "Hey, got a call from Timothy Turpen two days ago about you being up there for the wedding. My wife went to college with Timothy Turpen. He told her about the crazy wedding. That woman must be crazy to want to hike Pike's Peak for her honeymoon!"

He turned his attention back to Margaret, "Good thing we came along to get you out of the gate, huh?" He looked her up and down from her twinkling eyes to her slippers. Marcus stepped in front of his grandmother as if he was protecting her. Shaking his head, Mr. Gonzales said to Marcus, "Here's a copy of the receipt your father gave us. We want our money back. Too, there was no water source. Your father guaranteed a water source. I just looked again, there is no such water source." Pushing the paper forward, Marcus stepped back with his hands up, "This is between you and my father. I don't have anything to do with this."

Mr. Gonzales leaned forward with his left hand on the door frame, He put his hat back on his head, "Son, just give this to your father." Marcus abruptly turned, walked around Sophia to go back into the kitchen. Margaret reached out and took the paper from him. "Thank you, I am sure, Mr. Gonzales. My son will gladly return your money. Thank you for your help."

Quickly, she closed the door. "Marcus, Marcus, go and get me the box from the top of my closet. Quickly! Go!" Margaret stared at the paper. It was obvious she could not read it without her glasses. The paper was shoved over to Sophia who carefully took it.

Studying the receipt, Sophia said, "Margaret, this is a receipt for two hundred dollars. Added on in pencil at the bottom is a list of medical expenses incurred to one of the steers who was wounded going through the fence."

Marcus raced up the hall towards them. He tripped on one of the uneven bricks and went flying. The tin box landed within inches of Margaret's slipper. Sophia reached down and handed it to Margaret who asked, "All right, what was the total damage? Quickly, now Sophia! What was the final amount?" The paper was given back to Sophia who read, "The total amount is three hundred fifty-seven dollars and eighty-one cents."

The tin box was gingerly opened by Marcus who had recovered from his fall. He turned his back to Sophia, keeping her from knowing how much money was in the tin box. Margaret pulled out a wad of bills, counted out four hundred-dollar bills. She handed them to Marcus, 'Run, run, out there before he's down the driveway and give this to him.

163

TERESA PIJOAN

Oh, get him to sign this paper! Hurry, go!" The front door was pulled open, Marcus turned back, "I don't have a pen. What should I do?" Sophia pulled one out of her backpack to hand it to him. "Go. Just go."

Her backpack now back over her shoulder, Sophia studied her mother, "What type of game are you playing? One minute we are best friends sharing life on your bed. The next minute you throw around accusations that are completely untrue. What's going on with you?"

The tin box now held in Margaret's right hand was held close to her chest. Her left hand was closed over the handle of the walker. Margaret turned away from Sophia, "I don't know what you're talking about, Sophia. As I said before, you are always taking the negative side of things. We need to be good to Marcus. He's young, he needs support and confidence." Leaning on her right arm, she clanged the walker at an angle away from her daughter. "We can't turn him away from his father. Every son needs to worship his father. Just leave him alone!"

The back door was flung open. Marcus appeared out of breath, holding Sophia's pen high in the air. "Here, here's your pen. I caught up with him at the downed gate." Marcus pulled out a dining room chair to drop into it and catch his breath. "He said that he helped you out of the gate with his grandson. He said that Sophia didn't come until later." Pushing his bangs back, Marcus glared at Margaret, "Why did you tell me Sophia pushed you? Grandma, do you like Sophia? Do you lie, too?"

A harsh deep voice roared up and out at him, "You do not ever call me grandma! Do you understand?" The tin box fell to the floor. It fell open with wads of bills rolling out onto the bricks. "Pick that up, Marcus! Pick it up!" Margaret shook her fist at Sophia, "You do know I'm aware that you want to kill me!"

Shaking her head, Sophia quietly answered, "Why did you and Granger kill father? Margaret, you admitted it! Why is Marcus here and not taking care of his own home? Granger's the one who is after your money, not me."

Turning her attention to Marcus, Sophia softly added, "Your father only comes back here when he runs out of money. Perhaps if he made more than he spent, he would stay away longer, and we would all be happier."

Sophia stepped around the tin box, "You both have a lovely evening. I am going home. Margaret, thank you for a most entertaining afternoon."

Marcus stooped to pick up the dollar bills. He turned to Sophia and said, "Yeah, go to the home that Margaret owns. Since, you don't own anything, and you owe her everything." He smirked.

Opening the back door, Sophia glanced at her mother, "Margaret, perhaps you should be truthful. The truth shall set you free, don't you know?" Sophia walked out into the windy late afternoon. Leaves blew against her as she pushed her way through the wrought iron gate. There was a loud crash as a thick cottonwood tree branch fell squarely on top of the work shed's roof. The wind swept away the cloud of dirt and dust rising from the collapsed adobe walls. Sophia shook her head, "Hey, karma's a bitch."

165

## 15

Sophia stopped at the grocery store in Rincon. Farmers were unloading alfalfa at the back of the store. Two trucks were filled with watermelons and summer squash. Children, bundled in thick winter coats, were drawing with chalk on the sidewalk. An older woman walked out of the front double doors carrying a heavy bag of groceries and pulling a small dog behind her on a leash. The smell of fresh roasted chili filled the store. There were bags of steaming chili on sale by the cash register. The loud noise of a saw was coming from the butcher department. People were talking, sharing neighborhood news as they bought or searched for items.

Sophia loaded her cart with sliced ham, sliced turkey, sliced cheese, a loaf of fresh bread made in the bakery at the back, some whole milk from the dairy and a large container of orange juice. The freezers on the left side of the store had frozen dinners. Sophia knew Granger would throw a fit if he saw them in Margaret's freezer, but Margaret needed food. Sophia decided to pick out a tin of cookies and four peanut butter bars covered in chocolate. Studying chocolate bars, she wondered if mice ate chocolate.

Margaret needed food in her house. Marcus was driving her truck, which left Margaret unable to go anywhere, and even if she wanted to, she didn't see all that well to drive. Margaret was as thin as a rail and if she expected to be taken out for meals, well, Granger and his family were supposedly in California.

Walking down the cat aisle, Sophia questioned what she could buy for her mother's animals. The kibble in the bag would be eaten as fast as she put it down by the mice, unless she put it in the dog's tin container outside. She picked out kibble for elderly cats, a small bag. The tins of cat food would be safe, especially the ones with pop tops. The cans of dog food were mostly sold out, but way in the back of the shelf, she found six large cans. These would be good for Gizzie since he is a big dog. She picked out a small bag of dog kibble, not sure there was much in the tin on the porch.

Back at her mother's, Sophia had her arms filled with bags of groceries. When she tried to open the back door, it was locked. "Oh, no, now I have to find Mom." Walking to the window by Margaret's bedroom, Sophia knocked. Margaret was curled up in a ball on her bed with the quilt pulled over her. Sophia knocked again and called out, "Margaret, can you open the back door, please!"

Slowly, the quilt moved. Then Margaret sat up to stare at the bedroom door. Sophia knocked on the window again and called out, "Over here! Margaret, open the back door!"

Turning to the window, Margaret smiled and waved. Slowly, slowly she reached for her walker as she slid on her slippers. Gizzie appeared from around the barn. He was covered in dried leaves. Wagging his tail, he came up to Sophia for a good rub. Kneeling next to him, Sophia brushed off the leaves, kissed him on the nose and rubbed his tummy. His tail wagging back and forth with delight.

The back door opened. Margaret had fallen back on a kitchen chair. The walker had been tossed to the side and was lying on the bricks behind the chair. Sophia lifted the grocery bags, walking around her mother and the walker, she put them on the kitchen counter.

"What are you doing back here? I thought you went home. Where's Marcus? He's supposed to bring me dinner!" Margaret screeched at Sophia, "I don't want you here. Please, please, for God's sake go away!"

Ignoring her mother, Sophia put the groceries away. "I brought you food. I'm putting it away. You now have sliced ham, turkey and cheese. Oh, damn, I forgot the tortillas, but I did get you some fresh bread. It is going in the fridge since if I leave it out the mice will eat it. Also, you now have whole milk from the diary and food for your cat and dog. Why don't I feed them now and then you won't have to worry about them?"

Margaret turned in her chair. Her face was now mostly purple. She rubbed it with her left hand, which had cuts on it. Sophia grabbed a clean dish cloth from the drawer, soaked it in cold water from the sink and brought it to Margaret. "Here, put this against your cheek and part of your forehead. You are slowly turning purple. You must have hit the fence hard, but then you don't have much padding, do you?"

"That's it! You criticize and criticize! You can't say one nice thing about me or my home! I wish you would go! If you think for one minute I'm going to pay you back for those groceries, you are so very wrong! Please, Go!"

Sophia lifted the porcelain cat bowl. Tigger was dragging his body into the kitchen from the hall. The brick flooring had worn off most of the fur on his tummy. Sophia reached down to lift Tigger up to the counter. She opened a can of cat food, popped the top and dumped the whole lot of it onto the bowl. Before she could move the can, Tigger was chowing down. His tail twitched from side to side as he burped and ate.

Bending under the open counter, Sophia lifted Gizzie's metal bowl. She took the small bag of cat kibble with her as she went outside. The tin with the tight lid was where the dog kibble was kept. It took a few tries, but she finally removed the tight lid. The can was about half full. She used her hand to fill the metal bowl full of kibble. The cat kibble bag was dropped into the tin, as Sophia hurried back into the kitchen to get the small dog kibble bag before the mice got into it. Back outside she hammered down the tin lid.

Gizzie was now sitting on the kitchen floor by the counter. Sophia popped open a can of dog food, dumped it with the kibble and stirred a tiny bit of water into it. The water still smelled of rotten eggs and was the color of sludge. Sophia didn't want Gizzie to be sick. She chose to skip the water. Gizzie's nose was in the bowl before it was placed on the floor.

"Margaret, both of your animals now have food. There is no reason for them to be this hungry. Do you have canned food for them here? In the kitchen?"

"I'm not talking to you. Get me some orange juice. There's some in the fridge that Marcus bought. Pour me a glass." Margaret straightened as she sat at the kitchen table.

"You do have orange juice, now. I bought you some." Sophia poured her mother a large glass of orange juice and on a plate, she put four cookies and the chocolate bar. Placing this in front of Margaret brought another verbal bashing, "You didn't buy this! Granger bought this for me! Granger walks on water! All you want is my money! Get out. Go away. Get out!" Margaret's arthritic boney fingers grabbed the cookies and the chocolate bar at the same time. Crumbs fell in her lap. Sophia brought her a napkin.

TERESA PIJOAN

Once the groceries were put away and the animals fed, Sophia decided to straighten up her mother's bedroom. Margaret was too busy eating and drinking her orange juice to notice. Quickly, Sophia pulled off the bed sheets. Mouse poop flew all over the room. The stains on the sheets appeared to be more from the mice than from her mother. She pulled folded sheets from the linen closet. The sheets were high enough to where the mice didn't go. These were put on the bed. Getting the broom, she swept up the mouse poop from the floor and dumped it in the bottom drawer of the desk. "She'll never know, and she'll never look. If I put it in the trash can, she has a fit if she sees it."

The towels in the bathroom were exchanged for fresh ones. Sophia cleaned the toilet, the sink and scrubbed the bathtub. There was green mold around the tub on the floor, but Sophia felt that it would need to be another day. Tigger was making funny noises in the hall, coughing.

Hurrying to him, Sophia noticed the litter box at the end of the hall was overflowing. The hall was dark and with most of the paintings gone, there was no reason to turn the lights on. Tigger was lifted and held against Sophia's chest. The ancient cat began to purr. "Oh, you poor dear. You need loving, huh? Let's clean out your litter box and get some fresh litter in there. You want to help?" The cat was held in her arm as Sophia unlocked and opened the back door that went to the toolshed. Carefully, putting Tigger down on the soft sand outside the door, she lifted the litter box. The shovel was next to the door, which Sophia used to dig a hole. The dirty litter box was dumped in the hole.

There were two unopened bags of cat litter right inside the door. Cleaning the litter box with the hose outside, drying it off with a rag from the toolshed, the litter box was filled with fresh litter. Tigger was picked up to be put back inside the house. He sat down beside the clean litter box to wash his back paws.

There was a loud crash from the kitchen. Sophia hurried down the hall. Marcus was standing there with two other young men. Margaret was not to be seen. Marcus confronted her, "What the hell are you doing here? You were supposed to be gone!"

"I bought Margaret some groceries since she didn't have anything to eat. Did you bring her dinner? She is expecting you to bring her dinner." Sophia studied the other young man who appeared embarrassed to be there.

Marcus shook his head, "What am I? I'm not her slave! She didn't tell me anything. I don't have money to buy her food. She has that tin filled with money and do you think she shares it? No!" Nodding to his friend, he sat down on Margaret's chair. "She doesn't pay me back either, every time I buy her something she doesn't pay me back! Dad says she rich, but she doesn't share."

Sophia shook her head, "I'm going to check up on Mom. Then I will leave. Please, try to be quiet and let her rest or sleep. Remember, Marcus, she's old and the elderly need to be respected. Please, be kind."

Back in Margaret's bedroom, she found Margaret propped up in bed with magazines all around her. Gizzie was sleeping next to the bed and Tigger was curled up by Margaret's feet. Sophia patted her mother's leg, "I'm going to leave now. You have food in the fridge and the critters have food, so no worries about them, okay?"

Glaring cold blue eyes stared at Sophia, "Yes! I know! Granger takes care of me!" Sophia nodded, kissed her mother on the top of her head, to quietly walk out of the bedroom, down the hall and out the back door.

The wind had seriously picked up with tumbleweeds blowing down the road to crash into her vehicle. Cows were slowly walking toward their barns. A man on a bicycle was peddling frantically down the road with his beard flying over his shoulder. The geese were in fields searching for bugs or seeds. Dark clouds were moving across the sky to the west.

Sophia rolled down the window, "Oh, God, please give me patience!" The window was rolled back up and Sophia drove home dodging the tumbleweeds and crazy drivers.

## 16

Sybil and Ethan were having a serious conversation in the living room when Sophia entered her house. Sybil stood tall with her long hair pulled back in a ponytail. Her wide green eyes smiled as she noticed her mother walking into the room. Sybil had a flair for thick cozy winter sweaters while her husband Ethan was more of a button-down shirt type of guy. Ethan remained on the floor with the two dogs lying on either side of him. His thick curly bangs were low on his forehead as he rubbed the dogs' tummies. Ethan was very much a dog man while Sybil preferred cats. Both in their forties, both very professional and even after being married for more than twenty years, they were still very much in love.　173

Sybil hurried to Sophia, "Mom, we have an issue with Donna. Donna received a lot of money left for her through a will. The old woman who hired Donna to help her write her memoirs, left her a substantial amount. We felt, well, I felt Donna should share it with us since we helped her out when Fleur was a baby. What do you think?"

Ethan looked up at Sophia and shook his head, "Sophia, I don't want to have any part of this conversation. Would it be all right if I took the dogs for a run? Just a short run, say about twenty minutes? You two can talk." The dogs followed Ethan to the front door. He turned to say, "Donna left you a note on the kitchen counter."

Not waiting for Sophia to answer, Ethan and the dogs were out the front door in a heartbeat. Sophia studied Sybil, "Sweetheart, you told Donna not to worry about paying you back when you helped her twenty some years ago. Now? Now that Donna has money, do you want to collect? Am I reading this correctly?" Sophia placed her backpack on the front chest as she walked into the kitchen. The dishes had been put away in cupboards, the counters were wiped clean, and the note was placed up against the water kettle.

TERESA PIJOAN

Sybil leaned against the kitchen counter, "Mom, Fleur was a tiny baby, and Donna was stuck between a rock and a hard place. Now with all this money, don't you think she could pay us back?" Sybil looked out the window to watch her husband run the dogs on the ditch road. "Fleur is now twenty years old. I mean, Fleur has a good job and she's helping to support both herself and Donna. Wouldn't you think it would be all right for Donna to share her income now she has some?"

Sophia shook her head, "This is between you and Donna. I don't have anything to do with this. You and Ethan decided to help Donna, which was wonderful at the time since Donna was destitute. Have you spoken to Donna about this?"

"No. I thought you would be the one to mention it to her. I don't want to look like a greedy bitch and beg for money. Mom, couldn't you ask?" Sybil's eyes pleaded with Sophia.

The cellphone in Sophia's pocket chirped. She pulled it out and studied it and then answered it, "Hello, Dion, how lovely to hear from you. How is your son today? I cannot thank you enough for their help yesterday." Sitting the cellphone on the kitchen counter, Sophia put it on the speaker phone.

174     Dion replied, "Say, Sophia, I thought you should know that woman Karen was arrested last night. They say she was found dead in the holding cell this morning. No one knows what happened to her. Have you heard anything?"

Sophia quickly leaned on the kitchen counter, "What? Karen was found dead. How can that be if she was in a holding cell in jail?" Sophia stared out of the kitchen window, "Dion, what happened to her? Was she shot or knifed, what happened?"

Dion paused and then said quietly, "Listen, this is not a subject I want the world to hear about, how about we meet in town? Tomorrow, I will only work a half day. We could meet at three thirty at the optical office. Do you know where the office is? Today, I work the ICU."

Answering in the affirmative, the time and place were agreed upon. Sybil picked up her keys from the kitchen counter, "Mom, do not get involved in this affair with Granger. Leave it to Clementine and her legal team."

Sybil bent over and kissed her mother on the top of her head, "You're right. Ethan and I will speak with Donna. It's late. You've already had a full day with the horses leaving and grandma. Tonight, you can have some peace and quiet. The dogs and cats need to be fed. There is left over pasole in the fridge and some sopapilla dough is there if you are up to cooking."

Sophia stood to hug her daughter, "Thank you. Thank you, for all you and Ethan have done." Six cats strolled into the kitchen to sit in a line staring at the women. Sybil smiled at them, "Yes, I guess it is feeding time at the zoo. Say, Mom, who owns that cute little white kitten? If you feel you have enough felines, Ethan and I will take her off your hands."

Six cat dishes were taken from the dry rack next to the sink. The little kitten was now attempting to climb up Sophia's pant leg. "This one is called Mint. Fleur thought he looked like one of the mints Ethan is always chewing." Sophia reached down to lift Mint. She handed him to Sybil. "He's a handful. He hasn't quite learned how to use kitty litter or when to go outside and do his business. Careful, he will bite you with those sharp needle teeth."

Sybil kissed the small white kitten. "Ethan says we have enough cats. They seem to find us, we don't go looking for them. Perhaps our cat house is full of the seven we have now."

The large can of cat food was emptied into six cat bowls. The cats milled around Sophia's ankles meowing and purring. Carefully, balancing the bowls on her arm and in her hands, Sophia placed the filled bowls strategically around the kitchen table. Turning to her daughter, Sophia said, "Let's talk tomorrow when you get off work, you can give me a call and let me know about your day?"

The dogs and Ethan were now pushing open the front door to barge into the kitchen. "Sybil, we better get home. Sophia, perhaps you can have a quiet evening at home with some peace and calm." A warm threesome hug was given as Sybil and Ethan headed for the front door.

There was a loud knock as Sybil and Ethan were ready to depart. The two of them opened the front room. Standing in the open doorway was an older man looking ragged, exhausted and dirty. "Hey, guys, do you think I could crash here tonight? I seem to have missed my plane."

Sybil stood in front of this man with her feet firmly planted and her hands on her hips, "Sir, I don't know who you are or what you are doing here, but this isn't a hotel. Didn't you see the No Trespassing Sign?"

Ethan took his wife's arm, "Hey, I bet you're the guy who went with my mother-in-law to the famous wedding up north, huh?"

175

TERESA PIJOAN

Still glaring at the man, Sybil stated, "You know there are cellphones today? You can call ahead and let people know you are coming. What do you want with my mother?"

The clattering of dog dishes was heard coming from the kitchen. Sophia came around the corner, "Timothy! My God, Timothy, you look awful! Come in, come in, Sybil, let the man pass."

Sybil stood aside begrudgingly. Ethan lurched forward to catch Timothy as he fell forward into the front room. Holding Timothy up by his waist, Ethan exclaimed, "Wow, easy there, partner. Let's get you into a chair." Ethan half dragged and half carried Timothy into the kitchen, to the table and sat him down in a kitchen chair. His left shoe had come off in the process to show a foot with a dirty sock encrusted with dried blood.

Immediately, Sybil went into medical mode. She put her keys back on the counter, grabbed a clean cloth from the kitchen drawer, soaked it with water and rubbed soap into it. Kneeling to study Timothy's foot, she carefully pulled off the filthy sock. Blisters oozing pus revealed a painful foot. The big toe and second toe were blue with white lines running through them.

176       Gently, Sybil dabbed at the foot, "Mom, get some alcohol and the roll of gauze you have in the guest bathroom. This needs to be tended to right away." Looking up into Timothy's tired face, Sybil asked, "What have you done to your foot?" She then pulled off the other shoe, "What have you done to your feet?"

Sophia returned with the gauze, alcohol and antibiotic cream. "He hiked through the freezing snow in leather dress shoes to get frost bite. At the hospital they gave him a walking shoe after cleaning his feet. But this?" Sophia nudged her chin to Timothy's feet, "Were you walking? How did you get here? Timothy, where have you been for the last twenty-four hours since I spoke with you?"

A soft groan came from Timothy and then he tried to explain, "The jeep got a flat tire. I was stranded north of Trinidad. After several hours a cop showed up. He drove me into Trinidad, bought me a burger and fries with some coffee and told me to call someone. I felt so stupid. I was wearing Robert's pants, which did not have a back pocket. My wallet was in the jeep. It was in my backpack behind the front seat. The cop was willing to take me back to the jeep, but he got a call and had to leave me stranded."

His foot jerked as Sybil applied the alcohol. "When I tried to call Sal, who owns the jeep, I realized the battery on my cellphone was dead. The charger was in the jeep." Timothy rubbed his forehead, "All of this has been exhausting."

Sybil lifted his foot onto her knee as she cleaned it, "This is going to hurt. This antibiotic cream should help the foot heal, but it will sting." Timothy nodded. Ethan retrieved a bottle of ale from Sophia's refrigerator, "Here, drink this, it might help with the pain."

Timothy put his hand up, "No thank you, I am so hungry and tired I don't think booze is a good idea right now."

Smiling Ethan said, "Suit yourself, I'll drink it for you."

Sophia pulled out a kitchen chair to sit opposite Timothy, "So, there you were in Trinidad with no money and no cellphone charger, what did you do then?"

"I asked one of the young kids if I could borrow their cellphone. This one kid, who couldn't have been more than fourteen, loaned me his cellphone. Luckily, I remembered the jeep owner's cellphone number. I called Sal Melloy, the fellow Robert loaned the jeep from for the wedding. Sal was most kind. He said he would pick me up and I could go with them to the jeep."

Ethan raided the cookie jar. He put six cookies on a plate and placed it in front of Timothy who quickly grabbed two and stuffed them into his mouth.

Sophia went to the sink to return with a glass of water for Timothy who continued, "Sal brought his two sons with him. One was about twenty-five and the other couldn't have been more than nineteen. We drove to the jeep and then everything went wrong."

He picked up another cookie, "These are excellent cookies, thank you." He stuffed it into his mouth. "At the jeep, which had been left alone, Sal and his sons turned on me. Once Sal opened the jeep to sit in the driver's seat, the smell hit him hard. Sophia, we had become used to the Robert's vomit smell, but with the jeep locked up and left in the sun, the smell had intensified."

Sybil nudged off the filthy sock from the other foot, "This one doesn't look as bad. Why did you wear leather dress shoes to go hiking on a mountain?"

Timothy shook his head, "Who knows? Anyway. Sal erupted when he saw the vomit on the floor, the smell, all the clothes, towels, camping gear and dirt and mud inside his perfect jeep. He and his sons brought the spare tire. Evidently, we didn't have a spare tire with us in the jeep. Good thing we got down the mountain with Robert and didn't get a flat as we danced over the boulders, streams and thick mud."

Another cookie was taken as he continued, "Sal kept asking me questions. I didn't know how to answer except to say Robert was dead. Sal became a maniac. He didn't listen, he didn't want to listen. At one point once the tire was changed, he turned to me and hauled off and slugged me hard in the stomach. He called me every name in the book! At one point, I was sure he was going to leave me on the side of the road, and they would just drive away."

Ethan helped Sybil cut the gauze as she wrapped it tightly around his foot, "This is going to be tight. Try to leave this on tonight. What happened next?"

"Sal had me drive the jeep alone to Rincon, you know north of Calavera?" Timothy took a long drink of water, wiping his mouth on the back of his shirt sleeve, he went on to say, "In Rincon there is a homeless shelter run by an older priest named Father Michael. He and Sal know each other somehow. At this point, I was tired, my foot was hurting and I just wanted to be done with the jeep and Sal. Father Michael let me stay the night, gave me some stew for dinner and a cot to sleep on while he and Sal unloaded the jeep."

Interrupting him, Ethan asked, "Where did they put the stuff? I mean the stuff was Sophia's and Robert's and what about Karen's things?"

"Oh, well, Sal didn't want any of our stuff in his jeep. This was fine with me. Sophia, your rappelling gear and our cook oven and a whole bunch of Robert's things, as well as Karen's things, were in the back of the jeep. Sal paid Father Michael to have a man put the items in a closet in the shelter." Grabbing another cookie, Timothy explained, "Sophia, when you left and Karen was arrested, there was the hotel bill to be paid. The jeep was empty when I left Colorado Springs, and I had to fill her up with gas. My money was spent, so I put my wallet into the backpack in the jeep."

Rubbing his hands together, Timothy shook his head, "These last three days have been some of the best and some of the worst in my life! This morning, I knew I had to get to someone who could help me. My left foot was in serious shape, and I knew I needed medical help. The

178

cellphone was of no use because the charger was somewhere in all the stuff. The shelter phone cost money. My wallet was somewhere with the stuff in the closet. Sal and the sons were long gone. At least our things are safe."

He took another drink of water, "So, I did what I needed to do. Father Michael let me in the closet and slowly, piece by piece, I dug through all our vomit slimed things. Wouldn't you know it? My backpack was at the bottom under Karen's vanity pack." Twirling the glass of water on the table, he continued, "The woman at the front of the shelter gave me the number for an old-fashioned cab. Can you believe it? There are taxi cabs still in existence in this back wood country!"

Grimacing as Sybil rubbed the gauze to tighten it over his toe, he said, "The cabby guy took me directly to the airport rental lot. There I rented a VW bug. It's outside by the barnyard gate. I wasn't sure where I should park, but there it is." He nodded to the kitchen window.

Sybil stood, gathering the bloodied cloth, the gauze and the ointment. "Here, Mom, you deal with this. Timothy, thank goodness you're still alive. These feet, though, they need to be seen by a professional and I would recommend some penicillin." Touching his left foot with her hand, she said, "These two toes need care, right away care. I just hope you won't lose them." She patted Timothy on the shoulder as she turned to Ethan, "Honey, we need to get home. It's already dark and our children will be starving."

Ethan held out his hand to Timothy, "You are in good hands here, old man. Sophia will take care of you." He turned to Sophia, "If you need help with anything, just let us know. You both have been to hell and back." Ethan patted the dogs who were patiently waiting for their dinners. "Bon appetite."

Sophia walked Sybil and Ethan to the door, "Thank you both for understanding and helping. Poor Timothy, he's going to need to rest. Tomorrow, I'll call my doctor to get Timothy an appointment. Text me when you get home?"

When Sophia returned to the kitchen, "Would you like something to eat?" Timothy quickly looked up at her, "You know what I really would like? I would really like to be clean. Would you mind? Is there a place here where I could clean up? Oh, and my backpack is outside by the front door. It's filthy, but it has my clothes in it." Slowly, tears fell from Timothy's eyes as his voice cracked, "Sophia, I was so scared! I'm an old man not a young kid! Oh, God, Sophia! What has happened to us?"

Hurriedly, Sophia went to his side. She put her arms around him, "Come, Timothy, come, stand up and let's get you safely cleaned and perhaps put to bed in a nice cozy room. You are safe here! We will figure this out. Come, lean on me."

The dogs followed them down the hall into the guest room. Turning to the dogs, Sophia told them, "Yes, I know you need dinner, and you'll get dinner. First things first, you're my buddies and I know you'll understand."

The guest room door was opened wide to reveal a large room with a double bed. Gingerly, Sophia placed Timothy to sit on the bed. She turned on the bedside lamp. Going to the bureau in the corner, she opened the top drawer to take out a pair of blue sweatpants and a sweatshirt. "Here, these are clean and should fit you." These were placed beside him on the bed. Next from the second drawer down, she took out a pair of white cotton socks. "These are men's socks and should fit you. Also, if you need any other clothes, just search and you shall find."

Timothy fell back on the bed with a groan, "How am I going to take a shower when I can hardly stand?"

The door to the left of the room was opened, Sophia turned on the light. "This is your own personal bathroom. Here, let's make this happen before you become incapacitated." She unbuttoned his grey shirt, helped him pull off his pants as he was lying back on the bed. Timothy's eyes were wide as he watched her pull down his jockey shorts. "What are you doing?"

Not stopping to answer, Sophia grabbed his arm and pulled him to stand. "We are going into the shower, and you are going to get clean. You want to be clean. You shall be cleaned." His arm was placed around her neck, "You need to help me. Move your feet. One foot at a time. We'll need to remove Sybil's bandages, but we can redo them, no problem. Now one foot in front of the other."

A squeaky-clean Timothy, dressed in clean clothes, was neatly tucked into a bed of clean sheets and pillowcases. The hand sewn quilt was pulled up to his chin. A soft snort let Sophia know he was out for the count. Quietly, she whispered to the dogs, picked up a cat and closed the guest room door behind her as she went into the kitchen. "There, now it is time for my pups to get dinner." Tails wagged as the filled dog bowls were put on the floor in their proper place. Sophia cleared off the kitchen table, "Well, this has been quite a day."

Outside the crescent moon illuminated the empty barnyard. Soft fluffy clouds slowly drifted across the night sky. A steer called for his dinner. His bellow echoed through the cold night air. Under her breath, Sophia whispered, "At least for the moment, we are safe."

181

## 17

The smell of hot coffee woke Timothy. Sunlight filtered in through the open curtains in the bedroom. Slowly stretching out his legs, Timothy felt the soreness in his left foot. It still throbbed. Rolling onto his side, he cursed himself for wearing the leather dress shoes up on the frozen mountain. There was a soft thump on the bed. A fat orange cat walked up to his body to study his face.

"Well, hello there, fat cat. What's your name?" Timothy reached out to pet the green-eyed critter. The cat turned showing Timothy his bottom. "Oh, no thank you." Slowly, Timothy rolled out of the warm bed. Putting his weight on his right foot, he hobbled on the heel of his left foot to the bathroom.

Sophia blew on her mug of hot tea as she spoke to Clementine on her cellphone. Now that the conversation was over, she stared out the window. The day was warming with the heat from the sun and the absence of the wind. The cats had been fed and were all outside in the warm sunshine. Tucker and Sassy were roaming the property, looking for outsiders to bark at with vengeance. A door slammed in the back of the house. Limping into the kitchen came Timothy. He poked his head around the door frame. "I need my clothes. Can you get my pack?"

Smiling, Sophia shook her head, "Come in here, Timothy. You're in sweats that are decent enough for the farmhouse. Come in. Can I get you a hot mug of coffee or would you like something to eat?"

Still limping, Timothy hobbled into the kitchen. His hair was sticking straight up in the back and the black circles under his eyes gave him the appearance of a prisoner of war. Sophia motioned to a kitchen chair, "Please, have a seat. Now, I did make you some coffee." She poured the hot substance into a waiting mug. "So, what have you been up to today?"

183

TERESA PIJOAN

Slowly, he sipped the hot coffee. Then the mug of hot coffee was put on the table as he confessed, "I called Mr. Goldfarb again. Evidently, he has had a detective on the trail of Karen ever since her grandmother passed. There were curious outcomes from the autopsy of her grandmother." He took another sip of coffee, "The grandmother evidently had called Goldfarb prior to her death regarding her worries about Karen being mixed up with Granger."

Sophia returned to her seat at the table, "With Granger? We keep coming back to him, don't we? But, Timothy, from understanding my mother, Granger and his family are in California on vacation. At least that is what Granger told me when I called him in Colorado Springs, remember?"

Timothy shook his head, "Not all is what it appears to be. You do know the cellphone makes it impossible to know where anyone person is while they are speaking to you. A person can be in Texas and tell you they're at the grocery store down the street. Cellphones lie. They lie a lot."

"All right, I'll bite. What did this detective find out about Karen and Granger?"

184      "Karen contacted Granger to help kill her grandmother. The deed is done. Granger requested money from Karen. As we know Karen has no money and is in serious debt. She has numerous loans with not good people. She really is not a smart woman. I do believe she married Robert to save her from her debt. Although, if she would've found out that Robert wasn't filthy rich, well, that would certainly have put her off him."

Rolling her mug between her palms, Sophia asked, "Robert certainly wasn't rolling in dough, but he must have had a good savings account, and he does own the house near the university. Do you think she found out that Robert wasn't a millionaire that night in the tent?" Then Sophia, put out her hand, "Wait, Robert gave her the envelope at their wedding instead of a ring, right? Didn't the envelope have money for her?"

Timothy stretched out his left leg. He wiggled his foot. The bandage was still white with no bloody pus on it. He reached down to rub his knee, "Evidently, well, there is no evidently about it, I saw the envelope. I was with Robert when he sealed it and kissed the front of it. His remark to me was, 'My love is priceless. This envelope is filled with my love.' There was no money in it." He shook his head. "Karen must have been livid."

Placing her hand on the table, Sophia said, "Livid or not, she went on with the charade, didn't she?"

A black and white cat jumped in Timothy's lap. Startled, he picked up the cat and handed it to Sophia, "Here, I do believe this one is yours." He laughed. "This house is filled with cats! Everywhere I look there is a cat looking back at me!"

The cat purred in Sophia's lap. As she rubbed his fur, Sophia answered, "Yes, Karen fawned all over Robert at the campsite. She never showed any hostility or anger towards him." She looked at Timothy, "There was a man who seemed to appear at the hotel and then I thought I saw him at the train dock. Did you notice him?"

"I wondered if he was the detective following Karen." Timothy took another drink of his coffee, "When I called the police up north to find out what was going on with Karen, they told me she had died in the night from natural causes." He shook his head, "Natural causes seem to be going around lately. God, I hope we don't get it!"

"Timothy, the first order of business is to get you dressed and not in those stinky clothes in your pack. Check out the closet and the bureau. Some of Ethan's clothes are in there. He's about your size." She stood to put her empty tea mug in the kitchen sink. "Let's get your pack into the laundry room and we can soak whatever is salvageable. What do you think?"

Holding the edge of the table, Timothy stood awkwardly. "You know what? Let's dump a lot of my stuff. Do you have something we can just dump the clothes into and be done with them?"

"No, that wouldn't be wise. There are some clothes in the guest room that may suit you, but certainly we can save your own clothes. Tell you what, you go and get dressed in what you can find. I'll go through your pack. What you want after the clothes are washed, fine. What you don't want we can give to charity. There are many out there in need."

Timothy and Sophia were quiet on the drive to Rincon. Sunlight sparkled through the branches of the tall trees. The dirt road was rutted from being grated. A man on a tall palomino horse trotted alongside them for a time. Timothy pointed out the turn to Father Michael's Rescue. The parking lot was filled with vans. Many of them were from churches. As they walked around the building to the sound of singing, they noticed a large circle of people singing hymns.

185

A woman hurried out of the building to them, "Hello? Can we help you?" She wore a flowered apron over her yellow dress. Her hair was tightly pulled back into a bun. The thick lenses in her glasses reflected the sunlight, not allowing them to see her eyes. Her hands were frantically wiped on the apron, which was covered with white flour.

Sophia met her, "Yes, we are looking for someone who can help us retrieve our items from the locked closet."

The woman nodded to Timothy, "Yes, yes, I remember him. He was in bad shape yesterday." Putting up her hand, she said, "Let me get Eric. He knows where the keys are. We are having a special service today for one of our members. I'll find Eric." The woman disappeared into the building.

The singing stopped. A tall man dressed in a white shirt and white pants stood to greet the sitting visitors. Sophia and Timothy watched as the man said a prayer. Both bowed their heads, Sophia whispered, "Poor Robert."

"Excuse me, please. I'm Eric with the key." The young man spoke behind them. As the two turned, the young man dangled a key from his fingers. "Please, come with me. Hope you have a big vehicle for all this stuff. Never saw so much strange stuff in my life. Made me wonder what you did with all those ropes, hooks and smelly blankets."

The outbuilding was to the right of the main building away from the congregation. Sophia decided to drive to the building rather than having to carry it across the open space to the parking lot. The young man stood and watched as Timothy opened bedrolls to rewrap them tighter. The blankets were shaken out and refolded. Everything had been shoved into the back of the jeep in such a hurry, few items were neatly cared for in the confusion. Timothy placed each item carefully into the back of Sophia's SUV.

The drive back to the farmhouse was equally quiet. Sophia watched the road as she drove. Timothy studied the sky, watching birds. Finally, parked in front of Sophia's garage, Timothy jumped out to open the back of the SUV. "All of this needs to be aired. Some of the blankets and the bedrolls should go to the laundromat and get a washed. Do you have one around here? I could take them in this old vehicle."

Smiling at Timothy, Sophia questioned him, "Perhaps we should put things in piles? The rappelling gear can be put away since it doesn't need washing. The tents were covered with filthy towels. If we take them in the backyard we could spray them down with the hose."

Swearing under his breath Timothy answered, "Damn. I keep forgetting about the important things. Let's put everything in the garage. We can go through all the extra packs, the rappelling gear, blankets and bedrolls."

Items were strewn on the clean cement floor of the garage. Rappelling gear was put in one pile while bedrolls and blankets were thrown over the laundry line in the back yard. Karen's pack was put to one side. There was no point in going through it now. Timothy found his hiking pack. He did a little dance in the middle of all the fata. "Finally, my gear! I knew it was in here!"

Lifting a pile of clothes from Robert's pack, Sophia quietly asked, "Would any of these fit you?" Tears rolled down her cheeks, "Oh, God, Robert! What did you do to yourself?" Wiping her cheek, she stared at all the piles, "This is too horrible to imagine. Timothy, I believe I hadn't let any of this reality sink in until now! Robert's dead. Karen's dead. How is that we are still alive?"

Timothy hugged her, "Thank the Universe! We're still alive! Whatever just happened? Happened. We need to keep going and find out to right the wrongs. Sophia, come on! Keep it together, girl!" He took her arm, "Let's go in and get you a cup of tea."

Turning to look out the kitchen window, Sophia noticed the dogs barking furiously at the front fence. "Excuse me, it appears we have company."

The front door swung open without a knock. Granger Pino stood tall in the doorway. He watched Sophia walk to him. "Sophia, mom is in the ICU. She's dying and you need to come right away if you want to say goodbye to her."

Stopping between the kitchen and the front door, Sophia stared at him. "What are you saying?"

"Mother is dying. She's in the ICU. You need to come now." Granger did not move. He showed no emotion but remained leaning against the door frame.

"Granger, that's crazy. I just saw her yesterday. She was in excellent health. Marcus was with her."

"Sophia, I called your girls and their families and told them to meet us at the hospital. Are you coming or are you going to stay here and let your mother die without seeing you one last time?" His voice was smooth and calm. Looking over her shoulder, he noticed Timothy in the kitchen.

Sophia stared, "Well, let me get my things. You say you called the rest of the clan to meet us at the hospital?" Sophia turned back to the kitchen. Then as if remembering something, she said "My clean pack is still in the vehicle. Let's see, I better give Timothy the keys to house and the car."

Timothy appeared behind her, "What's going on?"

Granger gritted his teeth at Timothy. Then with a smile and a calm liquid voice, Granger put out his hand, "Hello? I'm Sophia's brother Granger and you are?"

Timothy remained behind Sophia who was fiddling with her keys, "Oh, Granger, this is Timothy Turpin. He was with me in Colorado," She handed Timothy the whole keychain, "Here. There isn't time to go through all these keys. The red one is for the vehicle and the yellow one is for the house if you should leave. Also, take the laundry out of the washing machine and put it in the dryer." Reaching around the front closet door, Sophia grabbed her jacket. "Okay, let's go. I guess we're going in your Mercedes, huh?"

Granger nodded to Timothy with a slick smile on his face. He followed Sophia outside. Timothy shut the door behind them. The dogs followed Sophia to the front gate, which she closed, keeping the dogs in the front yard.

188

Nothing was said as they drove to the hospital. Granger parked his precious Mercedes in the far corner of the hospital's parking lot. Tumbleweeds blew to crash against the west side of the hospital wall. Elm trees bent back and forth in the wind, spewing dried leaves in the air. The inside of the hospital was extremely warm. Granger took the lead, walking quickly down the hall to the elevators.

Once out of the elevators, Sophia was met by her family. Sybil was pacing back and forth in front of the waiting room. Donna and Fleur were holding hands, waiting for Sophia. When they saw her, they ran and hugged her. Ethan was sitting on a chair at the far side of the waiting room. He was on the phone.

Granger took Sophia's elbow, "This way. Come all of you, let's say goodbye." He steered Sophia down the hall, passed closed hospital doors to an open door across from the nurses' station. Sophia noticed Dion talking to a tall man in a white doctor's coat.

Inside the hospital room, Donna asked, "This isn't the ICU, is it? Is this a regular room? I thought you said Grandma was in the ICU?"

A stool was pulled out beside the hospital bed. Granger sat and took his mother's hand. Margaret was unconscious. There was a beeping monitor beside the bed, an oxygen cord going to the mask over her nose and mouth. Her eyes were closed.

Sybil gasped when she saw her grandmother. "What is wrong with her? Why is she here?"

Granger put out his hand, "Try to be quiet. We don't want to startle her, do we?" He patted Margaret's hand. There was an I.V. in her left arm, which was tied to a board. "She has intestinal issues. She fell at the farmhouse. Thank goodness Marcos was there. He called the ambulance and then he called me because he knows I'm a doctor."

Behind him, Ethan came into the room. He stood behind Sybil who was standing next to Sophia. "Granger, you are not a doctor. You work with Chinese herbs and acupuncture. You're not qualified to medically treat anyone in the hospital."

A nurse pushed her way through the family, "Excuse me, I need to check her vitals. Would you please wait outside until I'm done?"

Shuffling their feet, the family moved to the hall. The door was closed. Granger quickly walked to the nurses' station. Sophia watched as Granger spoke to the doctor. The doctor was shaking his head while Granger was forcefully speaking to him. Dion came around the counter. Sophia separated from the family to follow Dion down the hall.

At the end of the hall was a window that went from floor to ceiling. Dion jerked her chin to sidestep into a small kitchen area. Sophia followed her. "We have questions about my mom, Dion, what's going on?"

Dion shook her head, "Your mother was brought in here after she fell in her bathroom. Your brother feels she has a clogged intestine and is in severe pain. Our doc wants to do an MRI to be sure your brother's diagnosis is correct, but your brother does not approve. He feels she will not survive the MRI. Because she is in such pain, we have her sedated."

Leaning against the counter, Sophia asked, "Does anyone know what's really wrong with her?"

"We've taken an x-ray and there appears to be something going on with her lower intestines. We don't know if it is caused by inflammation or irritation from something she ate or drank or if she has a constriction. To know exactly what's going on, we need to do the MRI." Dion turned her head, "Someone's coming."

TERESA PIJOAN

Granger peered around the open doorway. "Hey, Sophia, mom doesn't need anything to eat or drink." He sweetly smiled at Dion, "I don't mean to interrupt, but the doc feels he can help mom, and we could move her to a nursing home for further treatment." Again, he took Sophia by the arm, "Let's go talk to the others and find out what they think."

Dion nodded at Sophia as she followed Granger down the hall. The family was back in the room. Donna and Sybil were singing one of Margaret's favorite songs. Marcus stood back by the window with his younger brother and his little sister who was reading a book. Julie, Granger's wife, was brushing Margaret's hair. Ethan was leaning against the far wall. The monitor beeped. The room smelled sterile and cold.

Granger moved back to his position on the stool beside the hospital bed, "The doctor believes he can repair Mom's intestine, but she will not be allowed to return home. She would need to be put in a nursing home. There are two problems with this."

He pushed back from the bed, "First, Mom would hate the nursing home. She told all of us she would rather die than go into a nursing home. Second, the cost. Nursing homes cost a fortune. They are impersonal and cold. Mom wouldn't know anyone there. We are all busy with our lives and our families. We would have a hard time taking care of her if she was in a nursing home. Sophia, you can't stand Mom, right?"

His vision turned to Sophia, "Do you have the funds to put Mom in a nursing home? The cost for her care would be around eight thousand dollars a month. How about you and Ethan, Sybil? Can you two afford to help?" He turned his attention to Donna and Fleur, "You two don't have any money, so I won't ask you."

Sophia touched her mother's foot under the sheet, "We could find a nice place. Perhaps she could come and live with me? I have room and I wouldn't mind taking care of her. I know she doesn't like being around me, but we would work it out somehow."

Sybil shook her head, "Mom, you and Margaret would kill one another. Granger, why don't you have your mother live with you? You're the doctor, right?"

The door opened. The doctor walked in oblivious to the family's dilemma, "The blood tests have come back. She does have an infection, however, without the MRI, we are unable to give a firm diagnosis. I recommend the MRI."

Standing abruptly, Granger took his mother's arm to begin rubbing it, "I have explained. She will not survive an MRI. Please, do not put my mother through any more pain." Julie reached across the bed to touch her husband on the shoulder, "Honey, he's only recommending. There's no need for anger."

Ethan stepped forward, "Why? Why can't she have an MRI? What's wrong with doing an MRI?"

The doctor studied Ethan for a moment and then answered, "We will need to give her chalk to drink and move her a certain way to find the exact location of the problem. This fellow, here, believes this would cause Mrs. Pino pain as we would need to have her awake to drink the chalk mixture."

Sophia continued to rub her mother's foot, "What is the alternative? What else can we do if not the MRI?"

Putting his hands in his white coat pockets, the doctor nodded to Granger, "He feels she has had a good life, and she should be let go and not have any more pain."

Silence filled the room. Donna watched Sybil who was looking at Sophia who was rubbing her mother's foot. Finally, Granger smiled, "Well, that's that then. I'll push the button on full release. The large amount of painkiller will stop her heart, and it will be over." He leaned forward, pushed on the beeping monitor as a flow of liquid flowed through the I.V. into her arm's vein and within seconds Margaret's body jerked and fell.

The doctor walked forward, pushing Donna and Fleur to the side. He pulled the stethoscope from around his neck to listen to Margaret's heartbeat. The oxygen mask over her face was carefully removed and placed beside her pillow. Standing erect, he turned to walk out of the room. Smiling, Granger said, "She's gone. No more pain, no more misery, she's gone."

Sybil sobbed and burst into tears as she fell against Ethan. Donna and Fleur stared at Margaret's body. Julie lifted the sheet and covered Margaret's face. Granger called his children to lead them out of the room. Sophia started to shake. Quickly, she moved to the top of the bed and pulled back the sheet. A puff of air came out of Margaret's mouth. Julie patted Sophia's shoulder, "Her soul has left her body."

Sophia slapped Julie's hand, "Do not touch me! She is my mother! Take your hands off me and off her!"

Teresa Pijoan

Ethan moved to Sophia who was still shaking. "Come, let's move out of this room. Sophia, come, let's go." She let him lead her out into the hall. Sophia took Sybil's hand, "Did you know about this? Did he talk to you before I arrived? What did he say?"

Sybil shook her head and pointed to Granger. Sophia took in his expensive suit, the ascot tie, trimmed beard and moustache. Julie was huddled over by her two younger children as Marcus walked behind. She herded them into the waiting room. Little Emma was crying, "I've never seen a dead person before! It was horrible!" Julie shushed her.

Ethan was leaning against the nurses' station counter. It appeared he was waiting to speak with someone. Sophia wished she would stop shaking. Finally, Sophia took Sybil's and Donna's hands and led them back into the hospital room. "We are going to sing the Lord's Prayer over her. She was a religious Christian. Let's show her some respect."

As they started singing, Julie returned. Quietly, she moved around Donna, "Margaret was a Buddhist! Granger helped her become a Buddhist!" Julie's voice became soft, smooth yet forceful, "Stop this! Stop!"

The three kept singing until the end. Julie was red-faced and angry. Again, her voice was soft, meant to be pleasant and smooth, "I' going to tell Granger. He will not approve." Sybil turned to face her. Mimicking her soft voice, Sophia looked Julie straight in the eye, "Yes, go tell your murdering husband. Just be sure you're not next?"

Julie turned on her heel and left the room. A nurse came in with Dion. The first nurse asked them to please leave because they were going to take the body down to the hospital morgue. Dion came over to Sophia and gave her a hug. "You're shaking. Would you want something to calm you down? I could ask the doc?"

Sophia hugged her back, "No, I'll be all right. It's just so sudden. I saw her yesterday and she was fine. Just fine. What was her diagnosis that caused her to die?"

Dion put her finger to her lips, "I'm not allowed to say anything. This was all arranged by your brother, the good doctor. I am not allowed to say anything, but it would be best if you would go to the waiting room and perhaps the doctor will speak to all of you there."

Out in the hall, Granger was speaking on his cellphone, "Yes, she's dead. We can be there tomorrow morning for the cremation. Yes, I want to push the button as she goes into the furnace. She is my mother after all, I have a responsibility to be sure her wishes are granted. Yes, thank you."

The cellphone was put into his jacket pocket. Sybil walked straight to Granger. She raised her hand only to have Granger speak softly to her, but loud enough for all to hear, "Careful there, I am the executer of Margaret's estate. You need to think before you act. You're upset. We all are but think about your actions." Donna took Sybil's arm and the two of them walked to the waiting room. Fleur walked over to Granger, she patted him on the back, "You're a nasty man. I don't like you, not at all." She followed her mother down the hall.

Ethan reached out to Sophia, "Sophia, come here. You need to speak to this doctor. He's not the one who was in the room, this is the floor doc. Sophia, talk to him."

A short, well-dressed man with a vest and a pocket watch nodded to Sophia. "Would you like to come into my office? It's right back here. Let's talk, shall we?" Ethan became her guide as he walked behind her. The office was a small room behind the nurses' station. There were four chairs in front of a large desk. Ethan and Sophia sat facing the doctor.

He lifted a chart from his desk. Thumbing through it, he spoke, "We had a long conversation with your brother Dr. Pino. He informed us of your mother's history of cancer, broken bones and how she is accident prone. Evidently, he has taken care of her alone for all these years and has the power of attorney over all her affairs. He decided it was in your mother's best interest not to suffer further."

There was silence in the room. Phones could be heard ringing down the hall. Nurses were chattering at the desk behind them. A clock was ticking on the wall behind his desk. Sophia stared at the doctor. Tears fell down her cheeks. Ethan was breathing slowly, his right foot was shaking. Sophia studied the doctor's face. It was pocked, probably from teenage acne. His short hair was thinning and grey at the temples. His dark tie was crooked.

Slow and steady, Sophia stood. Ethan stood beside her. The doctor put out his hand to her. Sophia shook her head. He dropped his hand to his side. Walking through the open door back into the hall, Sophia moved to the waiting room. She had stopped shaking.

Granger was talking, "Yes, I think that would be a good idea! Sophia, we are all going out to dinner to celebrate Mom's life. Since the dinner would be for her, about her and celebrating her, we can let her pay for the dinner, the cost would come out of her account. Where do you think we should go?"

Julie spoke up quickly, "We're vegans so we have to go to a place where the children can eat the food, and we need to eat, too, right dear?" Smiling as she took in everyone in the room, she added, "We could go someplace expensive and let her pay for it."

Donna was staring out the plate glass window. Fleur was texting on her cellphone. Sybil was with Ethan, the two of them were whispering. Granger spoke up again, "Where should we go to eat and celebrate Mom's life? Now, we can call her mom or Grandma, and no one can fault us for it. I'm starving. Where should we go?"

Sophia said to Ethan, "Can you drive me home?" Sybil answered for him, "Certainly, you can come with us in our car. Donna, Fleur, do you want to follow us?"

Donna shook her head, "No, I think we need to go home and take care of our animals. Thanks, though."

Grabbing Sophia's arm, Granger faced her. His silvery voice was soft, but firm, "Come on. Let's go and get food together. I'm your brother! You and I are now orphans, we need to stick together! Come on, Sophia!" He put out his arms to hug her. Sophia turned and walked to the elevators.

The others quietly followed her. Standing, waiting for the elevator to open, Sophia spoke more to the closed elevator than to a person, "You are not my brother, and I am not an orphan. I have a family. You had this all planned before I got here."

There was a loud ding and the elevator door opened. Julie pulled Granger and her children back, letting Sophia, Sybil, Donna, Fleur and Ethan go alone. Suddenly, Marcus pushed through and entered as the elevator doors were closing. Donna moved aside to let him be next to Sophia.

"Hey, I'm really sorry. Sorry about yesterday, too." He reached out to take Sophia's hand. She swatted his hand away, "Yes, me, too."

Marcus wasn't finished, he continued, "After you left, well, Bruce and I were hungry. I asked Margaret if we could eat what was in the fridge. She told me to help myself since I was a growing boy. I even called her Margaret. I remembered."

Staring straight ahead at the numbers on the elevator wall, Sophia asked, "Is that why when your father arrived there was no food in the house? You ate the frozen dinners, drank all the milk, scarfed down the cookies, the sliced meat and all that I bought for her?"

Marcus shook his head, "Bruce and I hadn't eaten all day. We were hungry. I was going to take her out to lunch today but got stuck at work. Can I pay you back for the food? We really shouldn't have eaten it all, even the frozen dinners although they were really good."

Fleur turned to him, "You're a pig. Your father is a murderer." Donna elbowed Fleur, "Shhh, let it go." Shaking her head, Sophia said, "You don't have to pay me back. You need to be careful around your father. People tend to die when he's around them."

Ethan pushed the closed button on the elevator when it reached the ground floor. "Marcus, what really happened at Margaret's farmhouse when you found her? What had she done?"

Marcus frowned, "I really don't know. I didn't get there at first. My father was there. He said he found her on the floor and carried her to bed. You know she was super skinny, light as a feather. She was unconscious when I saw her or at least that is what my mom said. Mom called the ambulance. They told me to wait in the living room with Emma and Billy. I drove Grandma's truck with Billie and Emma to the hospital. We followed Mom who drove the Mercedes and Dad was in the ambulance with Grandma."

Putting his hand over his eyes, he said, "Wow, the look on her face when my father pushed the button in the hospital room is a look I will never forget." He wiped his hands on his jeans, "I loved her, you know? Even her funny ways of wanting me to call her Margaret. I did try to take care of her even if we ate all her food."

Ever the logical one, Ethan still holding the elevator closed, asked the question, "Why were your parents at Margaret's? We were all under the impression Granger, Julie, Emma and Billie were in California, right? How did they get to Margaret's so fast if they were on the sunny beaches of California?"

Marcus turned completely around to look at the back wall of the elevator. "They weren't in California. Margaret gave them money to go on holiday, but my mom felt everyone needed new clothes. They were here. My father insisted I play along and take care of Margaret, we don't have any money now that my Mom has a new car."

Sybil pulled Ethan's hand away from the elevator button, "I think I'm going to be sick. I must get out of here! Please, let's get out of here!"

The elevator opened. Fleur pulled her long brown hair over one shoulder to ask Sophia, "What about Margaret's animals? Who's going to take care of Gizzie and Tigger?"

Marcus spoke up, "My father is going to take them to the pound and have the animals put down. He says they're old and sickly. My Mom doesn't want them in our house, she says they stink, besides we have cats who don't like dogs or other cats."

Granger stepped out of the neighboring elevator to greet Ethan, "Listen, man to man, since we are the calm gender, I want you to know that we didn't really have a choice here with Margaret." He laughed, "I still call her Margaret even after she's dead." Delicately putting his hand on Ethan's forearm, he continued, "Next week would be a good time for all of you to come to the farmhouse and pick out what of hers you would like to have. The farmhouse is on the market, and it appears we have a buyer."

Ethan removed Granger's hand from his forearm, "When next week? What time next week?"

Smiling his perfect white teeth at Ethan, Granger said, "Let's do all of this, say next Friday, that should give these women time to calm down. How about three o'clock on Friday and you can bring a U-Haul trailer, Sophia will want to take a lot of things that were both my father's and my mother's from the old house." Ethan nodded.

Fleur studied Julie's face, "My mother and I are going over to Margaret's right now. We're going to get Gizzie and Tigger and bring them to our house. We love animals and I've known both those animals all my life. Can we get a key or how could we get into the house to get Tigger and his litter box, food and his stuff?"

Marcus answered quickly, "Here, Fleur, you take my key. I won't need it anymore. I have the truck key on my other keyring. You take this one. It opens the backdoor." He placed a single key into the Fleur's palm. "Keep it, as I said, I don't need it."

Smooth talking Granger replied, "There, see, we can all be friends. There is no need for anger or hostility. Shall we have a group hug?" They walked away from him.

Sophia followed Sybil to her car to get into the backseat. Donna and Fleur disappeared down the parking lot to Fleur's vehicle. Sophia mumbled under her breath, "A group hug, really."

Sybil and Ethan dropped Sophia off at her gate as she wanted. The garage was closed, and the dogs were waiting for her in the front yard. Pushing open the gate, she knelt to hug them, "Let's have a group hug, you guys!" They gave her slobbery kisses.

There was a note on the kitchen table from Timothy: Thank you for my clean clothes. Washed the sheets from the bed. I called a cab and when you read this I should be flying my way home. Fleur texted about your mother. Too much death. I'm sorry. Call tonight, Timothy.

The barn was empty. All that remained was the smell of horses. Tucker and Sassy followed Sophia around the barnyard. The cats were absent, probably out doing cat stuff. Standing still, Sophia watched the wind blow the naked tree branches back and forth. She wanted to talk to someone, someone who would know what this felt like, this hollow gut hole in the middle of her body. There was no person, but there were her dogs.

Choosing to sit on the dry ground in the barnyard with her back against the steel pole fence, she called the dogs to her. Tucker sat right on her lap. The one-hundred-pound dog put his front paws on her shoulders and licked her face as tears flowed. Sassy sat beside her, chewing on a stick. "Pups, my Mama is dead. My brother killed her like he kills everything he cannot control. Oh, pups, I hurt. I hurt, really hurt." Sobbing, Tucker continued to lick her cheeks, her chin, her nose and her forehead. She hugged the large dog as the tears fell.

197

## 18

The wind had finally stopped sometime during the night. The clear blue of the sky meant no moisture was coming to the dry fields and empty ditches. Geese and cranes could be heard flying overhead well under the flying airplanes. The girls and Ethan had been wonderful with their openness of memories regarding Margaret, which somehow made it feel as if she was still a participant.

Sophia studied two of her cats chasing one another around the backyard. The plump Smokey ran up one of the thirty-foot-tall elm trees, disappearing in the bare branches up high. Oscar cat rolled in the dirt, letting his stomach warm with the sun. New Mexico would need rain or snow soon for the fields were becoming dirt with no sign of green or life. Sophia's cellphone chirped, she answered it.

"Mom, we don't know what to do with Gizzie, he won't eat! We've tried everything and he won't swallow. The food goes into his mouth, and he spits it out or he lowers his head and lets it fall out of his mouth. What do we do?"

"Donna, dear Donna, why are you calling me? You're the vet tech. What would you recommend to one of your patients?"

"We tried all the tricks. He won't even eat peanut butter. He smiles, wags his tail and looks at us as if we're crazy. I think he's laughing at us. It isn't the food because we give him cheese, peanut butter, like I said and even chopped beef. He won't swallow."

"Perhaps, you need to leave it on the floor and walk away, leaving him alone. He isn't used to attention. Margaret didn't have the time of day for him or for Tigger. How's Tigger doing?"

"Good old Tigger eats everything we give him. My vet says he's not that old, he's just thin and hungry. We gave Tigger all his shots. His teeth are clean and good for a cat, maybe because he didn't get much to eat. He's doing great with our cats, they all get along."

"Mom, tomorrow is Friday. Are we supposed to go to Margaret's to choose stuff or did she make a list of who gets what?"

"It's up to Granger. He's going to be there, you know it. He and Julie have already gone through everything. I thought there would be the reading of the will, but I guess not. Margaret left all decisions up to Granger. After tomorrow, he will give us our funds as required by her will. He's the one who will hand out the checks or put the money in our accounts. He's the head honcho now."

"Ethan called us yesterday, I guess he didn't want to bother you. He and Sybil are taking the day off from work. He planned with a friend to borrow their trailer. It's a small one. He was unsure what size to get."

"Donna, tomorrow let's meet up for lunch, all of us. I'll call Sybil tonight and we can meet up and go together to Margaret's. There's power in numbers. It would be best if we were all together rather than one or two of us dribbling in throughout the afternoon. What do you think?"

200      "I agree. How about lunch at our favorite restaurant The Range? We could meet there at one o'clock after the lunch rush and this will give us time to talk since, we're supposed to be at Margaret's at three."

Sophia put her cellphone away. Timothy had called every night, being a good friend. The Colorado police had been in touch with him over the last week, letting him know of their developments. The plan was to be interviewed on the first Monday of May. The New Mexico State Police and the Colorado Police wanted everyone to meet at the Albuquerque courthouse. The local sheriffs were not involved. Karen's lawyer had requested dissertations, although Mr. Goldfarb felt interviews would suffice.

Timothy had sent photos of Robert's ashes being spread over the old farmhouse, Robert had grown up near Alt Bay, New Hampshire. Thoughtfully, Timothy had placed an ad in the local paper there and several people who had remembered Robert from his childhood had come to the memorial service. Sophia could not attend, but she sent two large bouquets of flowers for the memorial service.

There had been many legal issues to deal with regarding her mother's death. Mr. Goldfarb had also contacted Sophia in that she was the only surviving daughter of Margaret Vivian McBride Pino and Mark Pino. Evidently, Sophia's father had an addendum in his will from years ago, leaving Sophia stock for when her mother would pass. Her father didn't want her to be totally dependent on Granger's judgement.

Mr. Goldfarb had replied, "Your father was a very smart man. He knew Granger and Granger's tendencies. You can come and pick up the stock certificates anytime it best suits you. The stocks have accrued a good amount, you might want to leave them alone for your granddaughter."

The day after Margaret's sudden death, Sophia decided to clean her own home. Her little farmhouse was filled with books from her college days, her research work and some written work of her father's. There were rugs she had inherited from her father that were now frayed and stained. Sybil and Donna had a section of children's books in the living room. These books had crayon pictures drawn in them, pages missing or were completely worn with broken spines. Many books were taken to the library's store or the dump. Some of her winter clothes were tattered and worn, those went to the dump, and others went to the thrift store. Pots and pans were examined as were table cloths, linen napkins and table mats.

201

Several trips to the dump and the thrift store made Sophia's house feel lighter, less dark. Driving from place to place helped to clear her head. At a stop light by the dump, she watched the clouds. Rolling down her window, she spoke to the sky, "Should I have said something to Granger? Do you think he would've let her live? Oh, God, I feel I let my mother down! I should've said something." She rolled the window up before the dirt blew across the road.

Sitting at the kitchen table, Sophia studied the family photo albums. Margaret was a beautiful young woman when she married Dr. Mark Pino. Both are now dead. Each page showed her mother becoming more bent, more wrinkled, more intoxicated with her love for Granger, her handsome boy.

Tomorrow was the day to clean out her mother's farmhouse. Sophia decided to put the albums away before she became too depressed. Seriously, she wasn't anything like her mother. Sophia hiked, mucked out stalls, travelled the world with her research and raised her two daughters with love.

Sophia's divorce had taken courage. Raising the two girls by herself had not been easy. Her father was impressed with Geoffry, her husband. The family was shocked when she divorced him until they realized Geoffrey had money problems. His problems were mostly between Mark Pino and Granger. Sophia knew she had to escape both her husband and Granger once her father passed away. Margaret felt men had the right genitalia and women were deficient because they didn't have the right genitalia.

All throughout Sophia's life she was told by her mother of her worthlessness. When Sophia earned her degrees, became a respected researcher, her father was proud of her. Margaret worked on condemnation. No one in the family could outshine Granger. No one. Margaret loved Granger to the end. The end of her life.

Tucker followed Sophia into the living room where she was putting away the memory books. He whined as Sophia slid the books away, "Yes, I know. It's dinner time. Let's call Sybil first and then you and Sassy get dinner. Where are all the cats?"

No sooner said, than in walked six cats with their tails held high. Each one complaining of their hunger and desperation for food. Patting Tucker on the head, Sophia answered the cats, "I'm coming, no worries, I'm coming, you cat cannon balls." After eating her own dinner, Sophia locked the doors, turned off the lights and moved into her office. The walls were covered with photos of her family, her crews of the past and closeups of her pets and horses.

Smiling as she turned off the light, she said, "I have had a very good life. No complaints from me."

## 19

The above sky was a clear blue. White chalk clouds spread out across the horizon. Birds chirped noisily as Sophia picked up her pace getting the dogs back to the farmhouse. They had done an eight-mile walk to the river and back. Tucker was in the lead while Sassy lagged with her tongue hanging out. Smokey cat jumped over the wood fence to join them as they turned the corner onto the driveway.

All her pets received a treat as Sophia locked up the house, grabbed her purse and was into her old SUV. She was to pick up Sybil while Ethan 203 and his friend with the trailer would meet them at the restaurant. Donna and Fleur were also taking the day off from work, having understanding bosses. Gizzie had befriended a neighbor's dog and was now living with the neighbor and their dog of equal age.

Sybil fastened her seatbelt as Sophia backed out of her driveway, "Mom, I don't like this at all. I told Ethan, we don't need anything from Margaret's. We have our own stuff."

"What did Ethan say to that?"

"He believes we might be able to sell some of her things to help us with the bills. My college classes are expensive, well, not the classes so much as the books. We've had to seriously tighten our belts. Our cats were told to stay healthy as we couldn't afford an expensive vet bill right now."

Turning with the blinker on, Sophia twisted to look for a parking place. She noticed the trailer was taking up three parking places. Ethan met them as they entered the restaurant. Donna and Fleur were already seated, talking to a man about food. Their plan was simple, no one would argue over anything. Whoever chose something, had dibs on it.

The concept was to keep everything simple, no fear, no emotion of any kind and the most important plan was to avoid speaking to Granger or Julie. Sybil handed everyone a scarf to cover their noses and mouth due to the large amount of dust in Margaret's house.

The trailer followed the cars into Margaret's front driveway. Ethan and his friend Eric turned it around with the back open to the wrought iron gate. Sophia led the group to the back door where Granger was standing talking on his cellphone. The dining room table and the matching chairs were gone. The kitchen appeared empty. The kitchen counters were graced only with mouse poop.

Granger turned his back to them as he spoke to someone on his cellphone. The group walked into the living room. It was empty. The bricks appeared more uneven. The whitewashed adobe walls were scarred from where the furniture had been placed against them. The Navajo rugs once hung on the walls, were gone. The Kachina dolls, which had been on the fireplace mantle for more than thirty years were gone, all that was left was their imprint in the dust.

Hall walls were bare as they had been weeks passed, what with Granger having already sold the paintings to dealers in Santa Fe. The front room with its bookcases from floor to ceiling, still contained most of the books. The Pueblo pots on the top shelves were gone. The room felt hollow. Sybil stopped to study the books, "Mom, I would like to take these murder mysteries of Margaret's. Should I go and get some boxes from the trailer or wait?"

Hearing her, Ethan ran outside and brought in boxes, "Here, my love, load them now before you know who arrives in here." He helped her pick the books, blowing the dust off them as they were boxed.

Donna and Fleur moved on ahead. They were standing in Mark Pino's office. It had been shut closed for many years. The oil paintings he had collected were only remembered by their outline on the walls. The heavy oak desk and the French carved office chair were not to be seen. The stained couch Gizzie had grown up on remained covered in mouse droppings. Mark Pino's medical books remained, again, covered in dust. Fleur spoke up, "Grandma, can I have grandpa's medical books? They may come in handy when I go to college?"

Dutifully, Ethan arrived. This time he was carrying several large boxes with smaller boxes inside. "Here you go. It appears Granger has a buyer coming here at six this evening and he wants us out by then.

Better take what you can while the going is good. We can divide things up better at Sophia's later."

Opening the closet in Mark Pino's office, Donna found a woman's finely embroidered riding jacket made of leather. Under it was a pair of high English riding boots. She took them both putting them in a box. Sybil stood watching them in the office, "I'm going into her bedroom. Mom, will you come with me? I'm not sure I will be able to hold it together. Please, Mom, come with me?" She held out her hands to Sophia.

The shock of walking into Margaret's bedroom and finding it empty, brought both women to gasp. The bed and bedside table were gone. The large mouse desk, the two bureaus were absent. Even the curtains were gone. Hurriedly, Sybil went to her grandmother's clothes closet. Empty hangers dangled from the poles. The brick floor showed mouse tracks. Heirloom boxes on the high shelves, missing.

The rocking chair - the famous rocking chair used to nurse generations of babies, gone. Ethan walked into the cavernous empty bedroom, "We have boxed all the books. Donna found some things in the guest room, she's boxing those things right now. Do you have anything more to box?" He walked around the bedroom, "Wow, this is 205 serious. Someone's done a cleanout, a complete cleanout. Too bad they didn't actually clean. Every room, every wall is covered in dust. This is going to take some strong muscle to clean."

Granger strode into the room, "Looks good, doesn't it. This room is so much bigger than imagined when she lived here, right?"

Sophia was staring out the window, "You must have worked fast to get all of this out of here? Did you notice the toolshed roof had fallen in?"

Granger stood beside her, ignoring her comment, "Most of the stuff in this room was beyond care. Every piece of furniture was filled with mice. It took eight trips with the moving truck to get this stuff to the dump. Nasty smelling, soaked with urine and feces, things no one should own. The bureaus were cleaned out and a concession company came and bought them. Got a pretty good price for them as a matter of fact."

Ethan spoke from the opposite side of the room, "You going to share that income, are you?"

"Hell no. We cleaned, scrubbed them, waxed them, Julie and I did all the work, we get the profit." Granger smirked in his calm, smooth voice.

Turning quickly, Sophia said, "That's good. Glad you were able to get some funds. The money can help buy your children some new clothes." She walked into her mother's bathroom. Not even the shower curtain remained. Sophia smiled at Granger as she walked back into the bedroom, "How much did you get for Mom's toothbrush and her toothpaste?"

"Now, Sophia, don't get spiteful. She made me her executor. Everything here actually belongs to me. I just let you pick what remains. What you leave behind will obviously go to the dump or the thrift store."

"Granger, there is nothing here aside from the books and we both know you aren't a big reader. What about the toolshed, have you gone through that as well?" Sophia walked down the hall to open the door to the toolshed. Granger followed, "Well, if you can get in there, more power to you, although you should know there are hundreds of mice living in there, in colonies." He peeked out the door, "We chose to not bother with whatever is in there. It's probably ruined or beyond saving. The new buyer can deal with that room."

206    Sophia pulled the door wide. The shovel she had used to bury Tigger's poop was still against the wall. Quickly, she handed it around Granger to Ethan, "Here, you can put this in the trailer." Granger shook his head and walked back to the kitchen. Sophia called Ethan, "Come with me. Let's get in there. Papa's paintings and his tools might still be in there."

He followed still holding the shovel, "Now may be the time to use our scarfs. Let's pull them up, the dust is thick in here and who knows what else is floating around?"

Ducking low, Sophia pushed aside spider webs as she pulled the scarf up over her face. The large room known as the toolshed room was still filled with items. Turning, as she ducked low over part of the fallen roof, she pulled out painting after painting. They were covered in dirt and webs. Behind her Ethan lifted a flashlight from a workbench. Behind it was another, he handed the second one to Sophia as she asked him, "Ethan, can you get out the front door of this room? Try and see if you can open the wedged door. Let's clean this place out before Granger notices we made it inside." He nodded and using the shovel like a crutch, he pushed the crooked door in, allowing fresh air to circulate.

Two hours later with the help of the girls, the trailer was filled with tools, mouse eaten chewed boxes holding baskets, clothes, a chest filled with artifacts and more paintings. The trailer was shut tight when Granger came out to tell them, "Sorry, you guys didn't find much, but I must ask you to leave. The buyers are coming here in about thirty minutes and Julie is here with a cleaning crew. You have to go."

Noticing Sophia covered in cobwebs, he laughed, "I see you wormed your way into the toolshed. It's too bad the roof destroyed everything in there." Sybil gave him a dirty look.

Granger's smooth syrupy voice added, "Oh, by the way, here are your checks." Each of them was handed a white envelope with their name on it. The last to be handed an envelope was Sophia, he said, "Don't spend this all at once, little sis."

"Sophia," Granger called to her as she was walking to her vehicle, "Listen, He pulled her gently to his right shoulder, "I love you, Sophia, you're my sister and I want you to be happy. Couldn't we bury the hatchet and have some time together? You can see I'm not the enemy, neither is my family. I love you. I love you so much and want us to be friends. Can't we just forgive and forget?"

Stepping back, Sophia stared at his shiny shoes, "You mean like in the Bible? Do as Christians do? Is this what you mean? For some reason I thought you were Buddhist?"

"Aww, Sophia, why do you have to make this difficult. You've always made this difficult. The Buddhists believe in forgiveness. They believe in generosity and love." Granger quickly glanced at his gold-plated watch. "Just think about it, Sophia, we are the only two of Mark Pino's and Margaret Pino's family. It's just us. We need to stick together. I do love you. Julie and I decided to let you keep your farm in the valley. We believe Margaret would've wanted you to have it."

Shaking her head, while breathing out, Sophia spoke directly to Granger, "You do know, I paid Margaret in full for that property ages ago. I paid her in a separate account you couldn't touch. Your limited allowance to her wasn't enough for her to live comfortably on nor pay for her personal bills, like the dentist."

"Oh, I knew about it. I moved it all over automatically into our joint account. Margaret told me all about you trying to undermine me. She knew how much you hated me, and she tried to keep things legal." Granger backed away to check the driveway.

Sophia smiled, watching her crew stare at them from their vehicles. The trailer was ready to roll. Ethan had his hand out the window, waving at her. Sophia nodded to him as she said to Granger, "Yes, you do love me like you loved Margaret. We need to go, and you can meet with the buyers and sell this place off before it is even cold from Margaret's death."

A hand clenched around her upper arm, "Sophia, damn, we need to work together on this. I need you to sign a paper, a legal paper, giving me your farm if anything happens to you. Just give me a chance to be your friend!" His front teeth gnashed with his bottom teeth. "Give us a chance!"

"You know what, Granger, I will. I will give it a thought." She opened the driver's door of her vehicle. Sybil was already in the passenger seat, "Okay, Granger, I've thought about it and the answer is no. Simple, quietly and quickly no. Hope all goes well with the sale." She started the engine to lead her group back to her farmhouse.

The vehicles followed to Sophia's house. The garage door opened to reveal three piles of miscellaneous things separated on the far side of the floor. Sophia explained, "Those are from the trip to Colorado. I have to keep them for the police investigation. I don't know about you guys, but I could use something to drink, also, a good hand washing after all that dust."

That evening, Donna and Sybil made a run to the drive through to bring home burgers and fries. Ethan and his friend had divided up some of the tools, putting some in Sofia's barn. The three women sat at the kitchen table, each with a mug of tea. Donna rolled the mug between her palms, "I had to laugh when we drove away. Granger thought we were leaving empty handed, hah, I think many of those boxes were things he never knew about."

Sybil pulled out her white envelope from Granger. "Hey, what do you say we open these and find out how generous Granger really is?"

Sophia retrieved her envelope from her new backpack. Three women, all dedicated to one another, opened their envelopes at the same time. Donna spoke first, "Well, well, look at this? Ten thousand dollars inheritance check. I am impressed. How about you Sybil?"

Staring at the check held in her right hand, Sybil laughed, "Yes! Yes! Now I can afford my university books! Yes!" She kissed the check, "Perhaps we did judge Granger too quickly. He came through with the inheritance. Mom, what did you get?"

Placing the check in the middle of the kitchen table, Sophia pointed to the paper, "You both can look. Granger paid me for the amount he felt I had given Margaret for this property. It's for fifty-four thousand dollars, eight hundred and nine dollars with seventy-six cents."

"Seventy-six cents?" Donna burst out laughing, "Seventy-six cents? He really counted the pennies, didn't he? Why wouldn't he round up to a dollar?" Sybil joined in their laughter. "What are you going to do with this money, Mom?"

Appreciating her daughter's humor, she answered, "I'm going to put this to good use. Right now, I need to think about it. There is so much that needs to be done here on the farm, getting it up to date, especially with the plumbing and the floors. Later, I shall make a list."

Sybil smiled as she held her mother's hand across the table, "You go, Mom, use this for you. Granger cheated you out of a job you dearly loved. You, use this for you. Right, Donna?"

Agreeing, Donna pushed the check back toward her mother, "Yes, I totally agree."

Fleur held her envelope unopened, "I think I'm going to open mine later. It is probably not much, and I don't want to know." Turning to Donna, Fleur handed her envelope to her mother, "Can you keep 209 this for me? I don't want to know, I don't want to spend it on just stuff. Would you put it in a safe place for later?"

Standing to hug her daughter, Donna said, "Now, I think we should help the guys in the garage because Eric needs to get home to his family."

Sophia had to agree, "The baskets Papa collected over the years must have something on them the mice don't like. The box was half eaten, but the baskets were untouched."

Giggling, Sybil nodded in agreement, "Granger can't sell them if he doesn't have them. We really cleaned out that toolshed. Although, why were those expensive things stuck in the shed? Wouldn't you have wanted to put them in a safe place away from the mice?"

Fleur answered, "I don't think there was a place safe from mice on the whole of the farm. I mean the barn is filled with mice from the horses she had once. The house was totally infested. At least in the toolshed, those things were out of sight out of mind."

Items were divided between families. Sophia kept many of the Native goods. She knew an appraiser who could help her decide what to do with them. Many of the paintings were too far gone to be sold or appreciated. Ethan said he would try to clean them or else take them to the dump. Sybil and Donna found small treasures they chose to keep while Fleur sat on the garage floor and studied the books. Finally, the adult children all received a hug as they drove off to their own homes.

It was time to be alone. To feed the critters. After a tiring day, Sophia read her book, turned off the bedside table lamp, said goodnight to all six cats and the two dogs and went to sleep. Tomorrow is another day.

Slowly, time moved to allow Sophia to get lost in new research assignments. Being off on mountains in foreign countries kept her mind busy with her work. Once home, Sophia had meetings to attend and her family. Life became balanced and good. The walks with the dogs were frequent when she was home and when she was gone Ethan took the dogs running. The six cats were not happy to sleep alone at night, but their mom always came home.

Winter passed into spring with little to no rain. The New Mexico sky was clear. There were few clouds over the last twenty-nine days. Farmers were worried about the lack of snow and the lack of rain. The water reservoir had emptied out in the middle of last summer with no irrigation from mid-July onward. Fields were going fallow. The price of alfalfa and hay for cows rose sharply, leaving many to sell their animals or go into debt buying stock food. A dry day in May was hopefully not a sign of what was to come regarding the weather.

Roaring airplanes shook the airport as Sophia walked to gate B. This brought back the memory of Colorado Springs and last November. The airport was filled with people coming and going, some with rolling suitcases, others with backpacks and all had cellphones.

A big smile crossed his face as Timothy saw Sophia standing among the greeters at the airport. Dragging his roll-along behind him, he hurried to the side of her old SUV. "Hey, hi, how wonderful to see you in this old thing!" He patted the top of the vehicle. He put his roll along in the back seat, he jumped in the passenger seat. "Sophia, you look great! You recovered from Colorado and your mother's passing?"

Sophia patted his arm, "Look at you? You've gained weight and you're not walking with a limp, how did this happen?"

"Antibiotics are wonderful things, let me tell you. It was wonderful to go home to the snow, the burning fireplace, the people who talk like me and walk like me and look like me." He took her hand in his, "But the highlights of my life were the evening conversations we had." Shaking her hand in his, he went on, "I'm not really looking forward to rehashing this whole ordeal about Robert and Karen."

Staring out the window, he explained, "The Colorado police have kept news of Karen and her demise quiet, as you know. This Bethany character, I feel, is somehow to blame as well. Although, I don't know how."

Sophia turned onto the main interstate to drive home, "We're just to give information, right? I don't believe we're guilty of anything anyway. The paperwork they sent me was about how we met, what we did once we were there, etc."

"I agree. If they felt we were guilty, they would probably have had us put in the clinker. Now, Sophia, you have not said anything about your friend Dion. You met her, right? She has some information for them, but she won't tell you?"

"Yes. Dion's son and her niece are good friends with Bethany and by association with Karen. Bethany and some of her gang separated from the wedding. All of them were students of Roberts at the university."

Timothy sighed, "Don't tell me, Robert failed them? They were out for revenge?"

"Who's to know? Collette, who is Dion's niece, is working for a correlator at the university. She's been discreetly looking into things there. We just have to believe the detectives. We can only hope to bring Granger to justice."

Timothy twisted in his seat to study her, "You are younger than the last time I saw you. Did you do something different with your hair?"

Sophia smacked his thigh, "No, life has been simpler, easier, now with my dear Mom in heaven. There isn't that constant worry over her health, her welfare or Granger. Life has been pleasant these last couple of months."

Timothy reached behind the driver's seat to pick out a piece of paper from his roll-along. "In this letter you sent me last year, wow, it's been last year already, you wrote Granger stood at the cremation doors of the burn oven and pushed the button for his mother to be burned to ash." He folded the paper. "Did you speak to a therapist about this? I mean, Sophia, seriously this man is deranged."

Sophia drove down her long driveway, "There was no point in

speaking to anyone about this. What would be the point? We all know Granger and his love of death. Really, there wasn't any point. What's done is done and cannot be undone." She parked her vehicle in the garage, "Come on, the dogs will be happy to greet you."

The dogs barked as she turned off the engine, "We shall find out tomorrow morning. Now, let's get you settled, eat some food and decide."

Legal papers were splayed across the kitchen table. Timothy was explaining, "These are the property papers. Donna and Fleur will be taking care of Robert's house near the university. It has a lovely backyard for their dog and their three cats with a lovely eight-foot-tall wall around it. The house itself has three bedrooms, two bathrooms and an office. The kitchen is small, but he was a bachelor and ate most of his meals on campus. There is Wi-Fi service, and it is within walking distance to Donna's vet clinic. I just hope she likes it, well, that they both will like it."

Moving to the long paper with blue underlines, Sophia asked, "What is this?"

"This is the educational savings account Robert had in the bank. This is going to go to Fleur for her education. I have moved all these funds into a trust to only pay for her education. All that is needed, and here you can see where this is needed, is her signature of acceptance of these funds."

Studying the numbers, Sophia glanced at Timothy, "This is all very extravagant. Are you sure you don't need this for your survival?"

"Sophia, I work for an accounting firm back East. Please, trust me, I will not go broke. Robert left me with a good chunk of change in his will. The old scoundrel had money put away in several banks and in several accounts. He was trying to outsmart his taxes. It didn't work, but he tried." Timothy smiled, "He thought he was being very clever, however, all the taxes paid were probably more than he wanted, but he felt clever. The old goat, God, I miss him so much."

Picking up another paper and pointing to Goldfarb's name at the top, Timothy explained, "This attorney worked for Edna Gilbert before she died. He has been sending me updates on her accounts. Copies of these were sent to the Colorado State Police and the New Mexico police. I believe these three points of information went to someone named Clementine. Evidently, she's a friend of yours in the force?"

Nodding, Sophia agreed, "Yes, we've known each other for years. She's great. Have you heard any more about this court proceeding we're going to tomorrow?"

Standing, stretching his back, Timothy shook his head, "No, don't know much. Granger is supposed to show up at this meeting at eight sharp tomorrow morning as we are. We received subpoenas, what about the girls?" He bent over to stack the papers in order, "Did they find Bethany?"

The dogs were let out the backdoor as Sophia answered, "They did find Bethany. Last I heard they were hoping she would lead them to Granger."

Lights were turned out, doors locked as Sophia bid Timothy goodnight. The six cats followed her into her bedroom. The two dogs licked water from the bowl as Sophia climbed into bed.

213

# 20

Emma Pino sat at her father's desk. Granger's laptop was open with words written on the monitor that Emma was trying to read. She was nine years old and learning how to use a computer. Her class had been told to practice during the summer break so as not to fall behind in their studies. The numbers were foreign to her, but she knew how to send.

Studying the round thingy in the middle of the laptop's keyboard, Emma knew enough to send. She used the round thingy in the middle of the keyboard to mark the words. They were now surrounded with a dark cloud. "Cool," she said, as she searched with the cursor thingy for send. She pushed it and watched, waiting for the box at the top telling her the message had been sent. Suddenly, the box appeared. "Cool," she said again.

Marcus walked behind her, "Emma, what are you doing?" Leaning over her, he read what was on the keyboard; 'Karen, I helped you with your grandmother. I helped you with Robert. They are both out of your way now you owe me. I expect to be paid for my favors. Watch what you eat or drink.'

Emma was shoved away from the desk, "What did you do? Who did you send this to? Emma, you shouldn't be messing with Dad's things! Oh, Emma, what did you do?" Bursting into tears, Emma fled from her father's office.

Grabbing the chair to sit on it, Marcus studied the laptop. The last email sent was to the Optical Center in Rincon. Granger had sent a message telling them they were moving to California and would no longer need a copy of Billy's eye refraction. Evidently, the letter on the monitor was a rough draft his father was working on and had not been sent yet. Marcus put the rough draft letter to Karen in the draft folder, closed the laptop, pushed the chair under the desk and left the room.

He found his mother and father arguing in their bedroom. His mother was furious, "Look at all the clothes you're taking? Look at that? You have four large suitcases filled with your clothes, your suits, your white medical jackets, your underwear, and your fancy shoes, all your things! What about me and the kids? How can you tell us to only pack two days' worth of clothes? Granger! What is going on here?"

Leaning on the doorframe, Marcus watched his father put his arms around his mother to kiss her on the lips, "Julie, my lovely, lovely dear wife, I've told you repeatedly how much I love you. I love you with all my heart, no, with all my soul!"

She shoved him away, "Answer my question, dear husband of mine, what's with all of your clothes and none of ours!"

Marcus smiled as his father's voice became honey smooth, "When we get to Mexico all of you will get new clothes. Every one of you. I shall buy all of you new clothes. Beautiful clothes to wear on the beach, to wear in town, to play and lounge in, when we get to Mexico. Right now, I will have my clothes, and I won't have to buy clothes. All my mother's money, all of it, will go to you and the children's comforts. I promise. Have I ever let you down?"

Running down the hall, Billy came screaming around Marcus and into his parents' bedroom, "Emma caught a horny toad! Emma caught a horny toad, and she won't let me hold it!"

Noticing Marcus in the doorway, Granger asked him to put all the suitcases into the rented vehicle out front. Julie followed Marcus, "Why do we have to cram into this small vehicle your father rented, when we have the large Mercedes and my brand-new SUV? I mean mine is new, hardly used and he wants to take this stinky little rental car to Mexico! What's with this? What is this all about?"

Carefully stacking the suitcases in the back trunk of the small car, Marcus answered her, "Mom, you need to trust Dad. He knows what he's doing. I'll be here, after all, and when he wants me to sell them, I will and then I'll come down there to be with you guys." Slamming the back trunk, he put his arms around her, "Mom, everything will be all right. You get yourself worked up over nothing. It will be beautiful in Mexico." Putting his arm around her shoulder, he added, "Dad knows what he's doing. He loves us and he'll take care of us. Besides cars are cheaper in Mexico."

Julie smiled at her tall son, "I know, I just wish he would share more. He keeps so much to himself, and I worry."

In the office kitchen, there were thermos bottles all lined up waiting for the steaming teas to fill them. Granger was lifting strainers from four different steeping bowls of tea filled with boiling water. Each bowl was made personally in China. The clay was from sacred land. The bowls had a handle on one side and a beveled lip on the other. Each had been given loose tea flakes chosen, measured and precisely set in the strainers to be a soaked product. Granger had been precise in his measurements.

As Marcus walked in through the backdoor, his father turned to him, "Each thermos has a name on it. Son, if you wouldn't mind putting the different teas strained, of course, into each thermos? This first bowl is for my thermos, the second for your mother and so on. The last bowl is for Billy. Got it?"

Marcus nodded as he noticed the thermos bottles. The pink one was for Emma, the smaller blue one was for Billy and the tall one with the flowers on it was for his mother. The dark grey thermos with the red top was for his father. Granger went on to explain, "I wasn't expecting this call until later, but the real estate agent just called to tell me the escrow is set up and she needs to know what bank to put all the funds into, she doesn't know we're moving to Mexico."

He handed the first strainer to Marcus, "This first bowl of tea is for me. It has caffeine in it, the kids and your mother don't need caffeine. Your Mother is already wired. Here you go, Son, now remember the first bowl, this one, is for my thermos."

Granger went out the back door to speak on his cellphone. Marcus took the strainer to start pouring the tea into his father's thermos. Emma came running into the kitchen bumping into him. The bowl splashed water all over the counter and around his shoes. His father's thermos was less than half filled. "Damn, Emma, look what you made me do! What do you want?"

She grabbed the empty bowl from Marcus' hand, "This! I can put all the Horny Toads in this." Taken from his hand, she ran outside past her father who was still talking on the cellphone.

Marcus took some of the hot tea water from the second bowl and poured it through the strainer into his father's thermos to top it off. "There, he'll never know." The rest of the thermos bottles were filled, Billy's thermos was topped off with tap water. Marcus carefully placed them in the box. He placed this box on the floor of the backseat.

217

TERESA PIJOAN

His father met Marcus in the kitchen, "Listen, son, you will need to wash out the herb bowls and put them back on the shelf when we're gone. Can you do that for me? We need to leave right now before your mother gets out of the car and starts fussing again. Please, remember, wash out the bowls. You can start right now, as soon as we're down the road. You understand? This is very important; those are my special medicinal bowls and they must be washed." Marcus nodded at his father, "Yes, Sir, right away."

Snacks were put into a tall brown paper bag beside the box of thermos bottles on the floor of the backseat of the car. Granger gave Marcus a slap on the back and a handshake before getting into the small rental car. "Remember, it is vital you wash out those bowls! I'll call you when we cross the Mexican border. Thanks, son." Emma was already coloring in her coloring book as she sat belted in the backseat. Julie was studying the map, still unsure of the direction they were going or how long it would take to get there. Billy waved to Marcus as they drove away down the driveway.

Entering the quiet house, Marcus let out a shout of relief, "They're gone! I have money! They're gone!" He jumped up to slap the ceiling.

A deep voice broke his celebration, "Who's gone?" An equally tall man walked into the living room. "The front door was open, thought I'd find out what all the shouting was about, son, where's your father?"

Shaken by this man's sudden appearance, Marcus backed into the couch, "Oh, no one. I'm here by myself, that's all. What do you want?" He sat on the couch.

The man walked to Marcus. Standing over him, the man pulled out a piece of paper and handed it to Marcus, "Your father received a subpoena to show up in court today. He's to be there in one hour. I have come to collect him as he is critical of this meeting. Would you happen to know where he is?"

The man walked down the hall. He tilted his head, "It is mighty quiet around here. Are you here alone?" The man walked into Emma's bedroom. Her bed was neatly made. Two dolls rested against the pillows on her bed. Some of her clothes were hanging out of her bureau drawers. The man turned to walk across the hall into Billy's room. Marcus could hear his heavy footfall on the wood floor.

Standing, Marcus made a run for the front door only to run into a woman with red hair, a face covered with freckles in a Sheriff's uniform.

*Granger's Demise*

"Can I help you, Marcus? Were you planning on going somewhere?" She pulled handcuffs from her back, swiveled him around to place them on his wrists. "We need your father, not you, but you'll do in a pinch." Marcus kicked the front step, "Shit!"

Emma studied the landscape as they drove down a small bumpy dirt road, "Dad, where are we going? This doesn't feel like the interstate?" She kicked the back of her mother's car seat. "Mom?"

"Hush, child, let your father drive. He said we're taking a short cut to a better road. It's here on the map. Arizona has all these neat little roads that lead from one major road to another." Julie put her hand on her husband's thigh. "Right?"

Granger nodded, "You know what, let's get out and stretch our legs? It's almost noon. You should be hungry. Let's drink some tea and have some sandwiches, what do you say?"

Immediately, Billy unhooked his car seat, "Yeah! I can look for Horny Toads!" The small car was parked on the side of the dirt road with a cattle guard to the right of it. There were no cattle insight. There were no tall trees, no grass, no sign of human life. Julie noticed some stunted cactus and a short juniper tree off on a sandy loam. It was a lovely temperature for being out on the desert in May. Julie grabbed the 219 tall brown paper bag with the food and Granger picked up the box with the thermos bottles. "I could really use a drink of tea!"

Julie and Emma opened a plastic tablecloth on the ground. The car gave them a small bit of shade. Julie placed the paper plates out, while Granger laid the container with sandwiches in the middle of the cloth. Each plate had a thermos placed next to it with the lid unscrewed and the top cups filled with the liquid within each person's personal thermos.

Billy grabbed his sandwich first. "Yummy, I love honey almond butter sandwiches," Emma reached for the blue corn chips. The open bag was placed in her lap as she stuffed the chips into her mouth. Granger and Julie lifted their cups of tea at the same time, "Here's to a new life ahead of us." They clunked the lids and took a long drink. Billy ran across the cattle guard with his empty sandwich bag searching for lizards. Emma crunched on the chips as she watched her parents.

Julie was the first to start gagging. Foam poured out of her mother's mouth to roll down her chin. Her eyes wide in terror, she reached out to Granger. He pushed her hand away, laughing, "You really thought I'd

TERESA PIJOAN

want you nagging me in Mexico?" Smiling, he took another long drink of tea from his thermos cup.

Emma stared at her mother, "Mom, Mom, what's wrong? Mom? Dad, help her!" Chips were held in her small hand as she shoved more of them into her mouth.

Granger went from kneeling on the picnic plastic cloth to falling on his side. His eyes wide. His finger was quickly put into his mouth to gag. He didn't need to bother. Foam gurgled out of his throat followed with blood. Frantically shaking his head, he tried to speak. His thermos was knocked over, spilling onto the dry dirt. Julie was no longer breathing, but her body was shaking, ripping the plastic cloth.

"Billy! Billy!" Emma dropped the chip bag, running to find her brother. "Billy, where are you?" The young boy slowly walked to her crying, "I found a lizard, but he wouldn't let me catch him. He ran off!" The clear sandwich bag was held out in front of him. It was filled with dirt. "I didn't get him!"

Carefully putting her arm around his small shoulders, she said, "We need to get back into the car. I need to find Daddy's cellphone and call Marcus. Billy, you need to come with me."

220         "I'm thirsty, can we get something to drink?" Emma shushed him, "No. We're not going to drink anything."

The little boy stared at his parents' limp bodies. Liquid continued to spew out of their mouths. Emma guided the small boy around the picnic area. His eyes wide, staring. Emma asked him, "How was your sandwich? Was it good? Why don't we eat the chips?" She grabbed the big bag of chips as she opened the driver's door of the small car, "Here, you sit in the front seat like the driver. You can turn the wheel like pretends." She slammed the door as he twisted the steering wheel.

Carefully walking around the picnic area again, she gingerly touched her father. He didn't move. The bloody foam was continuing to ooze out of his mouth. Changing her course, Emma knelt beside her mother. Reaching into her mother's front jean pocket with her two fingers and her thumb, she pulled out her mother's cellphone.

Jumping back as if bitten, she turned away, running to the passenger side of the car. Inside the car, she sat staring straight ahead. Billy squealed, "Dad won't mind, will he? I don't want to make him mad at me. He hates it when I pretend, I'm a grown up."

Rubbing the cellphone with her small fingers, Emma nodded, "No, he won't mind. He won't mind at all." Studying the phone and its black face, she asked Billy, "Do you know how to turn this on? I know how to play the games when Mom hands it to me, but I don't know how to turn it on, do you know?"

"Sure, it's easy." Billy grabbed it away from her, "See this thing on the side? Push it really hard. It will make a funny noise and this part comes light." He let the phone buzz and then he handed it back to Emma. Doing what she was taught by both her parents and the school, she hit 911 and listened. There was no sound. She pushed it again. The cellphone went dark. Nothing. There was nothing. No one answered. There was silence.

Emma put her head back on the seat. "Billy, nothing happened. What's wrong with this thing?" She showed it to him. His nine-year-old face lit up, "If you can't get anyone its cause there is no one there." He started honking the horn. The sound echoed across the land. Emma put her hand on his arm, "Stop it. Just stop it! There's no one here to hear you." Billy kept at it, honking and honking the horn.

Slowly opening the passenger door, Emma slid out around her father. Julie's cellphone was placed in front of her mother's white face on the ground. Inching her way to her father, she bent to reach for the cellphone in his front jacket pocket.

"Hey, what are you kids doing out here? Who's honking the horn?" A man on a tall horse spoke down to Emma. She jumped back, afraid. Then she put her hands up over her head and started to scream.

The man quickly dismounted. Billy hit the horn with one long honk and then stopped when he noticed the man by the car door. "You can stop that now, young man." Smiling at the man, Billy lifted his hands off the steering wheel. Emma continued to scream, scaring the horse. Quickly, the man who was holding the reins, pulled the horse away from the car, away from the girl.

The horse pawed the ground as the man walked over to Emma, "You can put your hands down now, please, stop screaming." He knelt and hugged her to him. Emma collapsed in his arms. Crying uncontrollably, she held on to his neck with all her might. Billy carefully stepped out of the car to walk to the horse who was watching him.

Gingerly, the man pulled Emma off his neck, "Can you stand by yourself now?" She nodded, still shaking with her nose running over her top lip.

TERESA PIJOAN

Remaining on his knees, he studied the scene in front of him, "Do you know what happened here?" Emma nodded her head. "Can you tell me what happened? Are these your parents?" Again, a nod. "Will you stand next to my horse? He's gentle, we may need to go for help. Will you help me?" She nodded again.

The man placed Emma on the saddle as the horse stood still. "If you get frightened, hold onto this. It's called the horn. If you hold onto the horn you'll be safe." He lifted Billie up, placing him right behind Emma. There was no space between them. "Hey, you're a smart young man. Hold on to your sister. Put your arms around her waist. She's not going to fall off and she'll keep you steady. Got it?" Billie nodded, "I've never ridden a horse before." The man smiled at him.

The man had explained his name was Rabbit. He lived over the hill where the cellphone would work. He would lead them on the horse to his home where they would be able to call for help.

It only took two hours for the BIA police to arrive at his home. The children were taken by one of the policewomen to Gallup where they were to be met by the New Mexico State Police from there they would be reunited with their older brother who was of age. The State Police had contacted the Sheriff's office to find Marcus being held there for interrogation. The Special Services had been called in to contain the area and to find out what exactly had happened to Dr. Granger Pino and his wife Julie.

Sophia walked into the county courthouse on Central Street. The entry room smelled of stale cigarettes and old coffee. The sign at the entrance of the main room stated that all cellphones, laptops and electrical devices must be stored in an allocated locker or left in the vehicle. She turned to notice Donna and Ethan talking as they entered the building. Evidently, Sybil and Fleur had decided to leave their cellphones hidden in their vehicles in the parking lot. Sophia opted to get a locker.

The flat keys to the lockers were given by a uniformed guard inside the main entry by the metal detectors. As she walked over to ask for a key, her cellphone began chirping. She stopped, smiled at the guard, turned and took the call.

It was Dion. "Dion, I can't talk right now. We are to be in a court room discussing what happened to Robert Glacie. I really can't talk right now." Her thumb on the button to end the call, she heard Dion screeching on the other end, "Okay, I'm listening. What! You received

222

an email from Granger? Yes, what? Can you send it to me? Yes, I have my laptop with me. I was about to put everything in the locker here at the courthouse. What? Oh, yes, the lawyer is Dr. Goldfarb. I think there is only one in Albuquerque. Please, send it to him, thank you, Dion! You are a dear friend." Using the key to open the locker, Sophia put her phone and laptop in and locked it. The key was put in her jacket pocket.

After Sophia made it through the metal detectors at the front of the large room, the five of them met at the stairs. Ethan nodded to the far corner, "There is an elevator over there, but the room we are supposed to be meeting the lawyers in is at the top of these stairs. Shall we?"

As they topped the stairs on the second floor, Timothy was leaving the elevator, walking toward them. "Fancy meeting you here" Sophia and Timothy hugged, separating when they came to the respective door.

Entering the large room, they found Mr. Goldfarb standing in serious conversation with Karen's lawyer. The conference table was almost as long as the room. There were fifteen chairs on each side with tall backed chairs at each end. The window was floor to ceiling and end wall to end wall. Hidden florescent lights were in the ceiling, reflecting in the well-polished dark wood table. The chairs on either side were of matching wood with woven Chimayo cushions on each seat.

The chairs closest to the door were occupied. Karen sat beside Bethany with their backs to the window, watching who entered. Sophia smiled and walked over to them. "Hello, Bethany, I want to thank you for the beautiful music you played at Robert's wedding. You certainly are a talented musician." Nodding to Karen, Sophia added, "I gather you are certainly not dead."

Bethany stood for a quick hug. Karen did not rise in greeting but glared at Sophia. Karen's hair was no longer a mango color, but now a mousey brown. Her bulbous nose was smeared with a light brown powder. More powder was caked around her face presumably to hide the numerous worry wrinkles. Bethany's long hair was pulled back in a tight ponytail. The tattoo of a heart with a capital K in the middle of it was on her neck. Both women were dressed in grey hoodies and jeans.

Across from them sat the man with the gray ponytail. It was obvious he was tall for his knees were pulled back where he sat from being under the table. His face was solemn. He wore a blue button shirt with an inlaid Kachina bolo tie. The wide silver Navajo bracelet was on his right wrist and an inlaid watchband was on his left wrist. He nodded his head at Sophia. In front of him was a black leather notebook.

223

Three young adults came into the room. Ethan studied them when they hurried over to Sophia for hugs. The tallest of the three was a young man of about twenty and six two. His hair was brown, long to his collar bone and in his face. He wore an ironed white button-down shirt with ironed black slacks. Collette flounced her way over to Sophia. She wore a colorful full dress, a flower print, belted at the waist to show off her slim figure. Matt wore an ironed chamois shirt, creased blue jeans and a tie. Sophia patted Matt's tie after she hugged him. Fleur shrugged, "Grandma hugs everyone. It's what she does." Donna laughed, "Yeah, Mom is a hugger, but this is a serious meeting, perhaps we should all sit down and get to it."

Mr. Goldfarb pulled out a chair for Sophia. Her back to the wall, she sat across from Bethany. The sky was overcast and grey with dark clouds, hiding the bright sun. Mr. Goldfarb pushed his laptop over to her, "I understand a person you know sent me an email regarding Granger Pino. How do you know this person and how did they know to send this to me and is it valid? It was forwarded from an Optical Clinic on the north side of town."

He watched Sophia's face as she answered. "Yes, Dion Aragon is a
224 friend. As a matter of fact she is Matt's mother and Collette's aunt. They are sitting right here opposite Bethany. Dion called me just as I was coming in the building to say she received this email at work regarding Granger and she thought you would be interested in it."

Karen's lawyer reached around Goldfarb, putting out his hand, "How do you do? I am Mr. Lawrence. I am representing Karen Gilbert. I work for the University doing pro bono work. How do you know this email came from Granger Pino?" His twenty-something voice was stern as his deep caramel eyes focused on her.

Shaking her head, she answered, "I have no idea. Perhaps you should ask her yourself." The woman sitting beside Mr. Lawrence stood to walk over to the large window at the end of the conference room. In her well-manicured hand she held a cellphone with her bright red nails. Her blonde hair was perfectly coiffed in a French roll. Her dress suit matched the color of her nail polish. Returning, she answered the question, "Mr. Pino and his family were leaving for a trip to California. He had emailed the Optical Office to let them know he would no longer was interested in his son William's eye exam set for next week. The email sent to her was evidently a rough draft that Mr. Granger was working on and had not finished expressing his wishes. It appears to be an 'oops.'"

The door opened once more. This time a worried woman rushed into the room. Her long brown hair was pulled back into a bun at the nape of her neck. Her dress suit matched the color of her hair. The perfume she used lingered as she hurried around the table to Mr. Lawrence. "Sir, there is an emergency phone call for you out front. I do believe you should take it immediately. It pertains to this case."

Mr. Lawrence in his dark blue suit, stood, nodded at everyone at the table and said, "Excuse me, I shall return shortly." He followed the woman's clacking high heels around the table and out the door.

Mr. Goldfarb held forth, "All of you at this table had something to do with Robert Glacie's death. We know this fact:

"Mr. Timothy Turpin is Mr. Robert Glacie's nephew.

"Sophia Pino worked with Mr. Glacie for over twenty-three years and was present at the wedding with Mr. Turpin.

"Bethany Abeyta was hired to play her guitar at Mr. Glacie's wedding. She was hired, paid and is a very close friend to Karen Gilbert who was the bride.

"Mr. J.J. Abeyta was the false minister of the wedding.

"Matt Aragon and Collette Aragon know Karen Gilbert and were to participate in the music at the wedding hired to play by Bethany Abeyta.

"Karen Gilbert is the supposed instigator in the death of Robert Glacie. Her advertised death was done to keep her safe from harm.

"Each one of you are now being asked to give a deposition regarding this relationship with Mr. Glacie."

Mr. Goldfarb nodded to Sybil, Donna, Ethan and Fleur, "You four are not relevant to this meeting and I will have to ask you to leave. Thank you." The four made a quick exit out of the room.

Mr. Goldfarb then nodded to the man with the notebook. "This is Mr. Yazzi. He is a private detective who has been following Karen Gilbert over the last four months. His information is vital to this case."

Taking his cellphone from his pocket, he punched in some numbers. "There will be a stenographer here to take down what you say. Remember, what you say in this room will be under oath and can be used against you in a court of law." An older woman came into the room. Her hair was gray and cut short. She had bifocals on and a very dark red lipstick covering not only her lips, but also her front teeth. She smiled at everyone as she took the chair at the head of the long conference table.

Mr. Goldfarb pulled a small tape recorder from his valise. "These conversations shall not only be recorded by Mrs. Garcia, but they shall also be recorded here." He patted the small box in the middle of the table. "We must wait for Mr. Lawrence to return before we may begin."

Right on queue, the door opened. Mr. Lawrence leaned over the table to hand Mr. Goldfarb a piece of paper. Everyone watched as Mr. Goldfarb read the note. He looked up, nodded to Mrs. Garcia and said, "Evidently, we will not be needing your services today. Thank you for coming." The elderly woman stood, gathered her small typewriter and left. Mr. Lawrence remained by the door, he studied each person at the table, "There has been a horrible accident. I will need Karen and Bethany to remain in this room. The rest of you may leave. Thank you."

Matt held the door as everyone else left the room. Mr. Goldfarb took Sophia by the arm, "We need to speak at my office. You know where it is around the corner from here? Good. Meet me there, now."

Sophia and Timothy joined the rest of the Pino clan, who were standing in the hall. Sybil was the first to ask her mother, "Is it over already? What happened? Mom?"

Timothy answered for her, "No, there is an emergency, and Mr. Goldfarb wants to meet with your mother right away. I guess the rest of us should head out. How about we all meet for dinner in an hour at the restaurant in my hotel. Here, here's the hotel's card. I took them from the front desk." It was agreed to meet and discuss what was going to happen next. Sophia went ahead of the others, out into the dreary day. The wind had picked up, radically shaking the tall bare trees. Dried leaves of brown and gold crunched under her feet as she walked. Other leaves blew against the walls of buildings to turn into slivers. Cars honked on the streets as drivers frantically moved around fallen branches in their path. Flags above the courthouse were snapping as the wind plummeted them with the ropes clanging on the metal flag poles.

Choosing to walk against the wind and not hassle with the traffic, Sophia crossed Mr. Goldfarb's parking lot. Her hands were thrust into her jacket's deep pockets and the jacket collar was pulled up to her chin. She watched the plastic bags fly into the bushes by Mr. Goldfarb's office. His dark green BMW was parked close to the heavy dark door.

Newspapers blew in front of him as he walked up the sidewalk to the entry door.

Mr. Goldfarb was just unlocking the door when Sophia ran across the parking lot. Hearing her call out to him, he held the door open for her. "You are brave to walk here. Has something happened to the ancient vehicle you drive?"

Laughing, Sophia said, "My SUV still runs well, probably as well as your BMW. Some things get better with age. What's going on?"

He closed the door behind her and locked it. "Let's go into my office first, before I say anything. I need to make a few phone calls and you're welcome to listen in on them."

The office room smelled of lemon polish and paper. There were stacks of long legal paper everywhere. Mr. Goldfarb moved a stack off a chair by his desk, waving for her to sit. "I'm going to put these calls on speaker. I want you to speak up whenever you have a question or have something to add. Feel free to add information or to ask questions. Got it?"

Sophia wiggled out of her jacket, twisting, she placed it over the back of her chair. The room had floor to ceiling books, neatly placed and dusted. Mr. Goldfarb had removed his suit jacket, sat down on his office 227 chair and punched in some numbers. He put the phone down on the desk and let the ring echo in the room.

A woman answered. Sophia knew that voice. It was Clementine. "Sheriff's office, Rincon Station. How may I help you?"

"This is Mr. Goldfarb Junior calling from Albuquerque. I have Sophia Pino here with me. We need to know what has happened in northern Arizona and what is being done about it?

There was a pause and then, "Hey, Sophia, its Clementine. I wish I was there with you to give you this news. We do have Marcus here in the cells, so he's not going anywhere. He has told us quite a lot and will be helpful in clearing all of this up."

Mr. Goldfarb's deep voice repeated, "What has occurred in Arizona and what is being done about it?"

Clementine answered, "A horseback rider's attention was caught by the sound of someone honking a car horn over and over again. When he arrived at the scene, he noticed two children. Both are under the age of twelve. Both of them are alive and well. There was a woman, and a man sprawled on a plastic picnic cloth, dead. They both had foam coming from their mouths. It wasn't until an hour after the local sheriff arrived when the foam stopped.

"The two children are known to be Emma Pino age eleven and Billy Pino age nine. The deceased persons, as far as the identification found on them to be, Granger M. Pino and Julie Sparks Pino, the wife. The Special Investigation unit found poison in all four of the thermos bottles at the site. The children had not drunk any of the liquid. The adults appeared to have ingested a full cup of poison. The Special Investigation unit found bowls in the Pino kitchen, each bowl had residue of poisonous herbal residue. The bowls, according to their son Marcus, held special teas brewed by Granger Pino."

There was a quick pause, Clementine continued, "The crew at the Pino home found a thermos in the fridge with directions for Marcus to drink it at bedtime since he says he can't sleep unless he has his father's tea. Fortunately for Marcus, Ignacio Cruz and I arrived at the Pino home with the subpoena for Granger Pino who was due at the meeting this morning. He had already departed with his wife Julie, his daughter Emma and his son William. Marcus did not have the opportunity to drink his tea. It contained poisonous toxins as well. The chemists are working on the types of poisonous herbs used. The odor was flowers, cinnamon and ginger. Thankfully, Marcus is of an age where he can speak for his smaller siblings."

Sophia leaned close to the phone, "Where are Emma and Billy? Are they with Marcus?"

Clementine cleared her throat, "Not at this time. They are in transport here. It is recommended currently they be with immediate family. Marcus recommended their mother's brother, their uncle, to be called. He had that number in his wallet. Mr. Larry Sparks is a lawyer in San Jose for a large tech company. His wife works with homeless children from the streets to find homes or safe havens. Rose Sparks answered the phone when they were called, and she is already on her way here via air. Larry Sparks was in a meeting. Evidently, according to Marcus, his Uncle and Aunt have a swimming pool and a two-story home in San Jose, California."

Clementine could be heard shuffling papers, "Marcus appears to prefer going to their place rather than staying in New Mexico." She could be heard drinking something and then added, "Emma and Billie are now in route to Rincon to be with their brother. Marcus is going to go with us to the house and explain to us what occurred this morning with the making of the teas found in the thermos bottles. We will keep you informed."

Mr. Goldfarb interjected, "Should Sophia meet you at the Pino house in Rincon? Perhaps she could be with the children until their aunt arrives?"

There was a long pause, "No. I don't think that would be wise. Currently, Marcus is blaming his Aunt Sophia for the deaths of his parents. He stated emphatically that because his parents hated her, she killed them. It would be best to keep everyone separate right now. Listen, I must go. Sophia, I'll meet up with you later. Don't take any of this personally, please." There was a dial tone.

Sophia studied Mr. Goldfarb's face as he leaned back in his leather office chair. He stated, "You go home. You wait. As far as your involvement in this case regarding Karen and Bethany, you are exempt. Karen is on her own as to the killing of Robert Glacie. According to the detective neither you nor Timothy were involved with Granger and Robert at the time of Robert's death. Timothy Turpin may wish to pursue further legal action against Karen since Robert was his uncle. This will be left to Mr. Turpin. Please, go home and wait for further information." 229

Shaking her head, Sophia asked, "What about Karen's grandmother? Who is going to pursue her death?"

"Edna Sullivan left me the funds to deal with her death. You are in no way involved in that case. This is something you need to leave alone. Go home. Try to find something to pre-occupy your time. All of this will pass quickly. Rincon Sheriffs are very professional. They will collect all the information and as Clementine is a friend of yours, I'm sure you will know all you need to know soon enough. Please, go home and let them do what they are trained to do. Leave it until further notice. Please."

Sophia picked up her backpack to put it in her lap. She studied her hands, "I feel terrible for those children. Isn't there something I could do to help them? After all, Granger is or was my brother. Some of this certainly must be my fault or have to do with me, right?"

Mr. Goldfarb stood to walk around his desk. He took Sophia's hands in his, "No. You had nothing to do with these deaths. There is nothing for you to feel guilty about and as for your mother, perhaps this was all done outside of your control." He put his arm around her shoulders as he led her to the door, "You have been a witness that is all.

You did not participate, nor did you incite any of this. Go home and have a strong cup of tea." He smiled, then laughed, "Go home. Take your dogs for a walk. We have to wait to find out more."

Sophia drove back to her farmhouse in a stupor. There was a strange car in front of the fence. As she pulled into the garage, Timothy came around the corner. He put his arms to her and she hugged him. "Damn, what a day."

Opening the smaller car door, Timothy said, "Come, let us meet the adult children, have a lovely dinner and enjoy one another's company. We need to let this day end on a kinder note. Mr. Goldfarb spoke with Sybil. She informed all of us about the tragedy. Your adult kids are already at the hotel restaurant, it's not far from here. Come, my lady, let's finish the day with gentleness. My treat."

## Epilogue

Clementine, Dion and Timothy sat around Sophia's kitchen table. Two weeks had passed since the devastating news of Granger's and Julie's death. Marcus, Emma and Billie were relocated to San Jose. Marcus had written Sophia a letter apologizing for his attitude. It was a short note probably requested by his Aunt Rose. Margaret Pino's ashes had been given to Sophia. Sybil and Sophia took a four-day camping trip to Monument Valley on Navajo land. Margaret's ashes were thrown into the wind over the land Margaret had loved.

Over the following weeks, Sophia became busy helping her elderly neighbors with their necessary chores. She was appreciated and noticed as a positive person while she took them to doctor's appointments, grocery shopping, checking out library books for them and helping with the house cleaning. Her life had taken on a new meaning with kindness returned. Sybil was now a full-time medical assistant, while Donna oversaw the making of surgical appointments for the veterinarians at their clinic. Ethan was still working as an IT tech on base and Fleur continued to work hard at the store whose owners appreciated her insight and hard work. Life was good and in harmony.

Timothy continued to call every Sunday to let the Pino clan know how he was doing. The lawyers found Karen guilty of murder in a court case decided by a jury. She was designated to eight years in the woman's prison near Gallup, New Mexico. Bethany was also involved with buying the poisonous herbs. She was slapped for two years in a prison in the south of the county. Matt and Collette were not implicated in any way. It was a good thing Bethany had stood them up and didn't have them participate in the wedding. Timothy was pleased with the outcome, yet angry those two didn't get more prison time. He signed over Robert's house near the university to Donna and Fleur, giving them the responsibility to pay property taxes on their new home.

As summer approached, the hope of rain came with the heat. Marcus, Emma and Billie were being adopted by their aunt and uncle. There had not been a memorial for Granger or Julie Pino and their cremation was quietly done with their ashes spread out over the desert.

On one cloudy afternoon, a group of people decided to meet at Sophia's home to discuss all the past events. Timothy shook his head as Clementine offered him one of Sophia's homemade cookies, "No, thanks. I couldn't eat another thing." He studied a paper held in his hand, "Karen has been convicted of attempted murder, not outright murder, since she didn't know the herbs she gave Robert would actually kill him. She believed they would incapacitate him enough to sign everything over to her and be a zombie for the rest of his life. He would then be taken care of by the state."

Taking a cookie, Dion asked, "What about Bethany's short term? Wasn't she seriously involved? Didn't she get the herbs to give to Karen? I thought that was how Karen received them in the first place?"

232    Clementine answered, "What a mess those two women made of so many people's lives. Yes, Bethany agreed to do the concert for free for Karen, While the two hundred dollars Robert gave Bethany and J.J. at the wedding went as a down payment for the herbs. Granger wanted a thousand dollars for Edna Gilbert's poisonous herbs and another thousand for Robert's. The two hundred dollars was just a down payment. Granger was seriously going after them."

Tilting her head, Sophia asked, "How do you know all of this? How could you possibly know this?"

Chewing a cookie, Clementine swallowed to say, "The computer. Our computer guy Liam Delgado was impressed at how incompetent Granger was regarding his computer. Evidently, Granger poured bleach into his hard drive box, believing it would ruin the hard drive. All it did was pool in the bottom of the box. The hard drive was untouched. There were numerous threatening emails Granger sent to Karen and several to Bethany. He wanted his money, and he wanted it right away."

Dion rolled her mug of tea between her palms, "What is going to happen to all the money Granger retained from selling his mother's farm? Where does that go now?"

Timothy answered this time, "The money goes to Granger's children. According to Mr. Lawrence the lawyer, Granger never finished moving the escrow with the money in it to Mexico. He wanted to finalize everything in Mexico. He even had a bank set up in Guaymas. The house in Guaymas was bought, along with a small office space next door. He paid for everything before they even left."

Shaking her head, Dion said, "This is all so sad. All for money. Just money. There didn't appear to be much love in that family. It was all about money."

Clementine agreed, "The tragic family was killed by a greedy father. The kicker is Granger made the teas to kill off his wife, his children and he even had placed a tea in a container for Marcus to drink at bedtime, since Marcus had difficulty sleeping in an empty house." Clementine went on to say, "Marcus was told to fill the thermos bottles with specific bowls of tea premade. Each bowl had a name inlaid with tiles relating to each thermos bottle for each person. The problem we ran into was only three bowls were found in the office's kitchen. Each of these Chinese tea bowls had names under them, but Granger's or Dad's bowl had the name, but we couldn't find bowl."

Dion asked, "What happened to Granger's tea bowl?"                    233

Clementine answered, "Well, Marcus explained to us what happened. As he was filling his father's thermos from the tea bowl, Emma knocked the bowl from his hand spilling the tea all over the place. Therefore, being a creative young man, he took some of the tea from his mother's, his sister's and his brother's bowls to fill his father's thermos. Of course, he had no knowledge that the bowls were filled with poisons. His little brother Billie, received basic tap water."

Again, Timothy asked, "What happened to Granger's bowl?" Laughing, Clementine explained, "Emma told us where to find the bowl. It was under the tamarisk tree in the backyard. There was a horned toad, a phrynosoma corntum or a Texas horned lizard from the Bufonid family of lizards. Say that ten times fast?"

Dion asked, "Oh, dear, was it dead?" Still smiling Clementine answered Dion, "No, as a matter of fact it was doing just fine. There was no poison in Granger's tea bowl. The little lizard was eating some grass Emma had thoughtfully put in the bowl and the herbal tea water remained in the bottom of the bowl. The little fella was doing just fine."

Timothy shook his head, "If Emma hadn't taken the bowl from

Marcus, then Granger would be living the good life in Mexico right now with no strings attached. His family would all be dead in the Arizona desert. But wouldn't they have been found? I mean corpses in the desert with sheepherders, and Navajo people riding their horses across the plains and the road? The road was there, right? People would've driven down the road to find the corpses."

This time Dion answered, "No, not necessarily. When Granger brought Billie in to make the appointment for his glasses, he showed everyone in the waiting room his new find. He bought a shovel, a folding shovel. When folded to its smallest size you could fit it in a suitcase, a backpack or in the tire well of the car. He was a very clever man. I'm sure he bought the shovel for the sole purpose of digging graves in the soft dirt of the desert. He had a plan, and he planned to keep it simple. Disgusting man!" Taking a sip of tea, she added, "Sophia, you would have been in real danger if he had lived. He appeared to be hell bent on killing off his family!"

Shaking her head, Sophia changed the subject, "Marcus is going to need lots of counseling. When I spoke to him last night, he told me that he felt this was all his fault since he filled the thermos bottles. Poor kid."

Drawing lines with the moisture from her tea mug on the table, Clementine agreed, "All those kids are going to need help. How can any kid get their head around their father wanting them dead? This is worse than a Greek tragedy."

Staring out of the kitchen window, Sophia sighed. Her horses were gone to a good home, yet the empty barnyard was saddening. She turned to her friends at the table, "You know what? I'm going to get some goats for the barnyard! I won't have to shovel their poop or have three-hundred-dollar vet bills every six months and the barnyard will be used again with hopping goats. Yes! I shall get goats. What do you guys think of that?"

Timothy's phone made a buzzing noise, "Opps, I must go. That was my alarm to get to the airport." Standing, he smiled at the women around the table, "Well, ladies, it has been interesting. Clementine, let me know about the wedding, if I'm able to make it back this should be a happier occasion."

They all stood for hugs, warm wishes as they departed. Soft white clouds continued to drift across the sky. Robins sang in the tall elm trees beside Sophia's driveway. The sun warmed the dry land. Sophia waved goodbye to the leaving company as she put the leashes on the dogs, saying, "Hey, pups, it is a lovely day for a walk. Let's talk about goats."

TERESA PIJOAN

www.ingramcontent.com/pod-product-compliance
Lightning Source LLC
Chambersburg PA
CBHW011118050726
47495CB00021B/2952

* 9 7 8 1 6 3 2 9 3 7 7 7 3 *